An Oath Broken

Also by Diana Cosby

An Oath Taken

An Oath Broken

Diana Cosby

LYRICAL PRESS
Kensington Publishing Corp.
www.kensingtonbooks.com

LYRICAL PRESS BOOKS are published by

Kensington Publishing Corp.
119 West 40th Street
New York, NY 10018

All Kensington titles, imprints, and distributed lines are available at special quantity discounts for bulk purchases for sales promotion, premiums, fund-raising, educational, or institutional use.

Special book excerpts or customized printings can also be created to fit specific needs. For details, write or phone the office of the Kensington Sales Manager: Kensington Publishing Corp., 119 West 40th Street, New York, NY 10018. Attn. Sales Department. Phone: 1-800-221-2647.

Lyrical and the L logo are trademarks of Kensington Publishing Corp.

First Electronic Edition: June 2015
eISBN-13: 978-1-60183-309-9
eISBN-10: 1-60183-309-1

First Print Edition: June 2015
ISBN-13: 978-1-60183-310-5
ISBN-10: 1-60183-310-5

Printed in the United States of America

At times in life we meet the most amazing people who touch us deeply. This book is dedicated to Cathy Papitto, a wonderful woman with an incredible heart whom I'm blessed to call my friend. Thank you for believing in me from the start.

Acknowledgments

I would like to thank Jody Allen and Cameron John Morrison for answering numerous questions as well as their insight into medieval Scotland. I would also like to thank The National Trust for Scotland, which acts as guardian of Scotland's magnificent heritage of architectural, scenic, and historic treasures. In addition, I am thankful for the immense support from my husband, parents, family, and friends. My deepest wish is that everyone is as blessed when they pursue their dreams.

My sincere thanks to my editor, Esi Sogah, my agent, Holly Root, my critique partners, Cindy Nord, Shirley Rogerson, Michelle Hancock, and Mary Forbes. Your hard work has helped make the magic of Giric and Sarra's story come true. A special thanks to Sulay Hernandez for believing in me from the start.

And, thanks to the Roving Lunatics (Mary Beth Shortt and Sandra Hughes), Nancy Bessler, and The Wild Writers for their friendship and continued amazing support!

CHAPTER 1

England/Scotland border, 1292

Lady Sarra Bellecote crumpled the missive and flung it to the chapel floor. "He can go to the devil!" She swept past the aged bench and halted before the stained glass window.

The angry slap of the January wind against the crafted panes matched the fury pounding in her heart. Her home, her decision to marry was being torn from her. She closed her eyes against the rush of betrayal.

How dare her guardian issue her such an ultimatum?

She inhaled deeply, a hint of frankincense and wood filling her breath. After a moment, Sarra regained a measure of calm and opened her eyes.

The stained glass portrait of the Blessed Virgin, crafted within the blue, pearl, and gray panes, stared back at her. Calm and reassuring at a time when she didn't know whom to trust.

Faith, her mother's voice of long ago whispered in her mind.

Bitterness curdled in her throat. As if after all of these years God would choose this moment to offer a token of hope?

Sarra clasped her hands tight before her, but she did not pray. Her belief in God, as in most things in her life, had long since fled.

Soft footsteps sounded behind her, accompanied by the swish of vestments.

"My child." Father Ormand's gentle entreaty spilled through the brittle silence.

For a moment the child whose faith had once guided her responded to his entreaty. Then, like her hope over the years, any remnants of her youthful beliefs flickered and died.

"Why should I yield to my guardian's request to marry his son or forsake my holdings and be exiled to a nunnery?"

Father Ormand cleared his throat. "Lady Sarra, your guardian knows not your feelings about—"

She whirled, aware her action bespoke poor manners toward a revered man of God, but at the moment hurt overrode decorum. "As if Lord Bretane would care?"

Thick lines sagged across the cleric's brow as his solemn brown eyes studied her. "Your father would have wished this, my lady."

"A marriage based on threats and conditions is not a union my father would have sanctioned."

"Lord Bretane was your father's best friend," the priest said quietly, as if she did not remember. "He was a godparent to Lord Sinclair, the man you are to wed." Father Ormand shook his head as his worried gaze searched deeply into hers. "Arranged marriages are expected. Feel blessed that your guardian, a man your father trusted enough to leave your keeping to, chooses your husband. With the wealth of your holdings, the king could have easily intervened and selected your betrothed."

A part of her acknowledged that she should be grateful. King Edward's matches often served his own gain. But her guardian's writ commanding her to wed his son by Midsummer's Eve was a directive she loathed to obey.

The past rose up in horrifying detail. For a moment, Sarra was again a child. She pressed trembling fingers against her temples as grisly images of her murdered parents flooded her mind. With their deaths her hopes and dreams had crumbled one by one. To think her last desire, to marry for love, would be lost because of a forced marriage to a Scot was unacceptable!

A shudder rippled through her as youthful images of her betrothed, a dark-haired child smashing falcon eggs, scraped through her mind. "Drostan was a contemptible lad."

"Lord Sinclair was but a child when you knew him," Father Ormand offered. "Boys make mischief, but boys turn into men. Ten and one years have passed since you have seen Lord Bretane's son. 'Tis unfair to judge what we cannot see."

Mayhap, but beneath Drostan's title of baron lay the blackened ugliness of his ancestry.

A reiver.

Lawless raiders who pilfered, raped, and murdered. The border savages who had attacked and killed her parents. *And for what?* The paltry pieces of gold they carried.

Wisps of hair slipped from her braid and the sunlight pouring through the stained glass illuminated the pale strands of gold. Sarra worked the wayward locks into the tight plait, her own life as confined by convention as the tresses she fought daily to keep within their bounds.

"Come," Father Ormand urged. "Lord Bretane's escort is expecting your reply. We have kept them waiting overlong."

However much she wished to send the priest to deal with the entourage of Scottish knights in the courtyard, as mistress of Rancourt Castle, 'twas her duty.

With a nod, she walked toward the exit. Determination and pride had allowed her to persevere since her parents' tragic death. The same resolve would serve her well in her upcoming confrontation with her guardian.

She abhorred the thought of the arduous travel ahead at this miserable time of year. For her sanity, she must believe the man she remembered, who had bounced her on his knee and had offered warm smiles during her childhood, would never condemn her to a life with someone she could never love.

Angry clouds boiled overhead, spitting fat flakes of snow. Wind, sharp and brutal, tugged at Giric Armstrong, Earl of Terrick's cloak. He remained motionless astride his destrier, positioned before his small contingent of men.

Waiting.

Through thick, black lashes, Giric scanned the courtyard of the English fortress. He took in the well-maintained grounds, the sturdy walls, and the skill of the knights training in the practice field as the clash of steel echoed throughout Rancourt Castle.

Envy shot through him at the quality of the swords they wielded. He smothered his discontent. The gold he would earn for this simple task would make great strides toward rebuilding Wolfhaven Castle, feeding his people, and furnishing his knights with sturdy blades of steel. With a grimace, he secured a loose strap on the side of his saddle. He was done proving himself to a dead man's ghost.

The slamming of the door to the keep at the far end of the castle caught his attention. A gust of wind swirled up, billowing into a white cloud thick with snow blocking his view. Two cloaked figures emerged through the wintry haze. Another icy burst exposed a hint of vestments worn beneath the black cloak of the larger form.

A priest? Giric studied the smaller figure lost within the rich folds of a burgundy cloak. The hem of an ivory gown peeked from the border. Lady Sarra Bellecote? He frowned. Aye, he'd expected the lady of the castle, but accompanied by her guard. Why would she require the aid of a priest? Only one reason came to mind—she'd refused the match and had requested sanctuary from the church.

Giric dismissed the notion, confident his desperation for coin spawned such dismal thoughts. Many reasons could exist for the vicar's accompaniment. Mayhap a devout Christian, Lady Sarra sought the blessing of her priest.

He relaxed in his saddle. 'Twould make their journey easier if his ward was a softly spoken maiden of God.

The pair closed on his entourage.

Several paces away, the woman motioned toward the priest. The vicar halted, yet the slender figure continued. A length before Giric, she stopped.

Wind tugged at the hood of her cloak as the woman slowly raised her head. Framed within porcelain skin, eyes as gray as a winter storm locked on his clan brooch, darkened as they cut to him.

Giric's breath stumbled in his throat. Draped within the oversize cloak, most women would appear nondescript within the numerous yards of wool. This woman's regal bearing, as well as the mix of innocence struggling against the fear in her eyes drew him.

With a muttered curse, he squashed his awareness. He was hired to escort the lass to her betrothed.

"I am Lady Sarra Bellecote, mistress of Rancourt Castle. You are in charge of these men?"

Her sultry voice flowed over him like peat-warmed air. "Aye," Giric replied, irritated this one slip of a woman, an Englishwoman at that, evoked such a deep response.

"Until I give further instruction, you and your men are offered shelter within Rancourt Castle." After a perfunctory glance over the rest of his party, she started toward the keep.

Dismissed! He bit back a string of oaths. With him staring at her like a green lad, 'twas nay wonder she treated him with such disregard. "My lady!"

Her pace remained steady, the whirl of snow consuming her with each step.

Never, in all of his years, had any dared to ignore him so deliberately. Giric dismounted in one controlled move. "Lady Sarra, I—"

"Sir Knight." The priest intercepted him, then shot a concerned look toward the mistress of Rancourt Castle before facing Giric. Wind tugged at his cloak, and he drew his hood tighter. "Please, you and your men come inside the keep and warm yourselves. Lady Sarra will speak with you once you have eaten and rested."

Giric started to correct the priest of his improper address, then remained silent.

A knight.

With his lingering status as an outlaw in the Western Marches and the shame of serving as an escort to earn gold, he'd decided to conceal his title of Earl of Terrick during this task.

Now, he must play the part.

The priest frowned at the exiting woman.

Curious at the cleric's reaction, Giric studied the fading figure through the whirls of snow. Escorting Lady Sarra to her betrothed in Scotland was to be a simple deed. Yet 'twould appear the bride was displeased by the match. "My thanks for your hospitality."

The priest signaled toward the stable.

A lad ran from the structure and halted before Giric's horse. "I will take your mounts."

After one last glance toward the keep outlined in the increasing fall of white, Giric waved for his men to dismount. Warmth and food were his first priority. There would be time to speculate on Rancourt Castle's intriguing mistress later.

Three days later, Giric sat down to supper with his men at the trencher within the great hall. He kept his hands clasped together, his head bowed, and waited until the priest finished the blessing. But the hearty fare of venison, onions, and sage did little to ease a temper that had grown shorter with each passing day.

While rich tones of a prayer echoed throughout the great hall, he covertly glanced toward the dais. Lady Sarra sat rigid in her chair and stared straight ahead. As during every other blessing before the meal, she neither bowed her head nor pressed her hands together in a show of faith.

Her indifference troubled him. If she was displeased by the match, 'twould seem she would seek answers in prayer. Yet, her lips remained still and naught about her countenance portrayed a hint of divine appeal.

If she indeed shunned the church and its beliefs, then why had she sought out the priest to accompany her during their initial meeting? Whatever her reason, it did nae excuse her poor manners. Each morning since their arrival, he'd sent her a request for an audience, all of which she'd ignored.

Though they'd yet to speak, her cool looks when he caught her glance served to aggravate his temper. He again looked toward her, damning his body's tightening as he took in her slender frame, porcelain skin, and rich golden hair. She was a task, nay more.

His respect for the priest who dealt with the mistress of Rancourt Castle on a daily basis rose a notch. The day Giric delivered his wary charge to her betrothed in Scotland would be one to celebrate.

After making the sign of the cross, the priest ended his blessing.

The servants stepped to the tables with bread as a page sliced off portions of venison roasting over the fire.

Another lad carrying a large platter of food halted beside Giric. "Sir Knight?"

Giric nodded and the lad placed a hunk of meat upon his trencher. Then he scooped onions and carrots alongside.

Once finished, the boy stepped to his right where a large man with whisky-colored hair sat. "Sir Knight?"

Colyne MacKerran, Giric's longtime friend and the Earl of Strathcliff, nodded.

The page filled his trencher then moved down the table.

Colyne speared the meat with his dagger, took a bite, then swallowed. "'Tis fine fare."

How could he let Colyne join him in this mayhem? Blast it, both of them nobles, yet playing the roles of knights. The matter was his to take care of, but Colyne had insisted on coming along. "Better than gruel."

Colyne lifted a brow, then laughed. "Aye, 'tis at that. Though with your surly temper, you would be deserving such."

With a grunt, Giric carved another bite.

Colyne reached for his goblet. "If asked, I would say your foul mood began with the arrival of Lady—"

"I did nae ask."

Humor flickered in his friend's eyes. "You did nae, but it has been overlong since I have witnessed a woman who has sparked more than a brief glance from you."

"My interest is in the coin this task will provide, naught more." He had enough to do in rebuilding Wolfhaven Castle. He didna need a wayward heiress to keep reined in as well.

"She has a fine figure."

Giric stabbed his dagger into the tender venison. "And the warmth of ice."

"I have known you to melt a few maidens' hearts in your days," Colyne said with lazy enjoyment.

"Even if the lady in question appealed to me, which she does nae, she is betrothed."

A glint of mischief sparked in his friend's eyes. "Betrothed, aye, but she could be wooed for a wee kiss."

"You are a blasted pain in the arse." His appetite gone, Giric shoved away the trencher. "I have nae figured out why I brought you along."

With a hearty laugh and his dimples giving a fine show, Colyne raised his cup in a toast. "Why, to keep you out of trouble, *Sir Giric*."

At his friend's emphasis on his title, Giric's irritation fell away. Indeed, 'twas best to remember the humility of his position until he'd delivered Lady Sarra to her betrothed.

The clank of tankards melded with the voices of the men. Smoke, thick and pungent, sifted overhead. Weariness swept him, and he rubbed his brow. "I am ready for this journey to be over. 'Tis long past time to return home."

"It will be quiet without your sister, Elizabet, in residence."

"Aye, but she is safe. Though English and sworn to serve King Edward, Sir Nicholas has proven to be a good husband and fair to the bordering Scots." Though Colyne nodded, Giric didna miss the shadow of hurt that crossed his face. Over the years when his friend had visited Wolfhaven Castle, the love Colyne held for his sister hadna escaped him, nor his intent to request her hand in marriage.

But true to her unconventional manner, Elizabet had fallen in love and wed a man who by rights should be their enemy. And blast it if Giric didn't like the Sassenach.

In these troubled times, where rumors of war between England and Scotland rumbled as often as thunder, that his sister had found a man worthy of her love, made their union all the more precious.

He glanced at Lady Sarra who maintained her regal pose upon the dais and toyed with her food. Regret sifted through his mind. It appeared she, like most women, would marry for obligation.

A knight slammed his fist upon the table several lengths away and laughter broke out around him.

Lady Sarra glanced at the warrior, then her gaze shifted to Giric.

Their eyes locked.

For a split second, hers darkened with awareness, then her mouth parted in surprise.

Heat stormed Giric's body.

Her finger touched her lips as if she could read his thoughts. Then, the warmth in her gaze iced.

An air of challenge snapped between them, and at her clear dismissal of him, Giric's regrets of moments ago faded. He held her gaze, refusing to be the first to look away. Her contempt toward him, for God knows whatever reason, was her affair. Like it or nae, with his duty to offer her escort, they would be traveling together.

A long moment passed.

Redness crept up her face, but from the hard set of her expression, it wasna from embarrassment.

Giric narrowed his gaze.

She tilted her head in defiance. Then, her nostrils slightly flared and she looked away.

His body thrummed with unspent energy, unsure if he should be pleased or aggravated by her bravado.

After a sip from her goblet, she leaned over, whispered to the priest, then pushed her chair back and stood.

"You will nae avoid me this time," he breathed. Giric snatched the cloth nearby, wiped the grease from his mouth and hands, then tossed it aside.

Colyne laughed as he watched the heiress depart. "Methinks the rose has thorns."

"A blasted bushel of them." Giric shoved to his feet. Rushes crunched beneath his boots as he strode after her. He kept his pace steady. Nae too fast as to alert the guards or her of his intent, but enough to keep her in sight.

Three blasted days now she'd made him and his men wait, and with her heading to her chamber, the lass would make it four. By God, he would speak with her this night!

Once shielded from the great hall, he took the steps up the turret two at a time. A wisp of her ivory linen gown twisted ahead of him with an elusive swirl, then was lost in the shadows.

Giric rounded the corner and caught her figure clearly silhouetted within the torchlight from the wall sconce. "Lady Sarra."

Leather kid slippers scraped over stone as she turned. The flutter of flames outlined her like a dark angel. Wariness flared in her eyes.

He took a step closer, damning her beauty, lured by her spirit.

Her hand slid to the side of her gown. With a flick of her wrist, she withdrew a slim dagger from the folds. "Halt." Her ominous warning echoed in the darkened void, edged with a hint of fear.

Saint's breath, did the lass think she could intimidate him with a mere blade? "I mean you no harm, my lady. I wish but a brief moment of your time."

That small pert nose lifted a fraction, like a warrior would raise his shield. "How dare you steal about and corner me in my own home."

"If you had talked to me instead of avoided me, I would nae have had to resort to such extreme measures."

A sliver of torchlight glinted off the dagger in her hands. "Leave me. I will grant you an audience when I deem the time appropriate."

If she believed he could be swayed by flashing a weapon before him or a terse command, she was about to learn otherwise. He wasna one of her servants she could order about. He took a step closer. "We need to discuss our departure."

She flinched, but she held her ground.

Determined to keep his temper, he drew a calming breath. "My lady, our acquaintance has begun poorly." Her narrowing eyes chinked at his hard-won control, and the fact that she hadna lowered the blade didna help either, but he pressed on. "Let us begin anew, this time in the proper manner. Let me introduce my—"

"No!" She stepped forward, the dagger tight in her grip. "I will leave Rancourt Castle at my discretion. Your name as well as your demands are of little consequence. Try my patience further, Sir Knight, and you will find yourself housed within my dungeon this night instead of on a pallet of straw." As regal as a queen, she sheathed her dagger and strode up the steps.

Fury slammed through Giric. He was wrong. With a woman like her, nae even a saint could keep his temper in check.

On a curse he bolted up the steps.

CHAPTER 2

The angry scrape of the knight's steps gave Sarra a second's warning as the Scot caught her arm, then pinned her against the wall.

The coldness of the stone seeped through skin as his hard, sculpted body leaned inches from hers. She stared at the large hand clasped against her skin, lined with scars. On an unsteady breath, she looked up.

His muscled frame blocked the light, casting his face in a partial shadow. Hard, unforgiving angles that served a fitting canvas for ice-blue eyes that held no quarter. And his devil's black hair added an ominous edge to his dark looks.

Fear surged through her, threatened to undermine her hard-won control. The man was dangerous, a fact she'd noted from the first.

So preoccupied by her anger over her guardian's news of her betrothal, she'd ignored the knight's request for a meeting. She'd struggled with the reality that once she left her home, if Lord Bretane denied her request and forced her to marry his son, she might never return to Rancourt Castle. And her intent to depart immediately to confront her guardian had become smothered by fear.

Shame filled Sarra at her poor manners. The Scottish knight was hired to perform a task. He didn't deserve her avoidance. "Apologize," he breathed.

His voice, as potent as thunder, rattled through her thoughts to the fore. Sarra shoved against his chest.

He didn't move.

"Release me." At his noncompliance, her mouth grew dry. She licked her lips, and his eyes followed the act.

The knight muttered a soft curse, and a new worry shot through her. She glanced down the spiral steps to where her men ate, oblivious to her peril.

The knight tilted his head and fragments of light spilled over his face. Anger still raged within his ice-blue eyes, but now desire churned as well.

Stunned, she shoved harder. "Comply or I will order you hung!"

With a look of disguist, the knight loosened his grip, but he didn't let go. "Rest assured, my lady, I have no personal intentions. A boar would offer more warmth than you."

"Ho—How dare you!"

"And how dare you ignore my requests for the last three days."

He was right, neither did he understand that his dark presence evoked painful memories of the reivers who'd murdered her parents, and reminded her of her future, promised to a Scot she abhorred."My decisions are those of the mistress of Rancourt Castle. And 'twas not I who skulked through the castle without permission."

"'Twas your rudeness that forced my hand."

"I am firm but fair."

He arched a skeptical brow. "Have you deluded yourself into believing that as well?"

Anger slid through her with a sharp bite. "You know naught about me."

His eyes narrowed. "Then we are even, are we nae?"

Again she shoved against his chest. To her surprise, this time he released her, but he didn't step away.

Silence clattered between them. She should be afraid. Terrified. Never before had a man dared touch her so. But she remained still, as intrigued as afraid.

"'Tis what you are good at, is it nae?" he pressed. "Ignoring those you do nae wish to see. Allowing others to deal with issues that you refuse to face?" The Scot leaned closer, one hand pressed against the wall where he'd held her trapped moments ago, his eyes riveted upon her.

The image of a wolf flashed in her mind. Dark. Wild. Untamed.

Refusing to allow him the satisfaction of discovering that he'd unnerved her, she angled her chin. "Once I leave, fate may never allow me to return."

"So you ignore me? Refuse to explain your reasons?"

What did he know about her and what did she care? "My reasons are not your concern." With as much dignity as she could muster, she turned, then walked up the stairs. The lonely shuffle of her slippers on the stone steps echoed around her, but she sensed he still watched.

Waited.

Though the writ from her guardian had tossed her organized life into chaos, 'twould appear that with the arrival of the Scottish knight, fate had thrown in another curve as well.

Whatever lay between them was far from over.

Blast it! Giric slammed the door to the keep. Air, bitter with cold, gusted against his face as he stepped into the night. Moonlight slashed through the shield of clouds racing overhead. The pale beams melded with the torchlight lending a majestic beauty to the well-kept stronghold.

One day his castle would stand as proud. Neither Lady Sarra nor any other would deter him from his goal.

Giric willed the English noble from his mind, but flashes of her vulnerability on the turret steps moments before haunted him.

Blast her. Why should he care about the quiet sadness that lurked in her eyes, a hurt that beckoned him when her wary manner foreshadowed a journey filled with naught but irritation? He didna need her problems added to his enormous pile. And let him nae forget that she was betrothed. The image of her mouth inches from his own on the turret steps lingered. A dull pounding began at his temples. And he thought only his sister Elizabet had a penchant for disrupting his sanity? He scoured the blackened nooks along the castle walls sure fairies lurked there and had addled his brain.

With a scowl, he tugged his hood over his head and strode across the courtyard. Snow crunched beneath his boots as he walked, but each step lingered on memories of the sorrow he'd glimpsed on Lady Sarra's face.

With an oath, he wrapped his hand around the hilt of his broadsword. This was why he'd ridden to Rancourt Castle, to wield his blade for gold, nae fall victim to another's plight.

Giric grimaced at the cloud-filled sky. As if Lady Sarra would ever seek him out for guidance? There was a thought to make a beggar laugh. He was a fool to contemplate earning even a token of her trust. Three days had passed and he stood at odds with the woman he had sworn to protect.

What had possessed him to touch her, much less challenge her? He desperately needed the gold this task would bring. As she'd threatened, she could have ordered her guard to cast him into the dungeon for his brazen act. A nightmare he'd sworn to never again endure.

The tap of his boots upon stone echoed as he ascended the steps to the wall walk. At the top, he nodded to a guard on his left then strolled along the snow-dusted path. Shafts of moonlight plunged through the crenellations like jagged teeth. As he walked through the play of light, beyond the castle walls, rolling fields gave way to a dense stand of trees. A thin layer of fog wove through the forest like a silken strand, lingered over the moon-bleached snow.

Though held by the English, the rough landscape of this northern stronghold mirrored that of his home along the border.

The grate of a window opening echoed from the tower ahead. Giric looked up to find the woman currently causing turmoil in his life lean into view.

Framed in the squared stone, her long golden hair fluttering around her, Lady Sarra leaned out the window and stared into the night.

He halted. On a silent curse, he waited for her to detect him, skewer him with a scowl of distrust, then slam the window as she withdrew. Her wariness he could handle, but nae this guileless maiden, still wearing the sad expression that lured him to care.

He stepped closer. His leather boots scraped to a stop on a patch of ice covered with snow.

She didna look down.

Then he realized he stood in the shadows, and with his movements muffled by the rush of wind, she was unaware of his presence.

A second passed, then another.

Giric damned himself for his indecision. He should walk into the light and make himself known, or leave. Struck by the pain in her expression, though, he could only stare.

As he watched, his chest grew tight and his every nerve came on alert.

Shaken by the feelings she inspired, he turned and walked away.

Two days later dark clouds churned overhead and spewed thick flakes of snow as Giric checked the straps of the saddle for the third time since they'd finished preparations to leave. A horse to his right pawed the ground, and he empathized with the steed's restlessness.

The bells of Prime tolled.

"Saint's breath, where is she?" Giric growled.

Colyne shrugged. "'Twould seem the lady will be here at her discretion."

Discretion? Blasted stubborn. He glanced toward the keep, already layered by several inches of freshly fallen snow.

Lady Sarra failed to appear.

At least she had finally decided to depart. Giric rubbed his hands together for warmth. "I told her we must leave at first light. After last night's storm travel will be slow, nae to mention make us an easy target if there are any about with ill intent."

Colyne adjusted his horse's halter. "Do you think we will be troubled by reivers?"

Giric sighed, too aware of the ways of those who raided to survive. "Nay, most should be home stoking their peat fires."

"Then what is troubling you?"

After a glance toward the empty entry of the keep, he turned away, irritated that he'd awakened with thoughts of Sarra on his mind. Giric released the leather straps of the saddle. "With King Edward making claims as overlord to Scotland, 'tis an unsettling time. The rumblings of an uprising could lead to war. The last thing I want is to run across English troops seasoned for a fight."

"Aye." His mail rattled as Colyne pressed his knee into his mount's side, and then drew the cinch tight. "I have had a clash or two in my day with the English king's troops. His knights are nae a discriminating lot. Once a king is seated upon Scotland's throne will be a day when every Scot can draw a deep breath."

"Our new sovereign should be Robert the Competitor. His claim for the Scottish crown is strongest," Giric said, concerned about the English king's next move. He prayed King Edward had nae unleashed portions of his army to the north in a show of force.

Colyne stroked his steed's withers. "Sir John Balliol's family ties are as strong, and he holds just claim to the crown as well."

"Balliol lacks the backbone to deal with the English king. The man would be naught but a pawn to King Edward."

"Aye, 'tis my worry as well," Colyne agreed. "I pray when the Scottish council meets and selects our king, 'twill be wisdom that guides them."

At the flurry of commotion near the keep's entrance, Giric turned and stiffened.

Lady Sarra moved among her people with tender smiles. At the foot of the steps, she paused and laid her hand upon the shoulder of the rail-thin man he'd learned was the steward.

A boy clad in often-sewed breeches and an old but serviceable brown overcoat squeezed between the priest and the burly candle-maker, held up a roughly wrapped gift.

With interest, Giric waited for her reaction. Nae only did she offer the scruffy lad thanks, but she knelt and embraced him in a fierce hug.

"She is taking her blasted time," Giric grumbled as she continued to move from one servant to another to bid her good-bye. But he lauded the warmth of her sincere farewells to each and every person.

With a critical eye, he scanned her travel garb. He'd expected her to exit the keep bedecked with frivolous attire. Yet, the worsted wool cloak atop her simple woolen gown and leather boots were an appropriate choice for travel. A choice he would have offered if asked.

Impatient, he shifted. He should be happy, pleased by this turn of events. Practicality was a trait he admired. So why was he as moody as a badger? Because the wary, at times rude woman he'd dealt with over the past few days didna match the sensible, gentle maiden standing before him.

The crowd parted and Lady Sarra turned in his direction. The tender warmth on her face faded, replaced by the cold, familiar distrust.

Irritation swept him, as well as a profound sense of regret. For a moment, he'd wanted her to look upon him with the same tenderness.

He clasped the leather reins and grumbled an oath at his foolishness. Even if Lady Sarra was nae betrothed, his finances allowed little room to consider courting a woman of her stature. Nor did he believe his years as a reiver would impress her.

Enough. 'Twas time to leave. He handed his reins to the stable lad and walked to Lady Sarra. "'Tis long past time we depart."

"I have one last errand," she announced, her voice cool.

"My lady, with the snow continuing to fall, we must nae tarry."

Gray eyes flashed. "You will wait."

A muscle ticked in his jaw. Through sheer will he refrained from giving her the set down she desperately needed. How could he have considered her genteel, even for a moment? Fairies were indeed playing tricks in his mind. The look of sadness he had perceived the night before must have been anger.

Emotions storming Sarra, she caught the flash of ire that darkened Sir Knight's eyes as she turned away. As if his judgment of her mattered? 'Twas her home that she was leaving, possibly forever, the only part of her that really mattered. Could he not see the personal cost?

Or did he even care?

Frustrated, she crossed the courtyard. 'Twould be a relief when Sir Knight and his men rode from her life. Once she reached the turret, she hurried up the steps. At the top she strode across the wall walk toward the waddle and daub building in the far corner.

A soft flutter of wings filled the small abode as she entered, and the rich scent of birds and hay embraced her. Memories of her father and their time spent here poured through her, and her heart squeezed. Fingers trembling, she closed the door.

A ruffled squawk to her right sliced through her potent thoughts. With a tear-filled sigh she crossed to the male peregrine. "Hush now, Sir Galahad."

The regal predator, secured by leather jesses, shuffled his claws over the wooden bow perch. He angled his pale blue bill to the side.

After donning a thick leather glove, Sarra reached into a leather pouch, withdrew a strip of meat, and held it out.

For a moment he eyed the offering, then snatched it from her hand.

"You were always finicky," she chided gently as he swallowed it whole. Her heart gave a hard tug. How could she leave Rancourt Castle? This was her home. In the aftermath of tragedy, she'd carved out a life on her own.

Now, with the arrival of the writ, the stability of her entire life was in jeopardy. What would she do if her guardian insisted on the union? Her independence would be lost. Even if she held her ground, she would end up in a nunnery.

Either way, how could she win?

Sir Galahad angled his head and stared at her expectantly, his black eyes alert.

A tear slid down her cheek as she recalled the day she and her father had found the raptor's mother sprawled on the forest floor, mortally wounded. Due to the time of year, her father was concerned that the falcon had a nest nearby. He'd explained that with the raptor's mother dead, and without their aid, any chicks within her nest would die.

After hours of searching, they had found the young raptor hidden inside its home of branches and mud. Once hooded, they'd carried him home. To her delight, her father had gifted her with the young bird and as Sir Galahad grew, her father had taught her how to handle him.

"Hek, hek," Sir Galahad squawked.

Sarra wiped the tears from her eyes. "I shall miss you as well." She gently stroked his blue-gray wings, closed her eyes, and let the warmth of her past fill her.

Happiness, pure and innocent, tumbled through her heart. The countless tales her father had told of King Arthur, Camelot, his devout knights, and their adventures rolled through her mind.

Though Sir Gawain and Sir Lancelot were among those knights most trusted by King Arthur, 'twas Sir Galahad, son of Sir Lancelot, who had earned Sarra's favor. That Sir Lancelot's son had chosen to hide his identity and had earned his knighthood on his own merit moved her. The trueness of the stalwart knight's heart had won her respect.

Pride filled her as she gazed upon the peregrine falcon that possessed the same fierce loyalty. 'Twas appropriate that his namesake should be drawn from an Arthurian legend. For men such as Sir Galahad existed only in tales.

A light knock sounded at the door.

Sarra swiped away her tears. "Enter."

The door opened with a muffled scrape.

And Sarra came face to face with the last man she wished to see.

Sunlight outlined Sir Knight's mail-clad form, and left his face masked in shadows.

A long moment passed.

"My lady, are you ready to leave?" His soft, rich burr wrapped around her like warm velvet. He stepped closer. "Are you ill?"

The tenderness of his voice threw her off guard. A sliver of her defenses cracked and tempted her to accept the compassion he seemed to offer, compassion that at this moment, she needed desperately.

She searched his face, the worries she harbored spilling out. "How can I go? Amice, my seamstress, is due with her first babe within a fortnight. I need to speak with the tenants to ensure their larders are full. Then, there is the upcoming planting season to discuss with the steward. Though I have tried to ensure that all is taken care of, what if due to circumstance I never return? What will happen then? I cannot . . ." Overwhelmed, she shook her head.

"My lady," he said with calm understanding. " 'Tis hard to leave those we love when naught but uncertainty awaits us."

His sage words hinted that he, too, had weathered such turmoil. But then, why wouldn't he? As a knight, he had tasted battle, faced death many times. She hesitated. What was she thinking to confide in this Scot, a man whose presence was bought with a few pieces of gold?

Sir Galahad squawked and fluttered his wings as he shuffled over his bow perch.

Sarra turned to the peregrine falcon and murmured soothing words as she stroked her hand across his wings. The raptor calmed, and she glanced toward the intruder who'd for a moment made her want to give him her trust.

" 'Twould be best to leave posthaste, my lady. The skies are growing dark, and another storm may be upon us before night."

"I need but a moment more."

"To ensure your safety, we canna delay further."

She wanted to argue, but realized logic, not her emotions, must guide her. "Then, we shall leave."

With a nod, Sir Knight stepped back and opened the door. "My lady."

She turned to the falcon one last time. "Take care, Sir Galahad. I will miss you." Without meeting his gaze, she swept past the Scot. Let them be on their way. The sooner she was free of his presence the better.

CHAPTER 3

Wind, bitter and sharp, ripped at Giric's body. He leaned lower on his steed's neck as his mount forged another drift. Swirls of snow darted through folds of his cloak and jabbed at his flesh.

He glanced toward Lady Sarra who rode several paces away. Through the gnarl of white he barely made out her form.

Another burst of icy wind pummeled him as he guided his mount around a large boulder. He looked up. Naught but endless white filled his vision. They would have to find shelter.

"My lady?" Storm-fed winds whipped away his words. "Lady Sarra!"

Her cloaked form remained stiff in the saddle and she didna reply.

Tugging on the reins, he guided his horse toward his wayward charge. From the start, she'd made this trip a test of his endurance. Why had he thought she might do something sensible and answer him now?

Giric tugged on her cape, which was dusted with a thick layer of snow.

She turned the slightest degree, her face shielded from his gaze by her hood.

"We need to make camp," he yelled.

Trees rattled overhead.

Her horse veered as it neared an aged oak, its barren limbs like bony fingers arching toward the sky, and she rode farther away.

A whirl of snow shot down his neck. He clasped the hood tighter and glared at her through the curtain of white. Blast if she didna have the sense of a pignut!

He scanned his men and Lady Sarra's maid following in their

wake. Then, he scoured the landscape camouflaged in numerous shades of white, barely able to discern the familiar landmarks.

The snow had continued throughout the day. Within the last hour, the flurries had grown into big, fat, blinding flakes. From the darkening clouds, it looked as if the storm would continue throughout the night.

They needed to find shelter. Now.

He nudged his steed and caught up with Lady Sarra. Giric touched her shoulder, then pointed ahead where rocks jutted out in a misshapen gray jumble. "Ride there."

Her horse trudged through the growing drifts. In a jerky, almost drunken motion, she turned. Wind whipped away the hood of her cloak.

Crystals of ice clung to her hair and her brows. Frigid tendrils slapped against her face, but she stared at him, her eyes wide and confused. She made no move to protect herself.

"We need to make camp!" he ordered, praying for a reaction, even anger.

Her eyes remained empty.

Blast it. She hadna answered before because she was freezing and her mind hadna registered his shout. Giric snatched her reins, then lifted her from her mount and set her before him.

She didna resist.

He hadna expected her to.

Guilt swept him as he drew her within the warmth of his cape and pressed her snug against his chest.

Her frigid body remained still, nae even a shiver.

He'd vowed to ensure her safety. Though he'd inquired about her condition several times during the beginning of their journey, her continual cool replies had deterred him from approaching her after midday. The senseless chit. Instead of alerting him that she was freezing, she'd remained silent.

He drew her tighter, prayed his warmth would begin to thaw the coldness numbing her slender frame.

"Colyne!" Giric yelled.

Cantering over, his friend shielded his face against another blast of the churning flakes. His brow arched as he spotted Lady Sarra bundled within Giric's cape.

"The lass is half-froze." Giric pointed to the outcrop of rocks he'd noticed before and prayed his memory served him well. An error at this point could mean Lady Sarra's death, and if she died, he could never forgive himself. "There should be a cave up ahead. Pass word back to the men that we are headed there."

Colyne nodded and rode back to inform the small party.

Her body remained still as Giric urged his steed through the thigh-deep drifts. "'Twill be all right, lass." And prayed he spoke the truth.

With care, he guided his mount up the steep, icy slope. Wind lashed in violent eddies off the ledges, and a fine dusting of snow sifted around them as Giric halted his horse beneath a shelter of jagged rocks. Thankfully, the mouth of the cave opened before them.

The stumble of hooves upon rock and snow announced his men's arrival.

Giric noted the woman half-bent over her mount. "Colyne, bring Lady Sarra's maid inside and tend to her. No doubt she is freezing as well." After commands to his men to secure the horses, bring in the gear, and to build a fire, holding Sarra steady in the saddle, Giric dismounted.

Her head tilted back, but instead of the wariness in her eyes that normally greeted him, he stared into a lifeless void.

"You have the sense of an addled gull," he growled, but his censure spilled out in a worry-roughened whisper. He lifted her down.

A muffled whimper fell from her lips as she tumbled into his arms.

His throat tightened, and he drew her against his chest. "There you go, lass." Leaning against the wind, he slogged through the ice-peaked drifts toward the entry.

Inside, the rush of wind muted to a deep, ominous groan. Bursts of snow churned at his feet, and he halted. Once his eyes adjusted to the dim light, he carried her toward an inner alcove devoid of drafts, but a space close enough to the outer cavern so that once a fire was started, and with her frozen garb removed, it should keep her warm.

Another soft moan fell from her lips.

He glanced down at her murky outline. "You are going to be fine, lass."

Fate seemed to mock him, for only the faintest of breaths fell from her lips. And like a fallen fairy, her face usually so alive and alluring lay chalky white.

Neyll, a knight with whom he'd trained arms as a child, moved ahead of him and stepped into the small inlet. He spread out a thick woolen blanket and an extra cloak.

"My thanks," Giric said.

"I will help the other men." Sir Neyll departed.

On edge, Giric gently laid her on the makeshift bedding. Colyne moved past with her maid in his arms.

Giric gave him a nod. "My thanks." He knelt beside Sarra while another of his men assembled sticks nearby to start a fire.

Moments later, the rich tang of smoke filtered through the cavern, and golden flames illuminated the cave.

Thankful, Giric withdrew his gloves, then removed her woolen gown along with the layers of linen underdress beneath.

Throughout the painstaking process, she never moved.

And his worry grew. Once he'd stripped her down to her chemise, he pulled the wool blanket around her.

She remained still.

He glanced toward the fire. The meager flames would take too long to heat the cave and warm her. That left only one choice.

Body heat—his.

He stared at the pale pixie that frustrated him to the point of insanity. He cursed himself. She shouldna have been allowed to deteriorate to this state in the first place. Because of him, she could die.

Bedamned if she would!

In quick, rough jerks, he shed his clothes.

Naked except for his tunic and braies, Giric slid beneath the covers and drew her body against his. Nae even a shiver rewarded his touch. Blast it, her skin was like ice. She needed his total body heat.

On a groan, Giric pressed his forehead to hers, the dire situation doing little to douse his body's awareness of her. Leather packs slapped the earth of the cave as his men, carrying in their supplies, filtered to Giric, but he focused on Sarra.

"Lass, I am going to have to remove your chemise." Nae to mention his tunic and braies as well.

Her shallow breaths fell between them.

Giric glanced down and groaned. Her taut nipples pressed against the thin cotton as if beckoning his touch. He gritted his teeth and within seconds she lay naked in his arms, her chest pressed against his, her legs wrapped protectively by his own. He covered them both with an extra blanket.

Heat.

It seemed to surround them, engulf him like the flames of the fire arching toward the cavern roof. Her scent mingled with his, intimate, alluring, and seductive. He tried nae to think. But how in the blasted Hades could any man do that with a naked woman in his arms?

Especially her?

Sarra's eyes, which had remained glazed and unseeing, began to drift shut.

Nae! "Come on, lass." He ran his hands over her back, up her arms and over her shoulders, then began again. "Where is that fighter who flayed my hide on the turret steps?"

Her eyes fluttered open, then lazily drooped closed.

He shook her. "Stay awake!"

Sir Neyll entered the alcove and held out a cup of steaming broth.

"She is nae alert enough to drink yet," Giric said.

With a nod the Scot returned to the fire.

The next few hours passed in a haze. Giric coaxed, cajoled, and threatened Sarra into remaining awake. Then she shivered, just the tiniest motion, but to him 'twas as if the heavens had poured down their blessings.

On a moan, her lids lifted. Confusion darkened her eyes as she stared at him, but the faintest recognition sparked within.

His throat tightened with emotion as he continued to slide his hands over her skin, feeling the next shudder. Then, her body began to shiver in delightful, uncontrollable bursts.

Thank God!

On an exhale, Giric buried his face against her neck, tasting the warmth of her life. As she roused, with the swells of her breasts pressed against his chest and her slender body encased protectively by his, need slammed through him. *Bedamned!*

"Wa—Want to sleep." Another tremor ran through her, and she leaned closer, frowning when her face pressed against the hard warmth of his skin. Then, her eyelids began to sag.

"Lass," Giric urged, trying to ignore the tempting vision of her curled against him.

A frown creased her brow, and she shook her head.

"Sarra."

She closed her eyes. "So . . . tired," she whispered, her words thick.

"You need to stay awake, Sarra." He threaded his fingers through her golden hair, then down her back in a gentle caress.

She released a gentle breath, and a faint smile touched her face. She snuggled closer.

His body hardened. Giric studied the jagged rocks overhead, counted the indents in each, focused on anything but what this woman made him feel. "Nay, lass, you canna go back to sleep."

With a grimace, she pushed her hand feebly against his chest. Sarra's fingers curled within the thick mat of black hair, stilled. Her eyes flew open. The grogginess of hours cleared into stunned realization.

On a gasp, she tried to break free.

He held her still.

"I am naked!"

As if he needed a blasted reminder.

Sarra tried to push away, but after a moment, her struggles ceased and the expression on her face shifted from anger to an emotion he nae wanted to see.

Desire.

As quick, he saw the confusion. God help him. An innocent, she didna recognize her own yearnings. But blast it, he did. And a virgin was a far cry from the type of woman who normally graced his bed. Neither was it his intent to change that situation now. The last thing he needed was for her to want him. One of them going blasted insane was quite enough.

"'Tis good to see you awake and full of cheer," he growled.

Her eyes widened. "You are naked as well!"

"I am."

Her gaze shifted to where the men sat by the fire, then to him. "Where are we? What did we—"

The futility of this entire situation eroded the last of his practical calm. "We have done naught but seek shelter," he explained, his soft burr rich with irritation, but he let it fuel him refusing to dwell on the intimacy of this situation. "You almost froze to death."

She swallowed hard, then closed her eyes.

Saint's breath, what was wrong now? "Lady Sarra?"

"Please . . . do not." On a shuddered sigh she glanced toward where her hand was curled on his chest, her body cupped snugly against his and his leg slung over the top of her thigh. She unfurled her trembling hand and laid it against her side. "My thanks, Sir Knight, but now that I am awake, yo—you cannot stay. 'Tis highly improper."

"Highly improper?" He stared at her in disbelief. "My impropriety kept you from blasted freezing to death."

Another shiver wracked her body. "I am doing this badly."

Giric arched a brow. "Doing what badly?" He could only imagine her explanation.

She sighed and her eyes grew soft. "Thanking you for saving my life."

He swallowed hard, needing her coldness, nae an apology that would weaken his defenses. "My lady, you have done most things badly since we have met, but I will overlook this as well." Heat filled her cheeks at his rude retort, but 'twas better if she loathed him. Her disdain he could accept.

Sir Neyll walked over and halted, two steaming cups in his hands.

Giric silently thanked his friend for the interruption. The whole situation between him and Sarra was plummeting onto dangerous ground.

"I heard voices," Sir Neyll explained, "and thought Lady Sarra might be ready for some hot broth now."

Wide eyed, Sarra gasped and drew the blanket up to her chin to cover herself.

"Aye," Giric replied as he tried to ignore her maidenly reaction. The warmth of the savory broth filled the air as he sat up and accepted the steaming cups. He set his own mug on a stone ledge. "My thanks."

With a nod, his friend left.

Giric glanced toward where Colyne tended to Sarra's maid. "How does the lass fare?"

"A bit cold," Colyne replied, "but with a night's rest she will be fine."

"My thanks." Giric looked at Sarra.

Shivering, she glanced toward Colyne. Concern darkened her eyes as she turned back to Giric. "How is Alicia?"

"She fared better than you."

A blush spread over Sarra's cheeks, the rosy hue enticing against her creamy skin.

Frustrated that he noticed, Giric held the cup to her mouth. "Drink."

Her lower lip wavered, but the familiar spark of wariness flickered in her eyes. "I—I am tired. Can you not let me rest?"

"You are weak. The broth will warm you and give you strength. After you finish it, aye, then you can sleep. By the morrow you should be back to full health. Once you are through, I will have your maid sleep near you tonight. You need warmth. I will nae risk your falling ill because you are thick-headed."

Her eyes narrowed. "I am not—"

"You are." At ease with her indignation, he nudged the cup against her lips. "Now drink."

"I shall drink it," she said, her words as frosty as the snow hurling outside, "but only to quicken the time to be rid of you."

"A thought that pleases me as well." He wrapped his hand over her own, ensuring she drank slowly. Once she emptied the cup, he set it aside. "Your maid will be over shortly."

For a moment she watched him, her face displaying all too clearly her emotions for him to see. The distrust clung like moss to the banks of a river, but within the eddies of emotion, desire surfaced as well.

"Close your eyes and try to rest." Then he wouldna see her yearnings, but unfortunately, he would remember. 'Twas the penance he deserved for wanting what he had no business thinking about.

With one last measuring look, she turned her back to face him, leaving her round, firm bottom in clear sight.

He gritted his teeth and willed his body nae to respond, but her every breath pressed her tempting bottom closer. He'd have to be a saint nae to notice or react, and God knew he'd long since lost any chance of pursuing such a spiritual vocation.

He rolled from the covers, shoved to his feet, and tucked the blankets around her. Within moments, her breathing grew slow and steady. With a frustrated sigh, he headed over to speak with her maid.

The next morning, after checking on his wayward charge, Giric scrubbed his hand over his face as he halted before the crackling blaze. Steam swirled thick and pungent when Colyne lifted the pot of herbed tea from the fire. "How is Lady Sarra?"

"She will live."

Mirth twinkled in Colyne's eyes. "'Tis good to find your spirits are up about the fact."

With a grunt, Giric knelt and picked up a long stick. Coals glowed red as he stirred them. "How long do you think the storm will last?"

His friend glanced toward where the wind howled with a fierce snarl. "A day, two at most."

Giric blew out a rough breath. "My thoughts as well."

"January is nae the time to be traveling in the lowlands." Colyne nudged a stray limb into the fire.

"'Tis nae, but we were given little choice. Lord Bretane's missive was explicit." Giric watched the snow whip past the entrance, his spirits sinking. "If the storm continues, it shall take a fortnight if nae more to reach Dunkirk Castle."

"Patience, my friend. We will make it."

Giric tossed the stick onto the coals and watched the flames engulf the dry wood. He had the rest of his life to right the wrongs of his past. A day or sennight more would make little difference.

After pouring two cups of herbed tea, Colyne stood and made a mock toast. "Alicia is awake and from the looks of it, Lady Sarra as well. I am off to save the damsels in distress."

"Her maid is of softer temperament," Giric said.

On a chuckle, Colyne headed toward the women.

Giric glanced at Sarra, who as Colyne noted, was stirring within the covers. Thank God she was safe.

Pulling the wool blanket tight, Sarra sat up and met Sir Knight's assessing gaze. Wariness streaked through her.

He turned away.

The tall Scot with the whisky-colored hair approached. He knelt before her maid with a steaming mug of tea. "Ho, lass," he said with surprising gentleness. He held up the steaming brew. "I have brought you chamomile tea. 'Twill help you to relax."

"My thanks," Alicia said.

Sarra watched with interest, intrigued by the easy manner of Sir Knight's companion, and sensing this man kept no dark secrets locked beneath an angry countenance. Still, he was a Scot.

He helped her maid take several sips.

Alicia smiled. "I shall hold the cup now."

"You are sure, lass?"

"Yes."

The Scot handed her the mug then turned to Sarra. "I have a cup for you as well, my lady."

The easy assurance in his voice far from swayed her to warm to him. "Do you need me to hold it?"

She cleared her throat. "I shall be fine."

He handed her the steaming mug.

"My thanks."

The Scot glanced toward Alicia who was taking another sip. "Drink it slowly."

A light blush touched her maid's cheeks. "I will."

The humble knight nodded. "I shall be back in a wee bit and check on you both."

Though she far from approved of the Scot, his actions were kind and did not deserve rudeness. "I—we appreciate everything."

He gave a slight, smoothly executed bow as if practiced many times in court. "'Tis my pleasure, my lady. With the storm still blowing, it looks as though we shall be here another day or two. Take this time to rest." He headed toward the center of the chamber.

She watched him go, surprised at his fluent grace. Confused, she scanned the rough lot sitting around the fire.

"He is a fine man," Alicia said. "I am sure he has set many a lady's heart aflutter."

Sarra shrugged, more interested in the fact that a man so well bred ran with the ruffians a few feet away, or more specifically, Sir Knight.

As if beckoned, her protector looked toward her, grimaced, and then glanced at the Scot as he approached. Sir Knight shifted to allow his friend room to sit within the circle of men settled around the fire. The knight who'd just left, a man with apparent unending patience, sat next to the devil himself.

"Aye," Sarra whispered, "he could give lessons to Sir Knight in gentleness."

Alicia's brow raised with surprise. "Sir Knight's demands are driven by ambition, not aggression."

"Ambition?"

"You are a good judge of people, my lady. I find it odd that you have not noticed. Then, with you upset over your guardian's missive, that you misjudged their leader is not surprising." Alicia sipped the

30 30 · *Diana Cosby*

last of her tea then gave a soft yawn. "The herbs are doing their task. 'Twill be a blessing to reach Dunkirk Castle and be in from the cold."

Sarra nodded and covertly glanced toward where Arrogant, Dark, and Brooding sat near the flames, oddly disturbed to find that she missed Sir Knight's presence. The kind Scot gave Sir Knight a hearty pat on the back, said something she couldn't hear, then the humble knight joined in as the men broke into laughter, all aimed at Sir Knight.

When Sir Knight merely shook his head without his expected terse retort, she frowned. Had she misjudged him? Unsure of anything this moment, Sarra pulled the blanket tighter.

The faint scent of man and wool teased her. She stared at the coarse wrap—his. Even in this icy prison, she would find no peace. Though she longed to shove it aside, it would keep her warm . . . as had he.

Frustrated, Sarra closed her eyes, refusing to ponder Sir Knight's gentle attention to her needs. His actions were offered out of duty, little more.

Giric inhaled a deep, icy breath and savored the freedom as his steed cut through fresh banks of snow glistening white in the morning sun. The jostle of spurs, leather, and steel, echoed behind as his men rode in his wake.

This morning, they'd crossed the border into Scotland. He longed to ride to Wolfhaven Castle, but that time would soon come.

He looked at Sarra, who rode in silence to his right. The last two days trapped in the cave with the wary Englishwoman had done naught to aid his temper.

It wasna because of the extra mounts required to transport her wardrobe of finely woven goods he could ill afford, or that his men had unexpectedly taken a liking to her. Nay, surely what spurned his foul mood was his need to return to his home and begin the much needed restorations.

Thankfully, they were once again on their way.

Giric's breath misted before him as he scanned the clear blue sky that had hosted the fury of the storm. The taut muscles in his body slowly relaxed as he rode past pine branches that hung low, weighted with crystals of ice that tinkled in the morning sun and sprayed shards of colored light upon the lush, pine boughs like fairy dust.

Anxious to make up for the distance they'd lost, he kicked his mount forward. Snow flew from his steed's hooves as he half-rode, half-slid down a steep, ice-glazed embankment and into the shadows of the trees ahead. At the bottom, a shiver of unease stole over him. On edge, Giric slowed his mount to a walk and searched the surrounding woods.

A hart bounded from a thicket.

After the deer disappeared behind the hedge, his edginess remained. With a grimace, he maneuvered through the path of snow-covered oak, pine, and ash ahead. Without warning, the forest fell away to a narrow valley.

Jagged walls raced skyward. Formations of blue-gray ice clung like talons from roughly hewn rock.

The shudder of falling snow echoed into the quiet.

Giric glanced to the end of the valley, where a slide of loose snow raced down the steep slope. As the tumble of white built, a deep rumble echoed through the valley like thunder. The rolling wall of debris slammed onto the basin floor, sealing off their chosen route.

Saint's breath! Giric halted his mount and signaled his men to stop. They would have to find another way around, the detour costing them precious days.

A glint of light flashed near the top of the jagged peak.

Instincts on alert, Giric made a slow, methodical sweep of the rim, cursed. Numerous figures lay flat against the mounds of snow on the upper banks.

An ambush.

"Colyne," Giric called, keeping his voice soft.

His friend's horse snorted as he moved up by his side. "Aye?"

"The avalanche that slid to block our path was nay accident. There are men scattered on top of the rim all around us."

Colyne's eyes narrowed and he scanned the top. "A sword's wrath."

"Sir Knight," Lady Sarra whispered.

"Silence," he quietly ordered. Her intake of air bespoke her dissatisfaction; thankfully she remained silent.

He scanned the crag. Ripples of energy crawled up his spine. "Why havena the men nae moved? This waiting is nae the way of reivers."

Colyne shrugged. "Aye, 'tis odd."

"We are going to turn back. Mayhap this trap was set for another and they will allow us to leave." Giric prayed he was right. "Colyne, lead Lady Sarra and her maid out. Everyone else, follow—"

"Terrick!" A deep, rough burr echoed through the valley.

Relief slid through him. They knew him, knew his pockets held nay gold. Their mark was another. "Aye?"

"Leave the woman and we will let ye and the others go, unharmed," the man called.

The woman? What could they possibly want with Sarra? Blast it, how did they know she accompanied them or of their destination?

"Terrick," the voice boomed again. "Our business is nae with you. Send the lass down. Alone."

His eyes narrowed as he glanced toward Lady Sarra. "Why do they want you?"

Uncertainty flickered in her eyes and her face paled. "I do not know," she replied, but he heard it, saw it in every curve of her face—the fear, the wonder if he would give her to them.

His hand tightened on his sword. What did she think he was? Never mind. He didna want to know. He'd given his word to give her safe escort. Though his background was mired with misdeeds, once he gave his word, he would back it with his life. "I will nae hand you over, lass."

She searched his eyes, then a blush stained her cheeks. "No, you would not."

Her trust in him at this moment was nae his greatest concern. With but a handful of men, they were greatly outnumbered. For Sarra's safety, they needed to get out of here fast. "My lady, you and your maid are to turn your mounts and make your way back into the trees."

"What about you?"

He stared at her in disbelief. Of all times for her to show concern. "Do nae worry about me, this is what I am paid for."

She hesitated, then guided her horse toward the woods.

"Follow me!" Giric yelled to his men and kicked his mount into action.

Snow flew from his steed's hooves as he led them into the shadows of the forest. Through the batter of hooves, a bloodcurdling battle cry ripped through the valley. Like a nightmare, men exploded from the pristine setting above, closing fast.

Giric withdrew his broadsword. "To arms!" He turned his mount hard, caught up with Lady Sarra, and reached toward her. "Take my hand and pull yourself behind me."

She hesitated.

"Now!"

She caught his palm.

Giric hauled her behind him onto his mount. "Hang on."

The battle cries grew.

Shadows of men appeared through the stand of trees, their fierce cries echoing through the forest.

Branches slashed against his body, stung his face. Giric urged his horse faster.

"To your right," Colyne yelled from behind.

Giric swerved and barely missed a leather-clad man charging from a thicket.

Behind them, the first clash of steel echoed throughout the forest. Grunts melded with the impact of bodies.

A horse screamed.

Another burst of battle cries exploded behind them. More mail-clad warriors poured from the woods at his side.

Blast it! Giric rode to Colyne's side. "We are going to have to split up. Take her maid. I shall head north, then round back. We will meet at Archerbeck. If I am nae there when you arrive, head east to your brother's and wait. I will come."

Colyne nodded and rode toward Alicia.

"Sir Knight," Sarra yelled from behind him.

Giric shook his head. "Hold on and prepare for a hard impact!"

"What?"

Her surprised question was lost as he let the rush of the fight fill him. Releasing his own fierce battle cry, he raised his broadsword.

And kicked his steed into a full gallop, on a collision course toward the warrior charging straight toward them.

CHAPTER 4

Snow whipped Sarra's face as Sir Knight's horse surged forward. Was this how her life would end, clinging to a Scot she barely tolerated only to be cut down by another?

Six lengths from the attacker, Sir Knight yelled another battle cry.

Long red hair streamed out in his wake as the aggressor raised his blade, leaned forward in his saddle.

Five lengths.

She held her breath.

Four lengths.

The muscles of their horse bunched and surged forward. Sir Knight's body tensed beneath her hands.

Three lengths.

Oh, God.

Two lengths.

This was it! She braced for the collision.

A second before impact, Sir Knight swerved his mount hard to the left. Steel merged with a vicious scrape.

She screamed.

Sir Knight raised his sword. "Hold on!"

"I am trying!"

"Do better." Sir Knight wheeled his mount toward the west and kicked him into a gallop.

Icy air rushed down her throat as they rode, trees blurred past, and hooves thudded on snow like muted thunder. Heart pounding, she glanced back, watched as their attacker raised his bow.

Sarra turned. "Sir Knight—"

An arrow hissed past, then another.

"Saint's breath! Hang on!"

She looked back.

Several men rode alongside their pursuer and were bearing down on them while reloading their bows. The man leading the scraggly lot withdrew another arrow from his quiver.

"There are five men behind us," Sarra warned.

Sir Knight urged his mount faster. "I know how blasted many they are."

They raced toward the dense swath of forest, the yells and clash of battle fading in their wake.

Another arrow hissed past, too close for comfort. With her entire body shaking, Sarra leaned against Sir Knight. Why did their pursuers want her? What would happen if they caught them? Would they kill her? Would Sir Knight let them?

"Duck!" Sir Knight shouted.

She lowered her head. Thin branches whipped across her shoulders.

Brush crunched, and then Sir Knight's horse broke free. The depth of the snow deepened.

She shifted to look back.

"Blast it, keep your head down."

Another arrow whizzed past, jammed into an oak a hand's breadth away.

The horse stumbled, and then regained his footing.

A scream built in her throat. Please, let them escape!

His steed began climbing. Fir trees engulfed them, the rake of pine needles harsh against her body.

Seconds passed.

She glanced back.

Naught.

"The men have lost sight of us for the moment, but they willna give up," Sir Knight said. "With us sharing a horse, they know we canna keep this pace up for long."

"Wh-what do they want with me?"

He guided his steed beneath a rocky overhang. "I was hoping you could fill me in on that."

At the sarcasm in his voice, she glared at him. "You think I would deal with those men?"

"Would you nae?"

"I do not want to be traveling to Dunkirk Castle, much less riding with you!"

"Lass, a desperate woman will go to many lengths to procure freedom."

"Desperate, is it?"

He met her gaze square in the eye. "And would you be saying that you are wanting to be married?"

"I—" Blast him. That much was the truth.

They rode out of the shield of trees and into the sun. Sir Knight guided his steed around a rock. "Nae worry. I doubt you are foolish enough to hire anyone to aid in a plan to escape wedlock. Especially those men."

She wished he could understand her reasons for not wanting to wed. As if he would care? He'd made his position concerning her life more than clear. And for an unexplainable reason, that hurt.

Now who was being foolish? "I assure you, if I did not want to be married, I would not have to go to such extremes as to hire ruffians to procure my freedom."

"If you say so, lass."

"Terrick," came a shout from below, lost somewhere in the thick firs.

She gasped.

He urged his mount higher. "Do nae answer them."

As if she was a fool?

"The lass is to marry Lord Bretane's son who is a strong supporter of Balliol," the man yelled up. "Is that what you would be wanting?"

Sir Knight stiffened in the saddle, and her panic grew. What did her marriage have to do with the choice of Scotland's new king? Regardless, by Sir Knight's reaction, the subject had hit a nerve. Would he now hand her over to them? "Sir Knight, what does his claim mean to you?"

A desperate second passed.

"Give her over," the voice called from below, "and we will let you go."

A shiver ripped through her. "You are not going to—"

"I have given my word to protect you," Sir Knight growled.

But he didn't look back, and her doubts grew. Would his vow matter? With their pursuers a short distance behind them, how long before they were caught?

They reached the summit and the landscape below, blanketed in snow, spread out before them.

Sir Knight halted, looked toward where the men below were closing on them, then back to her. "We will have to go over the edge."

Was he totally insane? "We will die!"

Ice blue eyes narrowed. "If we stay here we will be dead. If we go over the cliff, we have a chance."

Flashes of the men on their mounts flickered through the breaks in the trees below.

He was right. Sarra said a quick prayer, nodded.

"Slide back on the horse's haunches. If my horse begins to look like he is going to roll, jump."

She stared at him in disbelief. "Jump? Just like that?"

A muscle worked in his jaw. "There is nay time to argue."

It seemed a fine time to speak her peace. Sarra opened her mouth.

Sir Knight kicked his horse. With a snort, his mount plunged down the steep slope.

Air, bitter and cold, battered her in a dizzying rush.

The horse whinnied as he landed hard on the embankment, but kept his footing as he half-slid, half-stumbled along the sharp incline.

A third of the way down, the roll of snow that'd accompanied them from their initial impact grew.

With a curse, Sir Knight pulled hard on the reins. "Saint's breath, I was afraid of this."

"Afraid of what?" she yelled as she clung to him.

"We have started an avalanche."

Terror swept her as she turned.

Within the building rumble, a churn of angry white was engulfing all within its path, including them.

The valley floor below grew dim.

"Whatever happens," he ordered as his horse started to slide, "do nae let go of me!"

The churn of snow snuffed out the light.

The horse screamed.

Then, a sense of falling.

Snow and icy clumps battered Sarra as she struggled to maintain her hold. "Sir Knight!" Something hard jabbed into her side, then her world went black.

*   *   *

"Sarra!" Giric reached for her, but the rush of snow threw him back. Lost to the blur of white, he started to roll, then his body slammed to a stop.

Stars shattered in his skull and every inch hurt. For a moment he lay there, gasping for breath, stunned that somehow he'd lived. With a groan he peeked out. Sunlight, warm and blinding, greeted him.

Sarra!

Pain slammed his head as Giric tried to sit up, but from the waist down, his body was trapped in snow. "Saint's breath!" Several feet away his horse struggled to dislodge himself from a mound of snow. After several unsuccessful tries, his steed broke free. With a snort, his mount shook his head.

Sarra! Breaths coming fast, Giric scanned the haphazard mounds of snow.

Naught.

Blast it, where was she? He furiously dug at the snow trapping his body. "A blasted mess," he grumbled, but couldna ignore the fear edging through him like a knife. If he didna find her soon, she could die.

If she wasna dead already.

Nay, she was too stubborn to die. The blasted woman would cheat death and then some. And at this moment, he prayed he was right.

As Giric threw out another handful of snow, a movement from above caught his attention. He shielded his eyes. Glints of steel from the cliff reflected in the sun.

Blast it, 'twas Léod. Nay doubt he was trying to decide on the safest descent. That Léod, a man he'd reived with in the past, had set up an ambush to capture Sarra when he knew who escorted her, assured Giric the Scot wouldna negotiate.

One man gestured his way, and Léod shook his head. After several more moments, the riders wheeled their mounts and rode out of sight.

Giric didna delude himself. By daring to descend from the cliff, he'd bought himself and Sarra a bit of time. Once the Scots retraced their steps, they would round the base of the craig to where he now lay. And before then, he must find Sarra and escape.

He braced his hands on the bank, and his body trembled. With a grunt, he shoved. Pain streaked up his arms, and then they gave out. He collapsed. Blast it! Giric lifted his hand toward his steed. "Here, lad."

His horse gave a soft nicker.

"Come here now."

With a twitch of his ears, his mount picked his way toward him through the uneven ground. A pace away, he lowered his muzzle.

"There you go, lad." Leaning forward, he caught the reins. Giric wrapped the leather straps around his hand. "Back!"

With a snort, his steed lifted his head and stepped away.

The reins grew taut.

Pain hammered him like the blow of a mace, but he held tight.

His body inched forward.

"Back," he urged, and prayed he could keep hold of the reins without passing out.

Snow groaned.

His body shifted. "Back, lad!"

With a nicker, his mount took another step back.

Hands trembling, he clung to the taut reins, then his body slipped free. Now, to find Sarra! He struggled to his feet. Sweat soaked his brow as he stepped forward. Pain shot through his body. Giric leaned over, sucked in one deep breath, then another.

His horse eyed him and gave a soft snort.

Giric shot him a cool look. "Nae a word from you. The lass is enough trouble." And had been from the start. Now look at them. Guilt swept him as he scanned the toppled mounds of snow. He wasna being fair. She had nae chosen this marriage, to travel in the middle of winter, nor to be shackled with him.

"Sarra?" His legs trembled as he forced himself to move.

A moan sounded from behind him.

Giric whirled.

Another soft groan came from near a large, jagged bank of snow.

Thank God she was alive! Giric stumbled forward, cursing every ache, celebrating every step. He rounded the tangled heap of white and found her lying on her back. Shaken, he dropped to his knees at her side and laid his hand against her cheek. "Sarra?"

Gray eyes flickered open, and she stared at him as if unsure. "Si—Sir Knight?"

Her whisper, roughed by pain, shot another surge of guilt through him. He'd done a poor job of protecting her. "Aye."

"We . . . We made it?"

He nodded, scanned the slope of the land, and tried to smother a shot of unexpected need and the complications such could bring. "Aye." They'd made it, but at what cost?

Her brow scrunched, and she closed her eyes.

"Sarra, can you get up?"

Her lids flickered open. "What?"

"The men chasing us are backtracking. They will be here posthaste." At the flash of fear in her eyes, Giric damned the pending danger when the lass had already suffered so much. What other choice did he have? None. And that's what irritated him most.

Sarra started to sit up.

He lay his hand on her shoulder. "Before you move, I need to check that naught is broken." He ran his hands down her legs trying nae to think how good they felt. Confident she'd suffered nay more than minor injuries, he sat back. "Naught feels broken, but you will be bruised and sore for a few days."

The doubts on her face of moments ago faded. "I—Thank you."

He extended his hand to her. "We must go."

"You are bleeding."

He glanced at his chest. A small half-frozen stream of blood lay caked down his left side. "I will care for it later. There is nae—"

"Your wound needs immediate attention." Her eyes narrowed as if daring him to contest her. "I am not a healer, but I am aware that a wound untended can fester and become life-threatening."

He stared at her in disbelief. Of all times for her to give a damn what happened to him, now was nae it. "We have already wasted too much time." He reached for her hand, but she pulled away.

"Your wound needs—"

"Naught that we have time for."

Sarra scowled. "I can get up myself." Though her legs trembled, she stood, careful to avoid his touch.

Her defiance stoked his ire. "You do nae need anyone, do you?"

She lifted her chin in that all-too-familiar stubborn tilt. "I will make it fine on my own." She brushed off the snow that had plastered itself to her body during her fall, all the while keeping a wary eye on him.

Giric gave a disbelieving grunt. Alone he doubted she'd make it an hour. When she opened her mouth to speak he raised his hand. "Save your flattery for later. We must go."

On a *humph,* she followed him with an unsteady but determined stride.

He tried to ignore her stubborn pride, but admiration won over. Her rebellious nature reminded him of his sister, Elizabet. Giric slid an irritated glance toward her.

Her eyes narrowed as he continued to watch her. "I am fine."

Let her wear her foolish pride, she would find it a lonely companion. As had he.

Disgusted with the reminder that at times he'd allowed his pride to guide him instead of common sense, he strode to his horse. At its side, he cupped his hands and gestured for her to mount.

After a wary glance, she accepted his offer.

"Wait here." Giric retrieved a broken branch then returned and began leading the horse toward the river.

"Are you not going to ride?" she asked, her voice hesitant.

"Nay." Ignoring the pain, he strode at a brisk pace as he scanned the landscape for any sign of the men.

"What about your wound?"

"'Tis fine."

"If you move too much it will start bleed—"

He shot her a cool glance. "If we do nae get out of here before the men arrive, we will both be dead."

She stiffened in the saddle, her eyes growing cold. "I only . . ." Sarra focused straight ahead.

At her silence, he dismissed the edge of concern in her voice. She only cared about him because her blasted hide was involved. Nae that he wanted her to care. As far as he was concerned, when the day came that they parted ways, it wouldna be soon enough.

Hooves thudded upon snow as Giric led his horse to the river frozen over. He halted before the thick ice, studied the water rush beneath. Confident it was thick enough to support them, he led his horse onto a snow-free patch and dropped the reins, then he started toward where they'd fallen.

"Sir Knight?"

At the fear in her voice he turned. "I will be back in a trice." He hurried to where their tracks began, then, using the bough, he backed toward Sarra, erasing their tracks to the river.

A sharp crack echoed as he stepped on the ice.

"Sir Knight!"

Giric tossed the bough onto the bank. "'Tis the river making new ice. As long as we remain near the edge, we should be safe." He picked up the reins and headed north. "We will stay on the clear patches as we will leave nay tracks."

With a frown she scanned where he'd wiped away their trail to the river. "Will it work?"

"Aye, I have used this tactic many times before."

Her face paled.

Blast it!

They walked in silence. The clack of hooves against the ice blended with the rush of water below. The ripple of wind increased.

Caught within the gust, blustery white clouds swirled about them and sent a fine spray of snow into his face and down his neck. Giric tugged his cape tighter and shielded his face.

The muted thrum of men and horses echoed a distance behind them.

Bedamned, he'd hoped to have more of a lead. "Come on, lad." Hurrying his step, he led them around the curve of the river before their pursuers came into sight.

Another gust swept through the surrounding trees and shook the branches. The thick pelt of snow covering a nearby fir broke loose and showered them.

With disgust he glanced at their tracks in the freshly fallen snow.

"Sir Knight?"

"Shhh. Your voice will carry in the wind."

Sarra leaned forward. "If I dismounted," she whispered, "I could trail behind us with a branch and erase our trail." As much as he didna want her endangering herself further, her suggestion held merit. Léod and his men would deduct that he and Sarra could have escaped by the river. Any tracks he and Sarra left, however carefully they traveled, would lead their pursuers to them that much quicker.

Giric halted his horse and helped her down. After finding her a pine bough, he picked up the reins and started ahead. "Be careful and do nae stray near the middle."

They made their way north following the curves of the fast-flowing river. Sarra worked with quiet efficiency covering their tracks. Every so often the distant sound of men calling to one another confirmed their pursuers were conducting a desperate search.

He scanned the stand of trees on both banks. They had to find a way to lose them. But how?

A sharp crack echoed under his feet.

Giric jumped, then called himself every kind of fool. 'Twas naught but new ice forming—except he caught sight of a crack slowly working its way along the ice beneath his feet.

He sighed with relief as the fracture stopped a short distance away. Though several inches of ice lay below them, he led his horse closer to shore. With their pursuers so close, he wouldna risk a mishap now.

At his next step, another crack quickly split on his left. Then another arced in a wide vein to his right. The ice below him dropped a degree. Saint's breath! "Sarra, get off the ice!"

Another crack.

His horse snorted, and hooves clattered on the ice.

Another sharp crack streaked below them like a battering ram.

Giric tugged the reins; his mount refused to move. "Come on!"

"Sir Knight."

He glanced over and found Sarra gingerly heading back toward him. Was she addled? "I told you to get off the ice. Do it!"

Though her face was pale, she kept her hand on the horse's hindquarters and carefully edged forward. "You need help."

Muttering a curse, he yanked on the reins to drag his horse closer to the bank. "Then give him a push on his arse." Her stunned expression almost caused him to laugh, but to her credit, she hesitated but a moment before heading toward the horse's posterior.

The ice below them began to slowly rise and fall. Another crack echoed ahead of them, and a gash opened up exposing rushing water between them and the shore.

"Hold," Giric yelled back.

Sarra peered around the horse's rear, terror in her eyes. "What are we going to do now?"

CHAPTER 5

The ice shuddered beneath Sarra's feet. "Sir Knight, the ice is giving!"

A small fissure cut beneath the horse's hooves and fractured in erratic streaks toward the swirling water near the bank.

With a curse, he moved to her side. "We will have to jump to shore."

She stared at him in disbelief. The gap between land and the ice had grown to an arm's length. "We will never make it!"

"Nae if we wait." He held out his hand.

The churning rush pulsed beneath her. Her doubts soared. "'Tis too wide."

Impatience snapped in his eyes. "Take my hand!"

On an unsteady breath, she edged forward. A strong gust battered the ice. The surface gave beneath her next step, and she slipped.

Sir Knight caught her and hauled her against him. "Steady, lass."

Sarra clung, afraid, cold, but mostly bewildered that from this near tragedy she found not only strength, but comfort in Sir Knight's arms.

"Move toward the opening. When I tell you to, run and jump to the shore."

"What about you?"

Warmth flickered in his eyes. As if a trick of light it vanished. "This is nae a debate. Go on."

With a nervous nod, she edged toward the opening. On her next step, the ice below her fluctuated. She lost her footing. Off balance, she plopped on her bottom.

"Is that the blasted best you can do?" Sir Knight grumbled as he hauled her up.

She pushed him away, her pride hurt more than her posterior. "I am—"

The crack of breaking ice had her glancing shoreward. The gap in the ice now extended more than a body's length. Water rushed through the opening and slammed against the ice, widening the fissure along the bank. The sheet they stood on remained connected to the opposite bank.

He glanced toward the open water. "Blast it!"

Panicking, she caught Giric's cape, her mind already spinning back to the attack of her youth.

The screams.

Their wagon rocking precariously.

Then, how it had overturned. Icy water had seeped into the crevices, and then it had begun to pour through the windows and fill the luxurious interior.

Her father's calming words had surrounded her while he had struggled to free himself—then the screams of the attack had begun.

"Sarra!"

She fought against the hands that held her, for a moment a victim of her youthful terror.

"Sarra, look at me."

Sir Knight's voice dragged her back from her nightmare. The screams and images faded, but the anguish remained. She dug her nails into his cape. "We are going to die! Damn you. Why did I trust you!"

He caught her shoulders and gave her a hard shake. "Stop it."

Panic threatened to overflow. How ironic. A Scot like those who had murdered her parents now offered her hope. Hope? No, he would never offer her that. She fought his hold. "Leave me alone."

His grip held firm. "You canna fall apart now." His eyes narrowed. "I never figured you for a coward."

Her spine stiffened.

He pushed her toward the bank. "Move or I will leave your blasted arse behind."

The braggart! "You would like that, would you not? To be rid of me?" Who did he think he was? When he . . . Then she saw it, that hint of worry his anger couldn't hide.

He'd goaded her on purpose.

When she'd lost control, instead of helping him, she'd become a burden. And they both needed their wits if they were to survive. The anger of moments before shifted to guilt. By the rood, she'd almost cost them both their lives! "I am—"

"Later." He gestured to the opposite bank. "We are going to have to cross to the other side."

"But earlier you said—"

"I know what I said, but with the ice breaking up along the eastern bank, there is nay other choice."

Numb, terrified, but determined to live, she nodded.

His eyes held hers. "Are you ready?"

"Yes."

Sir Knight caught her hand. "If I tell you to run, go."

"I will." Sarra glanced at the horse who followed without issue. Mayhap the beast had known all along the ice was unsafe, which was why he'd refused to move.

With cautious steps, the Scot made his way across the remaining swath of ice with her on his heels, the clop of hooves steady in their wake. Fat drops of cold rain thick with sleet began to fall as they walked. The rush of water beneath them increased to a dull roar.

When they neared the middle of the river, Sir Knight slowed. "Keep an arm's length from me. We need to distribute our weight as much as possible."

She nodded, macabrely drawn to look down, transfixed by the seething current beneath the clear, frozen shield splattered by ice-laden rain. Sarra took in the distance to the opposite shore. This was ludicrous. Mayhap they should have tried to jump to the bank instead of chancing this crossing?

Sir Knight loosened his mount's reins, then walked at an angle to the bank.

A mix of wind and rain slashed her face. She willed away the fear threatening to erode her momentary calm, and began to walk.

A short distance ahead, an outcrop of rocks jutted through the ice. Thank God. Moments later they straddled the slippery mounds of rock near the shore while the horse followed.

A rumble echoed in their wake, then a loud bang.

She turned.

The remaining ice on the eastern bank gave way.

The sheet below them began to waver.

Sir Knight jerked her forward. "The ice is going. Run!"

Heart pounding, Sarra stumbled forward as the ice shifted below her feet. Fear rose into hysteria as she slipped. Sir Knight steadied her; she ran.

The horse whinnied behind them as his hooves hit the blanket of ice with an erratic clatter.

Ahead, the water-slicked ice near the shore cracked. Wind drove the shattered slabs together. They merged with a brittle crash, surged upward.

"Jump," Giric yelled.

With her muscles screaming, she started to push off, but her right foot began to sink into the collapsing sheet. "Help!"

Sir Knight hauled her onto firmer footing.

"My—"

"Go!" he ordered with a shove.

They both jumped.

She landed hard on top of Sir Knight, and her breath left her in a rush. But they'd made it to shore.

The horse stumbled up the snow-covered bank, halted by their side, and shook. Water puddled at his hooves while the river balked before them like an angry god.

A thunderous crack split the air. The scrape of splintering ice echoed as the river churned in a violent rush. White slabs collided. The frozen surface where they'd stood moments ago groaned, heaved, then collapsed into the raging torrent beneath.

"Saint's breath!" Sir Knight caught her face in his hands, and she forgot to breathe. The wildness in his eyes slid into worry. "Are you all right, lass?"

Whatever she was about to say, to think, fled. The intensity of how he watched her, the way he truly seemed to care, made her tremble. Not from fear. No, the heat stroking her body had little to do with fright.

"Lass?"

Stunned, Sarra stared at him. She desired him.

She wanted a Scot.

Trembling, she tried to roll free, but he held tight and the concern in his expression grew. "Let go of me," she whispered, the shame of her realization far from what he could ever understand, or what she would ever want him to.

"We need to be going. The men will be coming up the opposite bank." But he didn't move, watched her, his eyes growing dark, luring her to feel what she shouldn't.

A man's shout echoed from across the river.

Sarra gasped.

"Blast it!" Sir Knight shoved to his feet, then helped her stand. "Follow me." With a tug on the reins, he led his horse up the embankment and hurried toward a thick clutter of tall brambles that sheltered the base of an aged oak.

Sarra ran to keep up, the warmth he'd made her feel still hot and alive.

The yells of the other men grew.

Cold rain slashed across her face as she hurried, then the icy drops changed to pure sleet. She pushed through the thick branches, then scoured the river while ice pellets tinkled upon the ground like frozen tears.

Sir Knight knelt, pulled his mount's head down. "Let us pray they didna see us."

Flickering figures came into view on the opposite bank, and then faded in the growing haze of white.

"At least they are on the opposite bank," she whispered.

"Aye." He gestured upstream. "But the land narrows less than a league north of here, where a footbridge lies. If they suspect that we have crossed the river, they could catch up to us within hours."

Her relief deflated. They weren't safe at all. They'd bought a half a day at best.

A burly man wearing a thick cape, a fur hat, and sturdy leather boots with a scraggly black beard came into view. "I do nae see any tracks!"

Two more men walked into view. Several seconds later six others joined them. The band milled around the edge.

"Blasted cold," a smaller man grumbled. "We have nae seen a track since we left the base of the knoll."

The stocky man grumbled then spat on the ground. "I say we are on a fool's mission to follow the river north. Terrick would have gone south."

"That is nae for you to decide," the man with the scraggly beard said, his voice hard. "We will nae be turning back until we are sure that they have nae come this way."

"Aye," the stocky man replied, displeasure echoing in his voice.

The man with the beard kicked at a slab of ice with a grimace. "Terrick's nae earned his reputation for his stupidity. A sly one he is."

A red-haired man knelt beside the bank with a nod. He looked across the river straight toward the brambles where they hid.

Sarra held her breath.

Sir Knight looked over. "He does nae see us."

Heat crept up her cheeks from being read with such ease. Of course they couldn't. "I—I know."

"They will move on," Sir Knight said, turning toward the men.

She studied their pursuers, wishing she were as convinced. Though the river separated them, with the footbridge a short distance ahead, they were far from safe.

Wind blustered through the trees. The patter of sleet increased, the hard flakes slowing as they began to shift to snow. At least if they'd left any tracks since they'd reached this side of the shore, they would now be covered.

As if a prayer had been answered, the burly man with a scraggly black beard, who she'd deduced to be the leader, waved his motley group forward. Only when the ruffians rounded the curve and moved out of sight did she release a trembling breath.

Sir Knight released his hold on his mount. The horse lifted his head, and his ears flicked toward the direction of the departing men.

With the imminent threat gone, the man's use of Sir Knight's name bothered her. She turned. "Terrick."

His gaze grew wary.

Unease swept her, and she prayed that she was wrong. "You know them."

His eyes narrowed. Snowflakes battered them. Wind snarled around them like a curse. Ice blue eyes leveled on her. "Aye."

She didn't want to ask why he would be familiar with such a seedy lot. His assignment was to protect her. But for her own sanity, she needed to know. "How?"

His gaze deepened to a ferocious black, and the man she'd come to know over the past few days was lost to this intimidating stranger; a man she believed could kill without hesitation.

Her eyes widened with terror, and Lady Sarra started to scramble back.

Blast it! Giric caught her arm. "The men are my problem." He didna owe her a blasted explanation about his association with their pursuers, but her distrust of him made him want to explain.

What would he tell her? That he'd ridden on many a raid with the same men who now chased them? Had shared countless gains from their reiving? And when cornered, had killed in self-defense? Aye, he'd win the lass's complete trust with that admission, nae that he ever had any chance of earning it in the first place.

He released her, and she quickly moved away.

Regret fisted in his gut. Since the first night they'd spent in the cave, she'd begun to trust him. Until now, he hadna realized how much her belief in him mattered. Though an earl, and regardless that he'd vowed never to reive again, in her eyes he would never be a man she could turn to with complete faith, one whom she could look upon as a friend, or if a miracle happened to change her opinion of him, more.

With a curse he stood. To the devil with her. His people and their respect were all that mattered. Disgusted with the entire situation, he waved her forward. "Come."

She stared at him as if unsure.

"We must be long gone before the men search this side of the bank." She jumped at his harsh tone, but it was for the best if he kept her at a distance. A woman like her would bring a man naught but trouble.

After they mounted, he headed his mount northwest. As they rode, the temperature continued to drop and the thick flakes of snow erased their tracks. Weariness flooded him, but he pressed on, determined to find a safe place to hide and, however temporary, warmth.

The incline grew steeper.

Sarra coughed, a low wracking sound as if pulled from her chest.

Blast it. She'd barely recovered from near freezing. Between the avalanche, their haphazard crossing of the river, and now forced travel in this foul weather, she would be exhausted. They had to find shelter and soon.

She coughed again, the wracking sound ending on a quiet moan.

He leaned forward, took in her pale and withdrawn features, and his gut clenched.

"I . . . I am fine," she said before he had a chance to speak. She looked away.

The blasted stubborn woman. She would die before admitting her condition was growing worse. As if he was nae as stubborn? "The sun will be setting soon. We must find shelter before then."

Sarra lifted her eyes to his, and her cool gaze assured him that she had her doubts of finding anything warm, much less shelter this night.

"I know of a place." The men trailing them knew it as well, but he hoped they wouldna believe he'd head toward the deserted, broken-down hut. Or, with the weather deteriorating, if their pursuers ever did travel there, that he and Sarra would be long gone.

Suspicion darkened her eyes.

With a mumbled oath, Giric kicked his mount forward, tempted to add that the hut was a meeting place for a den of thieves. He grimaced. The description came closer to the truth than he'd like to admit.

The scent of pine, snow, and cold filled Giric's each breath as they crossed the next ridge. He pushed aside a thick fir bow, then guided his horse east. Through the snowstorm, the outline of a crofter's hut came into view.

The thatched roof sank sadly inward and several gaping holes exposed pieces of the dimly lit interior. A pile of wood half-covered in snow lay scattered on the left, and the collapsed, charred foundation of another wattle-and-daub hovel stood to the right. His memories of the sturdy cottages gave way to dismal reality.

"Sir Knight."

"Aye."

"There is a—"

"I know what is up ahead." As soon as he'd spat the words, he could have kicked himself. She didna deserve his poor temper. They would have to make do. "I didna mean to sound harsh. We are both tired."

Silence.

Blast it! He halted his mount, dismounted, and then helped her into their broken-down-yet-temporary lodgings. "We should be safe here." For a while. Léod and his men would come; the question was nae if, but when. Frustrated, he headed outside.

Sarra's breath puffed out in a cloud of white as the door slammed shut. How long would Sir Knight remain outside? Chills running through her, she rubbed her hands over her arms. Within the meager light, she made a slow circle of what the Scot had deemed a safe retreat.

A fine sheen of snow sifted through the cracks in the timber posts and the missing thatch in several places in the roof, and doubts lingered about the safety of this hovel.

An old but usable hearth sat centered in the single room. Shards of pottery lay scattered around the earthen floor. A broken bench sat in a heap in the corner nearest to the door, and a battered cauldron was tipped on its side beside the fireplace. In the far corner stood a well-worn bed filled with brownish straw. All smeared with a fine dusting of snow.

Another gust of wind pummeled the aged hut and whistled through the holes.

She shivered.

The door scraped open.

Sir Knight stepped inside carrying a load of wood, then shoved the door closed. "Colder than a . . ." He stomped the snow from his boots, then dropped the wood onto the floor with an unnerving clatter. "The horse is secure. Now I will start a fire."

A fire? Was he mad? They had just ridden for more than half a day over this godforsaken terrain and narrowly, only narrowly escaped the Scots who were determined to kill them. *Her,* she corrected. And now her glorious protector was going to build a fire? Why didn't he go outside and shout their location?

At this moment, any doubts of Lord Bretane's ability for rational thought were erased. Before her stood proof.

Her guardian had hired an idiot.

"The men will be able to see the smoke," Sarra said, unable to keep the temper from her voice.

The Scot shrugged, knelt, and then began to stack the wood in the hearth. "They are a ways off."

His unconcerned reply coated in a soft burr riled her further. When he pulled out his flint and used his dagger to scrape sparks into the small stack of dry timber, her control snapped.

Sarra stormed over and kicked the stack of tinder. Sticks clattered and shavings billowed up to glide back to the floor in a drunken heap.

Red slashing his cheeks, Sir Knight jumped to his feet. "Blast it, you have been naught but a pain in the arse from the start! Why had I deluded myself into thinking that at some moment during our journey that you would be of any help?"

Stunned by his ferocity, she started to take a step back, but indignation forced her to hold her ground. "The men will see the smoke."

He took a predatory step toward her. "If you have nae noticed," he drawled with uncensored sarcasm, "there is a blizzard raging outside. If the men are still attempting to find our tracks, I doubt if they can see a stone's throw before them, much less a wisp of smoke. That is if I can even get this blasted fire started!"

"Oh." She glanced through the holes to outside where the white haze of snow and wind obscured her vision, the same storm they'd traveled through for the past few hours. He was right, but couldn't he see that she was scared out of her wits? It wasn't as if being chased by a band of ruffians with intent to kill her was an everyday event.

His eyes narrowed. "Here I am carting around a high and mighty heiress. I should have expected that you would be dim-witted as a gnat in such dealings. A lad could have divined a fire was nae a threat!"

The apology brewing in her mind shattered. If he'd wanted to insult her, he'd hit her mark. She was many things, but dim-witted was far from one of them. "I was trying to be cautious."

"Cautious, is it?"

Scared, all right, she was terrified they'd be caught. But to the devil with him knowing that! She jammed her hands on her hips. "One of us needs to be on guard."

Sir Knight quirked his brow in a stormy tilt. "Is that so?"

Aware she'd stepped onto dangerous ground, she also realized that for whatever reasons, he insisted on pushing her to this point. A diversion he seemed to enjoy. By the rood, she was tired of his overbearing attitude. He wasn't a member of the gentry who could command her actions, and she wasn't a mindless maiden who would obey his every dictate or swoon at his feet.

"Aye," she replied. " 'Tis so."

He stepped closer. "And when it comes to being prudent, you have been a saint, exercising good judgment at every turn, have you nae?"

She angled her chin. "I have."

He gave a doubtful grunt. "You are nae worth the gold I am being paid. When you were freezing to death you did nae have the common sense to inform me."

"I—"

"And you found it essential to travel with three extra horses just to carry your goods?"

"They were necessary. How else—"

"Necessary?" He gave a rough laugh. "Nay, lass. A horse is necessary. A dagger is necessary. But when you haul trunks of extravagant garments and foolish trinkets across the lowlands in the middle of the winter, which will inevitably slow travel and possibly endanger our party, you are asking for problems."

Guilt surged through her. She hadn't known that the extra clothes would be an issue, neither had he mentioned it. Until now. And she hadn't packed frivolously. She'd only taken essential items. As if he would believe her? Sir Knight saw only what he wanted, and it wasn't her.

The night at Rancourt Castle when he'd pinned her against the tower wall and almost kissed her flashed to mind, and the excitement of that moment whipped through her. Stunned at the vivid memory, shamed by the unwanted thought, she went on the offensive. "If you had informed me the extra horses were going to be a burden, I would have—"

"What? Left them behind?" He shot her a cynical look. "If you would have bestowed upon me but a moment of your precious time instead of making me wait for several days, we would nae be discussing this issue now. But you did nae. Rest assured, you made your position clear about nae making time to discuss your plans, much less anything else, with me."

She'd been upset at her guardian's writ to marry his son, forced to leave a home she'd struggled to maintain and the people she loved, unsure if she'd ever return. And she'd been stunned by her attraction toward him, though she would never admit that. "You overbearing clout. If you had but acted like a gentleman instead of a heathen whose eye is on the gold he's to receive for this task, any issues would have long since been settled!"

Ice blue eyes plummeted to an inky black. The mood within the hovel shuddered with something dangerous. "And you would nae know a real man if he hauled you against him and kissed you senseless."

Her body's immediate reaction to that thought infuriated her further. "You would not!" she stated, cursing her temper at the same time. This wasn't good, and one of them needed to stop and latch onto common sense, but it seemed that right now it wasn't her.

Without warning he hauled her against him, their bodies snug, his face inches from hers. Sir Knight caught her chin in a soft but firm hold. His eyes sparked with dangerous delight. "Dare me now."

CHAPTER 6

Wind howled and slammed against the hovel's sturdy frame like the temper Giric fought to keep in check as he held Sarra's chin and waited for her response. He called himself every kind of a fool. Enough lay between them without adding to this lunacy.

Now, with her gray eyes fixed on his and shimmering with innocent yearning, he wanted her more.

She pressed her hands against his chest. "You dare not kiss me." Her reply fell out in a soft whisper, etched with need.

As much as he fought to deny it, he struggled to contain that same wanting—a desire that transcended common sense. And her soft plea, though she would never call it that, severed his good intent to walk away.

With a curse he lowered his mouth.

Sarra gasped as he brushed his lips over hers, and she stilled in his arms, but he worked her, drawing, teasing, luring her into the kiss.

A moment passed, then she relaxed against him and began kissing him back.

Lost to the intensity of her passion, he surrendered to her taste, to the heat of it. Wind whistled around them, the blizzard raged outside, but at this moment, with her body pressed tight, his thoughts were filled with her.

Her hands slid around his neck to pull him closer. Then her kiss changed, became demanding, almost frantic in its possession.

He'd had women before, was known for his ability to bring them pleasure as well. But naught in his life had prepared him for the desire knifing through him with a fine-edged precision.

Saint's breath!

He pulled free, his breathing unsteady, and his body trembling with the urge to take her.

"Sir Knight?" Her question fell out in a slumbered daze, her eyes hazed from passion, and her lips swollen from his kisses that invited him back.

"Giric," he rasped, already missing the warmth, the rightness of her mouth on his. "Call me by my given name."

"Giric." She worked his name over her lips, her sultry English accent making it sound as if a wish. And for a moment he'd become caught up in that dream. Saint's breath, what was he doing? He released her and stepped back.

The passion in her expression dissolved into stunned disbelief. Eyes wide, she swiped her hand across her lips.

At her overt rejection, as if what they'd shared was something foul to be cast into a cesspit, his ire ignited. Tempted to kiss her until she admitted that she'd wanted him as much as he wanted her, he didn't move. Even if she conceded, what would her confession serve? She would never accept him in her life.

As if that was even a choice? He'd been hired to deliver the lass to her betrothed, nae seduce her. What did it matter how she felt toward him? The kiss had been a mistake, an error he would nae allow again.

"I will make a fire," Giric said, the edge to his voice betraying his outward calm. He strode to the scattered mound of wood and shavings near the hearth and knelt.

Soft steps came up behind him. "Sir Knight, I—"

"Giric," he said without looking back. Though he may never have her, like it or nae, if she wanted to talk with him, she would use his name. At least he would have that.

She released a soft sigh. "Giric, let me help."

His heart pounding, he took a deep breath, turned. At the turmoil on her face, he wanted to draw her into his arms. Instead, he shot her a foreboding expression that hopefully would keep her at a distance. At this moment, with her taste still fresh in his mind, he wasna taking any chances.

Sarra squared her shoulders. "I kicked the wood over." Her cheeks pinkened with a light blush. "I acted foolishly." She knelt by his side and began to pick up the scattered kindling.

Saint's breath. The last thing he wanted was her understanding.

Disturbed by her humbleness and unsure how to deal with this confusing woman, he remained silent and applied himself to his task.

Once they'd restacked the kindling, he scraped his knife against the flint to send a shower of sparks into the tinder. After several tries, a puff of smoke spurted up. He gently blew into the shavings until flames flickered to life, then he added larger pieces of wood, enough to last a few hours. He rocked back on his heels as the fire continued to build. Though meager, blessed warmth began to invade his body.

Her face illuminated within the cast of firelight, she glanced over. Though her expression remained cautious, from her silence, he sensed her need to explain.

Why do you nae just batter yourself with a mace, Terrick. 'Twould be a blasted quicker way to end your misery of wanting her. He stood, needing to put distance between them. "I will be back."

Eyes unsure, Sarra stood with awkward hesitancy. "Where are you going?"

"I need to check on my horse before we can settle in for the night." He walked to the pack he'd carried into the hut. "There are oatcakes inside and a pouch of wine. I know you are hungry, eat." He strode outside, thankful for the blast of cold air as he stepped into the fury of the storm.

Unsettled by her actions, Sarra stared at the door as it closed. She wrapped her arms around her waist, startled to find her cape hard with ice. By the rood. So caught up in their confrontation, she'd forgotten about the cold she'd battled over the past few hours.

She rubbed her hands before the flames, thankful for their warmth. What had she been thinking? Never had she permitted anyone to touch her in such a bold manner. Not that she'd granted him the right. The arrogant Scot. 'Twas a wonder her guardian had hired the man.

Her guardian. This entire mess was his fault. If not for his decree to travel to Scotland in the middle of winter to wed, she wouldn't be stranded in this pathetic shack, in the middle of this godforsaken country, with a Scottish knight of questionable morals who'd likened her to a gnat.

A gnat!

Disgusted, Sarra tossed a twig into the fire. Greedy flames engulfed it then spurted out a belch of heat. She picked up another sturdy branch. The oaf. As if Sir Knight—Giric, she corrected—was her better. How dare he cast aspersions on her person?

Although she had provoked him.

And, he was right. Since they were attacked he'd acted honorably, risking his life for her many times over. And the truth be told, her earlier angry words were hurled not because she detested him, but because of her budding desire for this worthy knight.

Shaken, she dropped the branch and it landed on the floor with a soft scrape. A pounding began in her head, and she rubbed her temples. Somewhere in between her fatigue and disgruntled state, she grudgingly accepted that her attraction toward Giric had begun from the start. Perhaps 'twas why she'd avoided him, treated him in the unfair manner he'd claimed.

Giric. An unusual but strong name. Fitting for a Scottish warrior.

The old hurt, the pain of her parents' murder, and the cause—reivers—ripped through her soul. By the rood, how could she, in any manner, be drawn to a Scot? At least he wasn't a reiver. Then her mortification would have been complete.

A bang sounded on the side of the building.

She whirled.

Sticks and straw filled a hole that moments ago had allowed gusts of snow inside.

Guilt swept her at his unselfish actions. He'd left her inside to eat and rest, even after she'd treated him so poorly.

When had she grown so bitter? Is that what he saw when he looked at her, a cold, heartless woman?

The people of Rancourt Castle respected her. But she couldn't profess the heartwarming connection with her people that she'd witnessed between Giric and Colyne and his men when they'd stayed within the cave.

What was it about him that commanded respect, drew her to him, or made her aware of her coldness like no one else ever had? Regardless, when he returned, she owed him an apology. She'd attacked him unfairly. The men who pursued them weren't his fault. She paused. Exactly how did he know them? From the way he avoided her questions, he was hiding something, but what?

She frowned.

As Giric continued to plug the gaps within the hovel, Sarra looked around the shabby abode. She couldn't just wait here, she would go insane. After digging a pathetic, half-broken stem of a broom from near the hearth, she set herself into action.

With each hour that passed her guilt increased. Though chilly, she had a fire to keep warm and the sturdy wall to protect her from the howling force outside, while Giric endured the storm's brutality as he methodically filled every hole in the cabin wall and roof.

She fed more wood to the fire and dug out the oatcakes and wine he'd mentioned earlier, but she didn't eat. Once he'd returned, they would share the food. And for a reason she would rather not ponder further, she needed to prove to him that she was more than the cold-hearted woman he believed her to be.

The icy, snow-laden wind whipped Giric's face as he shoved a gob of straw and wood into the last hole in the roof. "That ought to hold you, you meddling tumble of wood." He climbed to the ground and surveyed his work, pleased considering the situation.

After checking several snares he'd set earlier, he checked on his mount before heading inside. His steed nickered when he entered the stall.

"Aye, 'tis a cold one, but I will be promising you oats when we return home." Although the gold he'd bring wasna earned in a fashion he'd brag about, it would allow him to begin repairs on Wolfhaven Castle. Wheat and oats could be purchased to sow in their now-barren fields, swords and other weaponry for defense, and he could help those within his clan who scraped for each pence. Then he would have taken his first step in becoming a man whom he could respect.

His thick-coated bay nudged his shoulder.

"I will see you in the morning, lad." He patted his withers. With a heavy sigh he started toward the hovel. Before he began to make plans for his future, he had to deal with the present.

Though subdued upon his departure, his absence had given Sarra ample time to convince herself of a myriad of despicable things about his character.

Prepared for the worst, he opened the door and hurried inside. As the door clicked shut, he stared in stunned disbelief. Flames roared in the hearth, and she'd cleaned the interior, or at least had straightened it a bit. Nae that much could be done with the decrepit state, but she'd tried.

Her eyes unsure, she glanced toward him from her seat near the hearth.

"You have done a fine job," he said, nodding toward the chamber. The soft flush of pleasure at his praise lured him.

"There was so much time and . . ." She stood and cleared her throat. "About earlier. I was rude, and I am sorry."

Of all of the things he'd expected, an apology was nae one of them. He eyed her, his defenses on alert. What did the lass expect from him now? And why did she have to keep looking at him that way, a cross between an innocent and a woman struggling to hold her own—a woman he could admire.

"'Tis forgotten," he replied, his response rougher than he'd intended.

"I . . . Thank you."

Giric shrugged. "I caught a rabbit." He withdrew it from his cape and struggled to guide his mind to safer ground. But the golden flames of the fire outlined Sarra in her wool gown and made his blood heat. "It will make a nice stew and help the food in my pack last us longer. Here. I will ready the pot while you skin it."

A blush slipped up her cheeks, and she dropped her gaze.

He set the hare on the wooden bench. "What is wrong now, lass?" Then it hit him. Given her station and the enormity of her wealth, he doubted she'd ever butchered meat for her table. "Never mind. You clean the kettle, fill it with snow, and then hang it over the fire to melt. I will skin the rabbit. After, you can use part of it to make a stew."

She lifted her eyes to his, but didn't move. Sarra watched him as if his opinion of her, this realization of her inadequacy, would matter to him. Saint's breath. He'd been out in the cold too long if he believed that.

Seconds passed, but she remained silent.

"Lass, if you would be telling me what the problem is, I would know how to help you."

The tender pinkish hue on her face darkened. "I do not know how to cook either."

"Then I will be taking care of the task as well."

She eyed him as if unsure of his offer.

He shrugged.

"'Tis nae a grand gesture."

Sarra interlaced her hands. "But I wish to help. You have done so much while I have waited inside, warm."

Warm he doubted, but aye, certainly more comfortable. As she watched him, realization dawned that her embarrassment truly came from her inability to assist in this simple task. Though raised with a golden spoon in her mouth, and the fact that she'd never learned the actual work involved behind the basic chores of cooking or most essential household tasks, her pride was wounded by her inability to help.

Sympathy for her filled him. Blast it! He didna want to begin to care for her. This softening could only lead to disaster. Had their kiss nae already proved that?

Their kiss. Saint's breath. He didna need to think of that with night falling around them, a blizzard raging outside, and him confined inside this hovel with nowhere to escape. Definitely nae a sane avenue to consider when the next few hours, perhaps days, they would spend together—alone. So he wouldna. He'd keep himself too busy to notice.

Sarra stood and firelight illuminated her slender frame, drawing his attention to her trim body that he'd embraced hours before.

Sweat beaded his brow. He grabbed the rabbit and stepped out into the cold. Somehow he would have to make it through the night without letting his thoughts drift to her. He muttered a harsh curse. As if he had a blasted chance of doing that?

CHAPTER 7

Dressed in her camisole, Sarra tugged the blanket closer. Until her gown hanging near the hearth dried, she should be warm enough. She stole a sidelong glance toward Giric who'd become unnervingly quiet since he'd returned from dressing the rabbit. He'd stripped as well, and now wore trews and a fresh linen shirt from his pack, the meager garb offering a tantalizing display of his muscled body.

Warmth slid through her at thoughts of a warrior like him. A man of fierce values who would fight to keep what was his. What would it be like if he wanted her?

Shamed by her illicit thoughts, she stared at the flames. Since when did she ponder a man's touch? Shaken by what feelings this Scot aroused, Sarra focused on their predicament. Thankfully the snow that'd fallen throughout the day had stopped, but the wind still howled. If it continued to blow throughout the night, it could build the layers of snow into impassable drifts and leave them stranded.

She tore a piece off the leg of the rabbit that Giric had roasted over the fire. Why had he only cooked half over the fire, then used the remainder to make a stew, which would make the meat last longer? Did he expect to be snowbound for several days? 'Twould explain why he'd become quiet.

A gust battered the hut.

"'Tis a fierce wind tonight," Sarra said.

"Aye."

How could he be so calm when she was barely maintaining her composure? "Do you think we will be stranded here?"

Giric glanced toward her, then shrugged. "We will find out in the morning."

The way his eyes darkened when they met hers reminded her of the ruffians who pursued them. A shiver of nerves trickled down her spine. And what of the men who wanted her dead, the surly lot Giric acknowledged that he knew, outlaws, who with the mention of Lord Balliol had left Giric moody and tense? Was this why he was quiet now? In light of her guardian's connection with Lord Balliol, was he reconsidering his agreement with her guardian to deliver her?

The lazy swirl of smoke, rich with the scent of cooked meat, sifted through the room. Wind howled outside. Though safe and warm, restlessness embraced her.

Giric's muttered curse had her looking over. He studied a thin red line along the side of his chest; his earlier cut.

Guilt swept her. So caught up in her worries, she'd neglected to treat the wound. "Let me look at that."

He scowled at her. "'Tis a minor injury."

Far from intimidated by his gruffness, she lay down her food and cleaned her hands. "Then you will not mind if I check how 'tis healing."

His eyes narrowed. She ignored his temper. A wound left untreated, however slight, could fester into a serious state within hours. The result could be deadly. "Take off your shirt."

"Now listen—"

"Who do you think you are?" she attacked. "If you die, I will be left in this wretched wilderness alone."

A muscle worked in his jaw. "Is that all you care about, your own blasted self?"

Let him think what he wanted. What did she care? But she did, more than she would like. "Take off your shirt. I will be checking your wound."

With a grumble about demanding, ornery women, he stood, tugged off his shirt.

Muscle, raw and lean, rippled from wide shoulders down to his flat waist, and she forgot to breathe.

"Are you going to stand there gawking?"

Heat rushed to her cheeks. "I—" She looked at the cloth he'd secured over the wound, now stained with a growing line of blood. Extending from the wrap, a long scar, not fully healed, ran almost the entire length of his side.

What in God's name had happened?

"Are you going to stand there, lass, or take a look?"

"I . . ." She stepped over. When her fingers grazed his flesh, she trembled.

"Do nae be taking all day about it."

Bother him for tying her up in knots. Not that he'd acknowledge that he needed her help, the thickheaded clout. Sarra unwrapped the cloth and examined the wound, but her gaze kept sliding over the long, angry scar. From the length and position of the wound, he could have easily died.

And she never would have had a chance to know him.

Saddened by the thought, she lifted her gaze to his.

For a second, something wild flashed in his eyes. With a curse, he snatched the bandage. "I will clean out the wound and put herbs on top. The method has served me well in the past."

A past riddled with battle and God knew what else.

"The wound needs to be sewn. Where do you keep your supplies?"

"In my bag."

Thankful for the familiar task, Sarra collected the necessary items. She handed him the wine flask. "Drink a long pull. 'Twill take off the edge."

Without hesitation, Giric drank a good portion.

After cleaning the wound, she threaded the needle. "Take another drink, then I will start."

"Blast it, lass, 'tis nae coddling I need but sewing." With a disgruntled look, he took another swig of wine then secured the top. "Be about it, lass."

In silence she started her task, finding herself curious about this warrior. At unguarded moments, there was something about his manner that hinted that he was more than a common Scot—a knight, she corrected. Exactly who was he? Or, did she really want to know?

Sobered by the thought, she finished the last stitch. Once she'd cut the thread, she rubbed a concoction of herbs he'd helped to select over the top, then rewrapped the injury. "You can put your shirt back on now," she said, her mind at odds with her tragic past and the man before her who left her intrigued. She began stowing the herbs.

"Thank you."

At his quiet words, her heart jumped, but as his hand lay upon her shoulder she stilled.

Giric turned her to face him, his expression a mix between sincerity and frustration. "I am nae fond of being plied with a needle."

He was apologizing. A jumbled laugh welled in her throat. What had she expected that he'd do when he'd laid his hand upon her? Shaken, she closed down every venue this thought could lead. The ground between them was already too dangerous. "You are welcome."

His face softened, and the mood shifted to something intimate.

With an unsteady breath she stepped back, gathered the last of the supplies, and stowed them inside his sack. She was going insane. How else could she explain how he twisted her feelings into knots?

She turned and thankfully he'd donned his tunic, but it didn't shield the memories of his hard, sculpted body. "Do you come from a big family?" she asked, stumbling to find a safe topic, then immediately wished the question back. She had no business prying into his personal affairs.

His expression curious, he studied her as if sizing up his answer. "I have a sister, Elizabet." With a wince, he knelt beside the fire, picked up a stick lying beside the hearth, and poked it in the coals. "Both of my parents are dead."

Her heart went out to him, having survived her own devastating loss. "How did your parents die?"

Giric raised the stick from the fire. A golden flame wavered on its end. He blew a puff of air. The flame flickered out, and then a curl of smoke wove toward the ceiling. "My mother died when I was seven. After, my father raised me."

"I am sorry."

He shrugged. "'Twas a long time ago."

Mayhap, but by the stiffness of his action, the memory haunted him. "When did your father die?"

A muscle worked in his jaw. "Several months ago in an English dungeon."

She looked away. That explained his dislike of the English. By rights, she would expect him to shun her country like the plague. So why had he volunteered to escort her? "I am sorry."

Giric caught the wash of sadness on Sarra's face before she turned away. "'Tis done," he said, touched by her sincerity. His father's death was nae the lass's fault, but until this moment, had he nae condemned all of the English, with the exception of his sister's husband? A man who served King Edward, but a man whom he admired.

Disturbed that she'd breached the anger he'd clung to since his father's death, he tossed the stick into the flames and watched it burn.

Ashes to ashes. He grimaced. As if she could make a difference in his life? She was betrothed to Lord Sinclair. "Last spring, Ravenmoor Castle, a Scottish stronghold, was attacked and claimed by King Edward," Giric started, finding a need to make her understand. "The English king installed one of his knights, Sir Renaud, as castellan. A brutal man, Sir Renaud brandished his contempt for the border Scots. His law consisted of using cruelty to control the neighboring lands." He paused, the upsetting memories all too clear. "Outraged, our clan chose to fight against his tyranny instead of losing our freedom."

She turned.

The understanding in her eyes made him ache. How many years had passed since he'd wished to seek comfort in a woman's arms? "'Twas in one of our attacks against Ravenmoor Castle," he continued, nae daring to allow his mind to wander further down this path, "that my father became mortally wounded by a bolt to his chest." He exhaled. "But fate wouldna allow him a kind death. He lay rotting in Ravenmoor's dungeon until he expelled his last breath."

Ashamed, Giric looked away. Locked within the cramped quarters of the dungeon, wrapped in the stench of death and fear, he'd been a coward to nae end his father's suffering. Instead, he'd watched his life slip away, his body cruelly caught in the throes of agony.

"You witnessed your father's death?"

The raw dismay of her words had him looking over, and his throat tightened with a fierce ache. He nodded, and her face shattered into deep sorrow.

And within this moment he sensed a kinship with Sarra. Only someone who had survived a personal tragedy could truly grasp the heartbreak of another.

Her understanding of his loss unveiled another layer he'd never expected. He'd thought himself a good judge of character. He'd pegged her as a cold and haughty heiress, but at each turn the woman he thought he knew transformed into someone almost elusive.

Intrigued by puzzles, he realized that he knew little of this complex lass. Who was this woman who harbored her doubts beneath a shield of defiance?

"How did you escape?" she asked, interrupting his thoughts.

"In an attempt to help our clan locked within the dungeon to escape, my sister, Elizabet, dressed as a lad and played the part of a squire to the new castellan of Ravenmoor Castle."

Disbelief spilled over her face. "She dressed as a boy?"

"Aye." Memories of his sister's exploits, the audacity of her daring rescue, shocked him even now. "Sir Renaud died in battle, and a new castellan, Sir Nicholas, replaced him."

Sarra leaned forward. "How did she set you free?"

"She didna. Sir Nicholas did along with releasing the rest of my clan."

Her brow dipped with confusion. "The new castellan?"

He nodded, proud of his sister's spirit. "You need to know my sister to understand that only she could make a muddle of it and come out smelling like heather."

Sarra's face softened. "Your sister sounds wonderful."

"Aye, Sir Nicholas thought the same. They were married several months ago." At her expression of disbelief, he held up his hand. "'Tis Elizabet's way, I assure you." Sarra's soft laughter sent a shaft of pleasure through him, and he joined in.

If a year prior someone had told him that he would allow his sister to wed a blasted Englishman, he would have cursed them to Hades. Looking back, his pigheaded sister's love for Nicholas, a man he trusted and respected as if his own brother, was her destiny. As his laughter fell away, the burdens of rough travel and the tension of being chased faded. A sense of contentment settled over him that he'd nae felt for years.

Sarra's eyes danced with intrigued delight. "So now your sister lives in Ravenmoor Castle with a dreaded *Sassenach*."

"Ouch, lass," he replied, intrigued she'd used the unflattering slang for an Englishman. "'Tis about the truth of it."

Her smile fell away. Somber, she stared at him. "And now you are saddled with a cold English heiress."

"Nay," he said, finding truth in his words. "I would nae be thinking that."

Her eyes watched him with a tender yearning, and he saw it then, along with the pain of past memories, her vulnerability.

Shaken, Giric stood, well aware of where an intimate situation like this could lead. "'Tis late."

She hesitated as if she had something else to say. With a nod, she ran her hand over her gown hanging nearby. "'Tis still damp."

He gestured toward the woolen cover folded at the end of the bed. "Use the blanket this night."

She frowned. "What about you?"

"I will be up for a while yet."

The questions, the quiet yearning simmering in her gray eyes tied a knot in his chest. "Be off with you now."

Sarra hesitated, and then walked to the bed. Hay crunched as she lay upon the sturdy but worn pallet. Stretching out, she tried to settle down for the night, but the fact that Giric's sister had married an English knight stuck in her mind. It would be easier to dismiss him if his family held no connections to the English. But they did, and at a great personal cost.

She pulled the coarse blanket up to her chin. That he could set aside his resentment toward the English and accept his sister's decision to marry his adversary left her confused.

Though Giric had witnessed his father's death in an English dungeon, somehow he'd found the forgiveness to embrace an English knight into his family. Yet, he made little bones about his aversion toward the rest of the English—which included her.

And why should he?

Sadness slid through her. What right did she have to feel regret for his decision to accept the man his sister chose to love? He'd made a choice that she'd never contemplated as an option, to forgive a people who by rights he should hate. Didn't that make her guilty of snobbery if not more?

Over the years her loathing toward the reivers had grown into a deep resentment. 'Twould seem that the Scottish knight, in his ability to move beyond his animosity toward the English, was a better person than she. He'd overcome his hate and had learned to forgive.

Humbled, she curled into a tight ball and tried to sleep, but the ache in her heart left her restless. She tried to find a more comfortable position, failed. Though somewhere in this storm-fed night she might fall sleep, she doubted she would ever find peace.

Sarra's continued shifting about had Giric glancing toward the pallet. She'd rolled over and now faced the wall. With the edge of the woolen blanket hitched up, it left him with a clear view of her tempting backside.

He muffled a groan and turned toward the fire. *Do nae blasted go there, Terrick.*

Hay rustled. Then her shivering melded with the chatter of her teeth. With a grimace, he glared around the room, sure he'd discover fairies, doubtless they tampered with his resolve to keep his distance from her.

A small whimper slid from her lips. Another helpless shiver rippled over her body.

On a muffled groan Giric scrubbed his hands against his face. *Ignore her.*

In answer, hay shifted as she moved again.

Blast it! He rose, grudgingly walked toward her. 'Twas for her warmth's sake, and wasna like he was going to lie next to her for his own good. The lass was cold. His body heat would warm her and provide them both with a much needed, good night's sleep.

Like a man led to the gallows, he paused at the edge of the pallet and stared at Sarra, his reasoning of seconds before strafed with doubts. With a sigh of surrender, he lifted the woolen blanket and stretched out beside her. "Here now, lass," he whispered, dismissing the intimacy of the thin linen chemise that did little to shield her body from his view. He drew her close.

A shiver rippled through her body, then another.

He rubbed his hand from her shoulder slowly down her back then up again. With each moment he soothed her, her trembling subsided. After a while, she lay peacefully within his arms.

Wind howled outside, and Giric smiled. Now that wasna as bad as he'd anticipated. All of his misgivings had been for naught. With the cozy haze of the night and the warmth of their bodies, his lids grew heavy.

On a sigh, Sarra turned and laid her head within the curve of his neck. On her next breath, she slid her fingers into the dark whorls of hair on his chest, her soft breaths caressing his skin.

The scent of woman and wool teased his senses and plunged straight to his groin. Bedamned! He tried to focus on the cold outside, the men who gave them chase, or how it would be sensible bedding down next to his horse. But her each soft breath eroded each and every attempt to put her from his mind.

Damnable seconds passed. Though he'd brought her warmth and allowed her to fall into a deep, resting sleep, that knowledge did naught for his disposition or his body's hard-edged need.

Only after several excruciating hours had passed did the exhaustion of the day settle over him in a hazy cloud. Fire crackled somewhere in the distance, a lulling, familiar sound, and the numbing warmth of sleep began to invade his senses.

Without warning, Sarra's scream ripped into the night.

CHAPTER 8

At Sarra's scream, Giric bolted upright and withdrew his dagger. Honed by his years of living as a reiver, his haze of sleep cleared to a sharp-edged awareness in a trice. His body vibrated with energy as he scoured the hovel for an intruder.

Gold and red flames flickered in the hearth and sent a shower of sparks to curl up within the twirl of smoke. Wind pounded against the side of the building. The faint aroma of cooked rabbit, hay, and of aged sod scented the air. After a thorough sweep of the dimly lit interior, he found naught amiss.

Another bloodcurdling scream echoed through the hut.

Giric glanced to his side.

Wrapped within the blanket, Sarra writhed on the bed, her face twisted in horror.

'Twas a nightmare, nae an attacker who threatened her life.

"No!" Her fingers clawed the air. An incoherent mumble grated through her teeth. Then she slumped against the bed.

Pulse racing, Giric sheathed his dagger and drew her against his chest. "'Tis fine, lass."

With a cry, her expression contorted into shock. She shoved her hands against his chest. "Stay back!"

"There now. All is well." He kept his tone soft, his words even, determined to offer her comfort.

She struck out and her nails dug into his chest. "You killed them!"

"Saint's breath!" He caught her wrists to prevent her from doing further harm, with a sickening suspicion that she was reliving her parents' death. He shook her gently. "Wake up, lass."

"Get away!" Her low, guttural demand spilled out like a wounded animal.

Stunned by the vehemence in her words, Giric released her, and immediately realized his mistake.

She flew at him all nails and fury, her body now a dangerous weapon.

And he was her protector? Blast it! For his own defense, he flipped her body beneath his and pinned her against the bed. "Sarra!"

The glaze of fear in her eyes slowly cleared, then became wary. She struggled against him. "What do you think you are doing?"

"You were having a nightmare."

Understanding dawned on her face, and the wildcat of moments before dissolved. But the fear lurking in her eyes lingered.

A woman alone, afraid to reach out. A woman who hid her fears behind a barrier of false bravado. He'd observed it last night to a degree, and now, with her mind raw from her horrific dream, and her defenses shattered by fear, he again witnessed her vulnerability.

His earlier physical desire for Sarra paled in comparison to another need so basic it made him tremble. The need to draw her into the very sanctity of his life.

Her eyes darkened with unspoken desire, luring him into the moment.

On a shaky breath, he skimmed his mouth over hers, and then settled against the soft fullness, tasting, savoring, and wanting her with every essence of his being.

On a soft moan she curled her hands into his hair and pulled him closer.

As their bodies entwined, he cupped the soft fullness of her breast, and she arched against him, her heated response a potent drug.

"Giric?"

Sarra's velvet plea threatened to sever the last thread of his rational thought. He lifted his mouth from hers, his breathing ragged. What he'd almost done, taken from her, slapped him like ice. His entire body trembling, he rolled to his side and pulled Sarra against him.

"Gir—"

"In a moment," he stated, needing time to subdue the rush of passion.

She looked away.

Did she regret what had happened? As if he needed a blasted answer? "What did you dream?" he asked, fighting to clear his mind and bring lucid thoughts to the fore.

She lifted her gaze to his. In the flickers of firelight, passion still simmered in her eyes, but now sadness as well. "My parents." She started to draw away.

Calling himself every kind of fool for trying to deepen their connection, Giric caught her hand. "Please, tell me."

She watched him with a wariness that made his heart ache, then nodded. "When I was eight," she began, a waver in her voice, "my parents and I were returning to Rancourt Castle from an important meeting my father had attended in Scotland. 'Twas winter and snow had fallen most of the day." Her eyes clouded with the memories, and her voice lowered to a rough whisper. " 'Twas beautiful with the hills covered with snow. As if we were traveling in our own fairy tale." She curled her hands into tight fists.

Giric pressed a soft kiss on her brow, feeling her pain as if his own.

"Then, bloodcurdling cries sounded, and from a nearby stand of trees, men attacked." She shook her head, her eyes wide with horror. "The stench of death was everywhere. Tainted everything." Her breathing quickened. Her entire body trembled.

"Shhh."

Sarra blinked then met his gaze. " 'Tis all right," she replied, but from her stricken expression, he had his own doubts. "Our carriage tipped on its side into the river. Water, cold with ice, filled our carriage, while our attackers slew our guard." She closed her eyes. "My father climbed out to defend us, but a blade ended his fight. Then they dragged my mother from the carriage and . . ." A tremor wracked her body, and she buried her face against his shoulder.

"God, lass." Giric held her tight, and her pain shuddered through him. The bastards! How could she nae feel this disgust, a loathing for the men who had stolen her whole life.

"Once they brutalized my mother and left her to die, th—they dragged me from the carriage. After searching my clothes and the carriage for valuables, they rode off." She looked at him, her expression that of a wounded doe. "I am unsure why they did not kill me, but I"—she swallowed hard—"I hated them for what they had done. For leaving me to freeze while I watched my mother die a painful and humiliating death. And for taking everyone I loved away."

Aching at the travesty she'd witnessed, Giric held her while the tears she fought rolled down her face. After a while, her tormented sobs slowed to a fragile shudder, and she clung to him as if a lifeline in a storm. And within this fragile moment, a bond formed, linking them in the most basic of ways. He understood the pain of loss too well, the damage it could bring.

Sarra sat back, her eyes troubled. "Th—The men," she breathed, and watched him nervously, "were Scots."

He struggled for a reply, but what could he say? There were good and bad men in his country. He would nae forgive their murderous act nor offer excuses. They deserved none. "I am sorry." Giric cupped her chin, but she pulled back.

"Reivers," she whispered.

His entire world stilled. "Reivers?"

Sarra exhaled, her eyes never leaving his. "The men who attacked my family were reivers."

An ache ripped through his heart, and the illusion of any tie existing between him and Sarra flickered out. He could imagine her revulsion if she discovered that he'd lived the sordid life of a reiver. His explanation that he'd been raised to the adverse trade and had followed his father's footsteps excused naught. He'd grown up a thief, stealing food and when necessary to survive, had taken a life. Nae that he was proud of his actions.

Blast it! Hadna he taken this mission so that he could put his past behind him, and to rebuild his life? He'd vowed to change his lawless ways and become a man he could respect.

Having learned of her past, and with him being a Scot, that she'd accepted him as a person was more than he could ever have asked or expected.

But she could never forgive the reiver.

"It has been a long night and you are tired," Giric said, doubting if there was anything more left to say. Either way in Sarra's eyes he was damned. He would accept this moment of closeness, mayhap a few more in the days ahead before he delivered her to her guardian. Then, however difficult, he would walk away. "Go to sleep."

She watched him a moment. With a nod, in the circle of his arms, she closed her eyes. After several moments her breathing slowed and she slept.

But sleep, like his peace of mind, would nae come.

* * *

The warmth sifting through Sarra lulled her to remain asleep. She nestled deeper against the heat, pleased at the reward of the firm, muscled body against her, and the possessive way a hand slowly curled around her breast.

She stilled.

Her heart jumped as she realized who she lay next to. On an unsteady breath, she opened her eyes and found herself staring at Giric's dark, hair-covered chest. Heat slid up her cheeks as she looked at his hand half atop her breast, then to where his very male leg draped over her hips.

By the rood!

Memories of last night flooded her mind. Their kiss. Her nightmare. How she'd crumbled before him in a pathetic heap. Then, his tenderness and compassion when she revealed her parents' tragic murder, a fact she'd told no one until now.

Until Giric.

A Scot.

Warnings flashed in her mind and urged her to pull away, but she found herself hesitating. With his unruly black locks, and his expression almost boyish in sleep, she found herself charmed. Somehow, incredibly, he'd touched a part of her that no one had ever reached before.

How could that be?

At what moment had he scaled her defenses and become important in her life? Stunned by the realization, she scanned the hard lines of his face, the contours of a seasoned warrior, a man who made decisions with a quick sureness. But she'd seen beyond his tough exterior. Beneath his fierce countenance lurked a man tender in his emotions and fierce in his love. Yes, this dauntless Scottish knight was a man she could admire and accept into her life.

The immensity of her acknowledgment, unthinkable until this moment, left her shaken. Her hand trembled as she stroked her fingers through his tumbled locks, felt the rough stubble that darkened his chin. By the rood, she wanted him.

As if bidden, his eyes opened, their blueness rich with the haze of sleep. Through heavy lids his gaze slid over her and darkened with passion.

Her desire ignited as if coals stoked by a smith. Before doubts could stop her, caught in the web of this dangerous attraction, she covered his mouth with her own, pleased when he crushed her against his chest. She lost herself in his kiss, in the way in which his mouth feasted on hers.

On a muttered curse, he pushed up on his arms.

She stared at him, her vision clouded, her lips swollen from their kisses.

He eased her away, scrubbed his hands over his face. "Nay, lass."

The coldness of his voice left her feeling exposed. Hurt and ashamed, she drew the blanket around her and sat up. "I . . ." What? Wanted him? Had acted the wanton? Oh, God. "I am sorry."

Like a cornered wolf, Giric stood and paced the room. He stopped near the hearth. A muscle worked in his jaw as he watched her, then he walked over and knelt before her, his nearness far from smothering her awareness.

"You are a fine lass," he started, then released a harsh breath, his eyes fierce as the devil's own, "but I canna be touching you, nor you me." He stood. "I am hired to escort you to your betrothed. I will nae be taking what rightfully belongs to another."

Heat raced up her face that he could talk of her innocence with such candor. As if she could forget her betrothed? But for a moment she had. What did that say about her, that she could block out responsibilities for a man she desired, something she'd never done in her life. Until now. Damn Giric for making her care!

"Get away from me." The pain of rejection and her own shame raked through her voice.

He didn't flinch or show any other outward emotion to her outburst, which cut her deeper.

"'Twould be for the best," he said with unnerving calm.

Again, the cold, dangerous Scottish knight she'd first encountered at Rancourt Castle stood before her. And for that she despised him—for all of her shattered dreams, and for the moment of hope he'd bestowed upon her. And, he was right. Naught but his escort could ever be between them. Humiliated, furious that she'd allowed her emotions to guide her, she withdrew.

Giric gestured toward their clothes that'd hung near the hearth overnight. "Everything is dry. You would be wanting to get dressed. Once I have donned my garb, I will ensure that we are nae snowed in and can depart."

He watched her expression of hurt spill into regret. How could he have been so blasted stupid? In her weakness, when nightmares had exhausted her strength to fight and left her helpless, he'd allowed himself to think that he could be a person she could rely on. At least for a while. And in his delusions, he'd almost given in to his desire.

Now he would pay for his foolish thoughts.

'Twas best that he allowed her to believe that he didna care. Bittersweet emotions curled through his heart. As if she could ever love him—a reiver.

The anger in her gaze brewed to fury. Once again she'd resurrected her icy walls, but he would have to live with that. To accept their relationship as anything but a sterile companionship would threaten the very essence of his mission.

And with the men who pursued them in addition to the dangerous winter conditions, they had problems enough to deal with without the complication of intimacy. And yet, with all of the reasons he shouldn't care, shouldn't want her, he still did.

She glared at him. "All you care about is the gold."

Giric shrugged and dressed with a casual ease he didna feel. "The gold will buy food to fill my belly on a cold winter night, but then you wouldna be knowing what that is like. With your wealth your larder stays filled."

Sarra stiffened.

"I will be back." The cold slap of the wind hit him as he exited. He pulled the door shut.

Good going, Terrick! He headed toward the makeshift stable, stopped. As he neared, his senses came on full alert. The hairs on the back of his neck prickled as he stared down the rambling hillside that opened into a long, tree-lined valley. On his initial scan, except for a Goshawk circling above the trees, he saw naught but the pristine lay of the land, ripples of snow blanketing the glen bound by a sturdy line of ash, oak, and pine.

Another wash of unease rippled through him. His instincts hadna failed him in the past.

A distant crack echoed from the far end of the field.

He turned, searched every shadow, every crevice of blackness for any sign of life and prayed it was a hart or another large animal.

A movement caught his eye. The fleeting cast of brown disappeared from view, but he didna need a second look to understand.

That's what you get for having your mind on a woman and nae your task.

On a curse, Giric scooped up an armload of snow and ran back inside. Kicking the embers, he threw the snow atop the glowing coals. Steam sputtered and spit with an angry hiss. With a gasp, Sarra grabbed the blanket and covered herself. "What do you think—"

"Get dressed—now!" Giric jerked her clothes from where they'd dried during the night, tossed them to her. "The men who are after us are about an hour away."

The blood rushed from her face.

"Move!"

The blanket fell to the floor as she tugged on her clothes.

He walked over to help her, and she froze. "Before you can give me any charming advice about your nae wanting my assistance, we need to get out of here."

"'Tis the only reason I would allow you to touch me," Sarra stated, wanting him as far away from her as possible.

Nerves whipped through her as his fingers secured her gown with familiar ease. No doubt he'd had plenty of experience seducing women with his practiced lines and devastating smile. At what moment had she lost her wits and deluded herself that he was different from other men? When he secured the last tie, she stepped away, unsure of everything.

His cold eyes held hers. "Put on your cape and come outside. I will be waiting." Giric grabbed the blanket and exited.

As the door closed behind him, a shudder ran through her for what she'd almost given him, for what she'd almost allowed herself to believe.

Sarra donned her cape and hurried to the door. But as her hand curled over the wooden handle, she paused to look behind her.

The simple abode was neat from her cleaning, and the bed tousled from where she and Giric had slept. For a moment she'd found happiness within these shabby confines, a place where her past no longer mattered, where she wasn't evaluated by her wealth, and with a man who'd soothed her fears.

No. Sarra shoved her foolish notions away. She'd but deceived herself into believing he was the man she'd one day hoped to find.

She again scanned the hovel, this time noting the tattered bed frame, the worn floor, and the blackened fire reeking with the smell of wet ash.

'Twould seem over the last few hours that only her dreams, spawned by her exhaustion, had come to life. Before her stood the harsh reality. Like the barbaric hovel, Sir Knight hadn't truly softened, only her delusions had made her believe so. A man, he'd seized the opportunity a young, naïve woman had offered. This room held only fragments of another's humble life, not memories she would ever wish to recall or cherish.

Tears burned her eyes, but she shoved them back. Tears were for a child whose life blessed them with hopes and dreams. Fate had carved her a path where she faced a guardian who would wed her to his son. Her escort was a temporary inconvenience, a Scot she refused to harbor in her thoughts, much less in her dreams.

With her heart secured, her mind refocused on her upcoming confrontation with Lord Bretane, and any silly notions of Sir Knight erased from her mind, Sarra stepped into the cold. She glanced to where Giric stood by his mount, irritation clear on his face as he waved her forward.

With a tug, she pulled the cape tighter, started forward, and promised herself she would not make that emotional error again.

CHAPTER 9

"The men chasing us are beyond the trees and to the left," Giric whispered to Sarra. His horse shifted beneath them and he murmured a soft command for him to still. Through the thick firs, he watched their pursuers advance on the hovel they'd departed a short while before.

The Scots had known where to look. It made sense that they would understand that with Sarra nae used to harsh winter travel, he would seek a known shelter, even if for a short while. But he'd hoped they'd nae find them so quick.

"I see them now." Seated on the horse before him, Sarra turned. "Do you think they saw us?"

"I canna say for sure. Though I erased the tracks for quite a distance, they will eventually discover our trail."

"Where will we go now?"

A question he'd pondered since their hasty departure. With the heavy snow, his plan to head east and meet up with Colyne was dangerous at best. To travel south would put them in jeopardy of meeting up with the other half of their pursuers. Nor would he choose to move farther north and into treacherous mountainous terrain. The best option was to travel a bit farther northeast.

He hoped Colyne had realized that due to the blizzard and time constraints to deliver Sarra to her guardian, their original plan to rejoin the group wouldna work. "We will travel to Colyne's brother's home. We can stay until the weather permits us to continue to Dunkirk Castle," Giric replied, irritated by the thought of her impending marriage.

Would Sinclair care if Sarra's haughty air was incited by fear? Or, would her betrothed find her resistance an annoyance, and demean her into subservience that would destroy her spirit? The thought of anyone breaking her left him cold. At least he had a reprieve in knowing that Sinclair, as most men in power, often kept mistresses. Odds were Sarra would suffer his touch only until she carried his child.

His grip on the rein tightened at the thought of Lord Sinclair or any other man having her. As if he had a blasted say? He prayed that the baron would value the woman he would wed. Frustrated by his thoughts, Giric kicked his mount forward.

Distant shouts of men melded into the gusty wind, and he thanked nature for that. With the snow swirling and drifting, though it would make travel difficult, 'twould cover their tracks as well. He wished he could erase his anxiety over Sarra's upcoming marriage with such ease.

For the next several hours they traveled in silence. The sun lent a false warmth, its rays dancing upon the cascading flakes like fairies at play. Wind, rich with the scent of pine and of the cold winter's day, stung their faces and slipped through their clothing.

As the morning wore on, they climbed the steep hills littered with fallen trees, clusters of bare bushes, and patches of open field. At the top of the next knoll, in the distance, Giric spotted what he'd been searching for, an overhang caked with layers of snow and half-hidden by a thick shield of evergreens.

He guided his horse through the snow-laden branches and into the rock's shadow, then drew to a halt.

Sarra turned. "What are you doing?"

In answer, he dismounted, held up his arms to aid her dismount. "Come."

She watched him with distrust.

Annoyed by her guarded expression, he caught her waist and hauled her from the mount. Outrage flared in her eyes as she stared up at him, her body inches from his, his mind already racing into forbidden territory. "We will hide here until the men have passed and are a safe distance away."

"You are sure they will not find us?" she asked, the doubts woven within her question making it more like a charge.

"Few know of this place."

She took a step back. "Like the hovel we stayed in last night?"

What did he expect after he'd reminded her of their journey to her betrothed this morning? In her mind, at least, she'd forgotten her sharing her fears, and their kiss hours before. When she looked at him now, she saw a Scot, a man she who incited naught but her suspicions.

"You are safe," Giric half-growled, then walked to the edge of the overhang. Snow crunched beneath his feet, and the breeze slid across his skin as he knelt behind a boulder and surveyed the glen below.

In the distance the tiny flecks of men grew. Thankfully the wind had erased any signs of their passage through the valley.

As expected, the Scots paused near the base of the glen and searched their surroundings. The Scot with the grizzled beard turned to the others and made an angry gesture with his hands.

Giric smiled, well familiar with their leader's quick temper. Obviously Léod couldna decide which route he and Sarra had taken.

"There is naught amusing about this situation," Sarra whispered as she knelt beside him.

He stiffened. "They are debating which way we went, and by the look of it, canna decide."

"What did those men mean when they linked John Balliol with my betrothed?" she asked, nerves in her voice.

"'Tis naught to worry about," he replied, irritated that his personal dislike for a contender for Scotland's crown should shroud his mission in any manner. Until their pursuers had stated the royal affiliation, he'd nae connected neither the father nor son's intent for marriage to Sarra to any political reason.

Now he saw the intent with biting clarity. Once wed, Lord Sinclair could use Sarra's fortune to support John Balliol's cause, with a political reward of being elevated to a higher station for his efforts.

"'Tis my life," she stated, jerking him from his musings. "If there are circumstances that affect my marriage, I should be told."

Through her anger, he saw the worry, and his heart went out to her. "As you know, with King Edward's guidance, the Guardians are in the process of selecting Scotland's new king."

She gave a curt nod.

"Lord Sinclair is a close friend of John Balliol, claimant for the crown. Though Robert Bruce, the Competitor, is the better choice for our Scottish king, Balliol is a powerful man who holds ties to his English counterparts including John de Warren, one of the English king's most trusted earls."

"And you believe 'tis my money and not I that is behind the betrothal?" she asked, resentment creeping into her voice. "That he wants to use my wealth to bolster John Balliol's claim for the crown?"

"You are a beautiful woman," Giric said, irritated to be caught in a position to defend what could be the truth, and to realize that her dreams might include romantic notions. "His motivation for a union could easily be due to his desire for you."

"Save your praise for another. I need not pathetic words to flatter me. I am an heiress," she said, her gaze unwavering. "I realize my value to the man I wed. 'Tis learning that I am a political pawn for Scotland's cause that catches me by surprise." Her last words ended in a bitter clip.

"I do nae need to craft false words of your beauty," Giric snapped, irritated she would dismiss a man's reason to wed her for her looks. She was breathtaking and didna even realize it.

Sarra's eyes darkened with anger. "Is that not part of your task? Deliver the heiress safe and sound. Mayhap keep her happy as well? Or does the fact that Lord Sinclair intends to use my fortune to support Sir Balliol and not Sir Robert Bruce, the Competitor, raise your ire? Tell me," she said, her words ice, "how far would you go to halt what you believe is Lord Sinclair's intent?"

Damn her. "I have nae—"

"Like it or not," she pushed on, "you have given your word as a knight to deliver me to my betrothed. Except I do not believe sleeping with the prize was part of the agreement."

Saint's breath, now they were back to that. "I was trying to keep you from blasted freezing to death."

"Were you?" She folded her hands over her chest. "I wonder how Lord Sinclair would view your *caring* act? Or is it common for an escort to climb half-naked into a woman's bed or for her to awaken with her protector's hand on her breast?"

The lass was so blasted smug. On an oath, Giric caught her shoulders. "What is it that bothers you? That I lay in bed with you and touched you or that you liked it?"

Sarra shoved against his chest. "You self-serving—"

"Or the fact that this morning you instigated the kiss?"

She opened her mouth to reply.

"The truth. Or canna you admit that you wanted me?" He arched a brow and witnessed the silent battle in her eyes, understanding her value for the truth, a value he cherished as well. From her recount of her past, he understood the cost, but for a demented, self-tortuous reason, part of him needed her to confess that she desired him as well.

"I was exhausted."

Giric cupped her chin in a gentle hold. "And now?" He lifted her mouth to within inches of his, the silent draw to claim her lips humming through him. "If I kissed you here?"

With a hard jerk, she pulled from his grasp, her breathing fast, and her expression unsure. "Leave me alone." But her demand trembled with fragile need.

"As I thought." He waited for her to refute his words, then her shoulders slumped. The denial in her eyes faded to acceptance.

She stared at the valley where the Scots now circled at the base as they tried to discern which direction he and Sarra had taken. "You are not what I expected," she finally said. "I wanted to hate you."

Her tender confession moved him. "I know." Turning her to face him, he slid his thumb along the curve of her jaw, and she trembled beneath his touch. He wanted her. He could already taste her mouth, warm and willing, soft with the wanting. Her eyes darkened with need, and he was tempted to make his fantasies reality.

A hint of vulnerability shimmered in her gaze. "I still think you are obstinate, overbearing, and a bit smug."

"Some have said the same." With regret Giric slid his hands along her shoulders, and then released her. He drew in a deep breath sharp with cold. He wanted to believe that naught had changed between them, but one look at her told him otherwise.

Shaken, he glanced where the Scots were searching for tracks along the valley floor. "A compromise," he said, calling himself a fool to invite camaraderie between them. 'Twas a bargain with the devil and he knew it. In a fortnight at most she would be gone from his life. Why couldna they at least depart as friends? "Trust me to take care of you." Even as he said the words, he realized that above all else, her trust was what he wanted the most.

"Why should I?"

"Because I give you my word." She hesitated, and he held his breath, her decision holding more importance than he would want.

"I will trust you—on that."

He nodded. "Agreed."

Below, the men had regrouped with several pointing toward the north. They started riding away.

"After they are out of sight," Giric said, "we will head toward a small village where I am known. We will remain there for the night, and then continue to Colyne's brother's home."

Her eyes widened. "Are you insane?"

Aye, for allowing her to get under his skin. "Those trying to find us will nae be expecting such a bold move."

"You are right, 'twould be the decision of a lunatic."

He took her hand, finding he needed to touch her. "Though a risk, a minor one comparatively, and by staying in the village, we can rest before continuing on. Trust me."

She took a deep breath. Her hand trembled in his. Sarra nodded.

Elation surged through him. As much as he wanted to draw her to him, he let her go. He had what he wanted. In this she'd given him her trust. It would be enough.

The sun sat high in the sky as Giric guided them from their safe haven, but she agreed they'd used the time wisely. While they'd remained beneath the cover of the overhang, they'd eaten and rested his mount, plus with their pursuers headed on a northward trek, they'd increased their chances to escape.

For a while.

The Scots chasing them would not give up so easily, nor had she forgotten the other part of the band that rode to their south. The men's determination to ensure she never reached her guardians was spawned by loyalty, not gold. With a frustrated sigh, she turned her attention to their travel.

Deep snow, persistent wind, and sheer exhaustion had her leaning against Giric's muscled chest. He draped his cape around her, and she snuggled against his solid warmth, but doubts left her uneasy. Had she erred in offering him her trust, even to a small degree? A part of her wanted to reject the Scot who reminded her of her past, but another was drawn to the man whose actions and genuine concern lured her to care.

He guided his mount along a stand of ash, then up a steep incline littered with clumps of brambles glazed with snow. They crested the hill and a small village came into view.

The last streaks of the setting sun bathed the misshapen community within its golden rays. Sod homes, similar to the hovel where they'd stayed last night, but in better repair, lay clustered together on a narrow flat of land crowded around an aged rowan tree. The tree's tangled limbs sat barren of leaves, and clawed toward the sky.

The simplicity of the setting touched her. Like the gnarled tree, the people within this mountain village endured the fury of life, and against the odds, persevered.

As did Giric. In their discussions he'd shown her that he would bend when the cause demanded it, but when the need came to protect, he was steady and strong.

Hooves crunched as his mount trudged through the crusted drifts. With a shiver she glanced skyward. A hint of stars glittered through the wash of purple. Without the cover of clouds, 'twould be a bitter night.

The smoke curling from the holes in the roofs promised warmth. Mayhap his decision to stay at this small village was wise. Indeed, 'twas only for a night.

As they entered the outskirts of the humble village, a burly man, dressed in a thick woolen cape, stepped from the largest home, a claymore secured in a leather sheath strapped on his back.

A dog barked from the shadows as Giric guided the horse toward the man. The scrape of hooves on the hard snow splintered into the silence.

The man whirled. With the swiftness of a seasoned warrior, he withdrew his sword. "Halt," he ordered, his burr rich, thick, and filled with threat. "State what would you be wanting."

"'Tis Terrick," Giric called out. "We are seeking shelter for the night."

Sarra tensed as the man eyed them. By the way the fierce Scot studied them, even if he agreed, she doubted she could sleep one wink this night.

"Terrick?" the man charged, his voice cautious.

"Aye," Giric replied.

The Scot stepped closer. The ferocity of his expression warmed to a welcoming smile. He sheathed his claymore, and Sarra sagged with relief.

"You are an ugly sight on such a cold winter's night," the burly man said.

Giric gave a hearty laugh that eased her fear a degree further. "'Tis not saying much from a man who would kiss a sheep."

"A blasted upstart." The Scot chuckled. He met her gaze, and Sarra held her breath. He arched a thick brow and glanced toward Giric. "A might fancy piece if you be asking me. You didna steal her for ransom did you?"

Sarra stiffened in his arms, and Giric muttered a silent curse at Fergus's jovial charge. The last thing he wanted was to bring up his past and incite Sarra's suspicions. "Do I look like the type who needs to be stealing a woman?"

"'Tis a jest, lad." With a chuckle, his friend motioned them down. "'Tis colder than a witch's toes this night. Both of you come inside. From the looks of the lass, her teeth should begin to chatter any moment."

With a nod, Giric dismounted, but he saw the silent questions in her eyes along with the fear. Understanding her nervousness at staying in an unfamiliar Scottish village, he slipped his hands around her waist and set her before him. Before she could speak, he turned to his friend. "Fergus, this is Lady Sarra."

She slid him a surprised glance, and then nodded toward the burly man.

"A pleasure to meet you, my lady." Fergus rubbed his hands together. "Come, 'tis too cold on me bones to stay outside." The Scot walked to the nearest hut. He shoved the thick oak door open, and the rush of smoke and cooking meat greeted them. "Look who I found outside," he called as he stepped inside.

Sarra hesitated at the entry. Wind tugged at a strand of hair that had come loose in her snug plait as her eyes searched his with a quiet desperation.

"'Twill be fine," Giric assured her, and she followed him inside. The haze of smoke and cooking meat melded with the dried grass and herbs tied overhead to dry. Several beds were shoved into the far corner, and a loft that Giric knew held another pallet lay above.

A sturdy oak table with rugged benches sat to the right, and the hearth, filled with wood, burned near the far wall. Several chests lined the left wall, and he knew these would hold coin, silks, sugar, or any other valuables they owned.

A short, plump woman, stirring a pot over the fire, turned. When she spotted Giric, delight sparked on her face. She trudged forward and gave him a fierce hug. "'Tis a blessing to see you again." She held his face in her hands, her eyes scanning every inch. "Are you faring well?"

Embarrassed by her mothering, but helpless when it came to this woman who was more like a mother to him than a friend, he smiled. "I am fine, Esa."

She huffed. "I have known you since you ran around in your trews all sass and what for. Fine indeed." Aged eyes lined with crow's-feet narrowed. "I will be the judge of that." Then her sharp gaze found Sarra.

"Esa, this is Lady Sarra."

The elder woman paused at her title.

Sarra gave a hesitant nod.

"There is nay reason to be shy." Esa glanced at Giric. "I had nae heard that you had found a quiet lass to be courting?"

"She is nae . . . We are . . ." Blast it! "We have journeyed a distance," Giric said, disliking the speculation on Fergus's and Esa's faces. The less they knew of his escort, or of the man she would marry, the better. "I would be grateful if you would be sharing a bowl of stew. Lady Sarra is weary and hungry."

With a tsk, Esa nodded. "'Tis poor manners I am showing. Remove your cloaks and hang them by the fire."

After, she gestured toward the table, Esa moved to a huge kettle hanging over the fire. Inside a brown liquid bubbled that smelled like heaven. After ladling out a bowl of stew, she set it on the roughly carved table. "Sit and eat."

"Go on," Giric said when Sarra glanced toward him.

She cleared her throat. "But you need—"

He laid his hand over hers. "I will join you in a moment. I need to stable my horse. Do nae worry, all will be well."

On a nervous sigh, she sat and began to eat.

Aware of Esa's keen eye, he prayed she'd nae question Sarra in his absence. "Thank you, Esa." Giric exited the hut, Fergus on his heels. Night edged through the winter sky as he stepped outside, the air, void of the sun's warmth, already bitter cold.

Fergus closed the door and walked by his side. "Are you going to tell me why you are away from your castle in the dead of winter carting around an Englishwoman and a noble at that?"

"'Tis a favor," Giric answered, but he didna add it was for his people and his pride. Walking to his mount, he caught his reins and led him toward the stable.

Fergus gave a grunt. "The lass doesna carry your child?"

Stunned by the question, Giric halted. His horse nudged at his shoulder.

His friend gave him a firm slap on the back. "I will take that as a nay." He started forward, and Giric fell into step, the horse's muffled clops echoing behind him. "That you would be liking the lass is obvious. Only a reason of dire urgency would force anyone to be out in this blasted cold."

"Aye, we have already traveled through two snowstorms."

"Which way are you heading?"

"East."

The elder Scot shook his head. "You will nae make it far. Several men returned from a hunt late this morning. The blizzard sealed off the pass."

Saint's breath! The pass after Colyne's brother's home was notorious for becoming impassable in poor weather, but he'd hoped they'd make it through before the snow had grown too deep. Now they would have to wait a few days, a sennight, perhaps more. For as quick as heavy snows sealed the pass, the winter sun would open it. If nae, they would have to travel south and take their chances of running into the other half of Léod's men.

Inside the stable, his friend's breath misted before him as he leaned against a sturdy beam. "I have known you too long, Giric. More is weighing on your mind than the lass or the difficulties of travel." Sadness crept into his gaze. "'Tis difficult to bury loved ones, more so when you are given the responsibility of your castle and its people."

Hay rustled beneath his mount's hooves as Giric led him into a stall. "I am adjusting," he replied, though time had far from healed the pain of losing his father. He loosened the saddle then pulled it free. After removing the blanket, he began to brush him. "I didna see Ihon," he said, nae wanting to discuss his personal life.

The elder man's face sagged into a displeased grimace. "Ihon has become entrenched in politics, and I believe his own aspirations. Nae that I agree with the English king sticking his nose in our affairs, but I do nae consent with the men Ihon has entangled himself with. Rabble-rousers, the lot of them, all headed to the Highlands to make plans. Nay good will come from his association, I will tell you that."

Giric nodded, thankful their son rode with those far to the north. At least he wouldna be among those who had followed them up the river and were determined to kill Sarra.

Unease filtered through him as he thought of the men who chased them. Sarra needed rest. They would remain here overnight, nay longer. He returned the brush to its rack, then used a wool blanket to rub his mount. After, he added a fair amount of hay to his horse's feed bin, then walked over to his friend.

"He is a fine horse," Fergus said, his eyes filled with appreciation.

"Aye." And up to this point, he hadna been forced to sell him. "Let us be going in." As they walked toward the house, Giric glanced toward the thick of trees blackened in the shadows where men could easily hide.

"Come on in, lad," Fergus said as he opened the door.

With one last look around, Giric strode inside. He was being foolish to think Léod and his men had trailed them here or would arrive in time to catch them. Within hours he and Sarra would be gone.

CHAPTER 10

Later that evening, standing at the outskirts of the village, Sarra stared at Giric in disbelief. "Why do you not want me to mention the men who are after us?"

He laid his hand over hers. "'Tis best if they do nae know." The muted shadows lent a grim twist to his expression, and unease slid through her. Through the clear, star-filled sky she glanced at the hut where they'd left Fergus and Esa sitting beside the fire. Ever since Giric had returned with Fergus after caring for his mount, he'd remained somber. The evening had passed without event, but an unexplainable tension hung in the air.

Though she'd known Giric but a short while, 'twas enough for her to sense when something was wrong. "It has something to do with why you did not tell Fergus and Esa your true reason for escorting me, does it not?"

His breath exhaled in a rough cloud. "Aye. 'Tis best if Fergus doesna discover that your betrothed has any connection to John Balliol."

She stared at him in stunned disbelief. "What?"

"This shouldna be a problem," he assured her.

"Unless the men who are after us arrive and expose the truth, is that not what you are saying?"

He shrugged. "The chances that they will find us are slight, otherwise I wouldna have taken the risk."

"Are they?" she demanded, anger sliding into her voice. "Your friends live here, and you have admitted to knowing the men who chase us. Why would they not search this village?"

"Because the men rode off to the north. By now, they should be too far away to be any threat."

Far from convinced they were safe, Sarra snatched her hands from his. "So why did you not inform me about your concern of your friend's position with my betrothed?"

"Lass, I do nae—"

"Tell me!"

"Blast it. I didna wish to cause you undue worry."

"Undue worry?" That he'd withheld his friend's loyalties toward Bruce, for whatever reason, hurt. "I have been on my own since the age of eight and have made decisions that affect a stronghold," she stated, anger riding her voice. "I am far from a green girl who cannot handle herself."

"Sarra—"

"You will hear me out! I am tired of men interfering with my life because they believe they know what is best for me. That includes you!" She stepped closer. "From now on, you will tell me exactly what is going on if it involves me. Understand?"

He arched a brow. "Are you finished?"

The wisp of humor mixed with pride in his expression incited her further. The day she banished men from her life, especially Giric, would be none too soon. "You—"

"Sarra." His voice gentled into a soft burr. "Wait," he said when she made to speak again. He reclaimed her hand, wrapped it in his own.

She attempted to pull free, but he held tight. "I would never treat you as anything less than the woman you are." His grip eased, his silken words firm with conviction. He stroked his thumb over the back of her hand. "My hesitation comes from my own indecision. I care for these people. The last thing I would wish is to place them in a situation where no one wins."

"You mean if they discover I am to wed Lord Sinclair, they would seize me to aid Robert Bruce, the Competitor's cause?"

Giric's thumb paused. "They would nae harm you, nor would I let them. 'Tis that when I agreed to the task of escorting you, I didna realize your betrothed's political loyalties or his possible intent for your wealth."

"Now do you regret your decision to offer me escort?" He must. How could he not? Unwittingly, he'd placed himself in a position against his own political beliefs, and put himself at odds with those he cared for. She shook her head. "Never mind."

A dog barked from the other side of the village. Somewhere in the distance a wolf howled with a mournful cry.

Giric's gaze, steady and strong, searched hers with a tender desperation. "If I had known of your betrothed's connections to Balliol, I am nae sure if I would have accepted the task. But now . . ." He muttered a curse. "Now I wish I hadna." He cupped her face with a tenderness that made her heart ache. "Because now, God help me, I find myself nae wanting to let you go."

Anticipation rippled through her. He was going to kiss her. She should pull away. 'Twas foolish to remain near, to be regretting that in the end he must leave. But as he leaned down, she moved into the kiss, soft like the petals of spring, warm like the sun on a lazy summer's day, tender with an urgency that had her head spinning.

His hand cupped her neck and drew her closer, his tenderness destroying her defenses until her entire body trembled beneath his quiet seduction. And with the night surrounding them, filled with stars like slivers of hope, she poured herself into the kiss.

On a sigh, Giric pulled away, leaned his forehead against hers. "I had nay right to kiss you like that."

She closed her eyes, wanting to disagree, but finding the words elusive. Somehow wrong and right had become jumbled, twisted so that what she thought she wanted was becoming confused with an ever-growing need for him. A choice forbidden. But the concept of a life without him left an emptiness inside her, the intensity one she hadn't experienced since the loss of her parents.

He stroked his fingers through her hair then pressed a soft kiss on her brow. "I have made a mess of this, but I promise you, until I am nay longer a part of your life, I will protect you."

In a time where a man's word could be bought for the price of gold, he was a man of honor. Any doubts she'd held toward him fled. "I know."

Silence filled the moment, broken by the whisper of the night. The scent of the cold entwined with the rich aroma of smoke and a hint of evergreen.

With a nod, Giric released her. "To bed with you now. We will be leaving at first light, and the travel will be rough."

Shaken by the depth of emotions Giric made her feel, Sarra walked toward the hut. Though they had no future, the day he rode from her life would leave a stark void within her that she doubted anyone would ever fill.

At the door, Giric watched as Sarra stepped inside. When she paused at the entry, his heart stopped. *Go inside.* It had taken every ounce of his willpower to send her away.

After a brief pause, Sarra entered.

He started toward the stable, but instead of the door closing behind her, it opened wider. He paused.

Esa stepped outside. The elder secured the entry, tugged her shawl tighter, and then looked around. When her gaze landed on him, she walked forward with purpose.

Curious as to her reason to leave the protection of her home on this cold winter night, he met her halfway.

The light breeze sifted through the snow, tossing shards of white into a senseless twist as Esa halted before him. She glanced toward the edge of the trees where the moon seeped into the sky. "A fine night."

"'Tis." Giric followed her lead as she started toward the rowan tree. He scanned the homes, noting several new buildings since his last trip. "It has been a while since I have last visited."

"Too long," she replied. They strolled in companionable silence. As they neared the gnarled tree, Esa halted, and then laid her hand on the weathered bark. "I remember when you were a lad and played upon the boughs."

The memories filtered through his mind. "I remember you chasing me when I swiped a sweetmeat."

"And I would have caught you if you hadna climbed the tree."

The smile came unbidden, and for a moment, the warmth of the past embraced him. "It saved my life."

"Your mother would have liked Sarra."

Giric shrugged, but his gut twisted. He'd purposely avoided pondering how Sarra would have been received by his family. Any thoughts of a future between them were a delusion. "Mayhap."

The folds upon her brow arched, and she chuckled. "Lad, though the lass is a bit cold, which I owe to Fergus and I being strangers, a blind man could see that you care for her." The mirth on her face fell away. "You have nae told her of your feelings for her, have you?"

He swallowed hard. "Her parents were murdered by reivers."

"Ouch. I am sorry for that. What did she say when she learned of your past?" She stared at him a moment, then shook her head. "Blessed, Mary. You have nae told her that you are a reiver?"

"Was," he hissed. Blast it. He'd left his past behind him, or tried to, but at every turn his days of lawlessness lived. "And I willna be telling her."

"Why? She cares for you as well." Esa gave his shoulder a gentle squeeze. "Give the lass a chance. Time heals wounds, but love allows us to forgive."

Love. The word scraped across his mind. "How could Sarra ever forgive the people who killed her family, or accept me, a reiver?"

"Giric Armstrong, never have I heard such sot-witted nonsense. You have nae given the lass a chance to make her own decision, but have condemned yourself first."

He muttered a curse. "You do nae know her."

Sage eyes narrowed. "And you are making sure that she will never know you."

"What difference does it make?" he asked, the exhaustion of his emotions sapping his will to fight. "There could never be a future for us."

"Because you willna let there be?"

Because I am nae her destiny. He remained silent. Let her believe 'twas his stubbornness that stood between him and Sarra. To say more would invite further discussion.

Esa was a romantic at heart, had married the man she loved. He could never explain that beyond Sarra's dislike of reivers, a greater challenge arose. Even if she accepted him, knowing his past, he had naught to offer her. His acceptance of this humble task as an escort showed with clarity his desperation to raise coin. Nor could he forget that she was betrothed to another.

Shrewd eyes searched his face. "You still blame yourself for your father's death, do you nae?"

Her question sliced his heart like a knife. He stiffened. "My father's death has naught to do with this."

"Nay? You have never forgiven yourself for his death. Or, have you even tried and add the loss of your father atop what you consider your mountain of faults?"

On a curse, Giric stared at the rowan tree, the gnarled branches resembling the futility of his life. "There is naught to forgive." Even as he said the words, they were untrue. Saint's breath! The attack on Ravenmoor Castle, witnessing his father wounded with a bolt to his chest, then later, with them both caged in the dungeon, he'd watched his father die a slow and miserable death. A death he'd lived a thousand times over, and each memory pummeled him with self-condemnation.

"Listen—"

"I should have stopped him from attacking Ravenmoor Castle," Giric interrupted. "We were outnumbered and without proper arms. Instead, I rode by his side."

"Do nae flatter yourself."

Giric whirled. "I should have done something. Nae have allowed him to rot in an English cell."

"And what could you have done?" She made a dismissive gesture when he made to speak. "I know how thickheaded your father was. Stubborn as a mule if an idea got into his head. And if you think you could have changed his plans of retaliating on the English, you are wrong." Her expression softened. "You fought by his side for loyalty, for the belief in what was right."

"I should have somehow saved him . . . If only I had—"

"What? Taken the bolt instead of him?"

"Aye!" he rasped, the accuracy of her words matching his own thoughts a thousand times over.

She crossed her arms over her chest. "What good would the both of you dying do?"

He shook his head and looked up. Stars twinkled in the ebony sky so bright and filled with hope. "I do nae know. 'Tis just that somehow I feel I could have done something different. Imprisoned, I should nae have allowed him to suffer."

"Do nae be so hard on yourself," she said, her words quiet. "At the time, you did nae know if you would be rescued. I think you did everything you could, and that is all anyone could have asked. 'Tis time to stop carrying the guilt of your past."

The belief in him shining in her eyes left Giric humbled. How could she believe in him when he couldna believe in himself?

"Aye there's work to be done now that you hold the title of the Earl of Terrick and have responsibility of Wolfhaven Castle and those within," she continued, "and you will do what is needed. Have faith and persevere. In the end, everything will work out for the best."

As much as he wished to agree, at least with issues concerning

Sarra, doubts persisted. Her destiny was set, but Esa didna know that. And she was right, for his people he would do what was needed.

A sliver of peace crept through his tormented thoughts. He may never have a future with Sarra, but that with his people burned bright. That would be enough. It had to be. "My thanks," he said, his voice somber. Like the rowan tree battered by time, Esa stood a solid force, her wisdom ageless.

A light gust feathered her hair, streaming it against her brow. She pulled her shawl tighter. "I am getting a wee bit chilled. My old bones are nae as sturdy as they once were."

"Go on," Giric said. "I will come inside in a bit."

"Nae too long now."

He smiled. "I will be but a wee bit."

With a nod she headed toward her home. The moon's glow splayed her shadow on the silken snow as she walked like waves of silver light entwined with darkness.

Giric scanned the remote village set in this quaint, rugged surrounding, bordered by hills, tempered by harsh winters and brief summers. Esa would always live a humble life, but it didna negate her stout heart.

Nor would he give in. Though he may have a struggle ahead of him in rebuilding Wolfhaven Castle, he would persevere.

Hours later, Giric glanced out the stable to where the sun inched into the sky. Rays of burnished gold crept through the purple-gray shadows, illuminating the earth within its muted light. With a sigh, he checked his mount's cinch. "We will travel to Kirkshyre Castle and remain until the pass opens."

"You are welcome to stay here longer," Fergus said, his breath white puffs in the cold morning air.

A hawk's cry echoed in the distance. Other horses secured in their stalls shifted.

"My thanks, but we canna remain longer." Giric double-checked the rest of the tack. "I will stop by on my way back."

His friend nodded. "You—"

Sarra's scream pierced the morning.

Terror shot through Giric, and he bolted from the stable. As he rounded the corner, his heart dropped. Léod and his men encircled Sarra outside the hut.

Her eyes wide with terror, she brandished a dagger in her hands, waving it at whatever man dared to step toward her.

Furious, Giric drew his broadsword, bolted toward the motley group. "Get away from her!"

The men glanced toward Giric, but held their positions, their swords readied.

Sarra glanced toward Giric.

With her distracted, the redheaded Scot caught her hand wielding the blade. With a quick twist, he pulled it free, subdued her against his body, then pressed her dagger against the soft column of her neck.

Fear for Sarra's life slammed Giric. "Release her!" On a curse, he swung the flat of his blade against the largest man.

The man's eyes rolled and he slumped to the ground.

Giric turned to take on the next aggressor. Before he could focus on one, three of Léod's men grabbed him, one clamping hard upon the hilt of his sword and preventing him another swing.

The leader strode up to Giric. "The lass is ours now."

"Release them!" Fergus yelled as he rushed toward them.

"'Tis naught for you to worry about," Léod spat.

"Fergus," Giric warned as the elder halted before the group, "go back inside. 'Tis my affair to deal with."

"They are on my land and threatening my guests!" Fergus's shrewd eyes studied Giric. "And what affair are you talking about?"

Léod's eyes widened in understanding. "'Twould seem you are as ignorant as Terrick when he first accepted his task," he stated in a low, fierce tone. "Because neither you nor Terrick knew of Lady Sarra's political connection, we willna kill you."

Giric struggled to break free, trying to think of a way to save her. "She is nay threat to you."

"Nae any longer," their leader replied. "Without her, Sinclair willna be using her dowry." He gestured toward his men. "Take her away and be done with the task."

The red-haired man dragged Sarra toward where their horses were tethered near the outskirts of the village.

Panic slammed Giric's gut. "Nay. I forbid you to take her. She is—" His mind went blank with possible arguments that would save her life. Then, his gut wrenched as a way came to mind. Blast it! "—my wife."

The red-haired man dragging Sarra whirled. He glanced at Léod, who eyed Giric with keen interest.

"Blast it, all of you hold," Fergus boomed. He shoved his way through the burly lot until he stood within the circle of men. He glared at Léod, Giric, then to where Sarra stood within the rugged man's grasp. He turned to their leader. "What the Hades is going on?"

A sated smile edged Léod's mouth. "Terrick was just telling us about his new bride."

If Giric could have wrapped his hands around Léod's neck, he would have cheerfully wrenched the last breath from his miserable life.

Confusion on his face, Fergus stared at Giric. "The lass is your bride?" He shot a curious glance toward Sarra, whose face had blanched as pale as the winter snow, then he faced Giric.

Blasted trapped. Nor would he involve Fergus and his wife further. Giric nodded toward Sarra. "Aye," he said, his voice rough with anger, "she is my wife."

An unwitting partner in sealing Giric's fate, Fergus met Sarra's gaze. "Is it true, lass?"

Her eyes wild with desperation, Sarra stared at Giric.

With his blood humming through his veins, Giric steadied himself. If she verbally concurred with his declaration of marriage, by Scottish law, they were legally wed. Mayhap he could somehow spare her the opportunity to say the words.

"Tell him, lass," Léod pressed.

"Leave her alone!" Giric yelled, but Léod stepped toward Sarra, his face ripe with menace.

"Answer me," their leader demanded.

Sarra floundered, then gave a clumsy nod.

"What was that?" Léod demanded. "You will speak to me when I am talking to you, lass."

Giric fought against the men who held him. "Sarra do nae—"

A shudder rippled over her body. "Ye—Yes."

CHAPTER 11

After Sarra's confirmation that they were wed, a satisfied grimace edged Léod's mouth. He nodded to her captor. "Let the lass go."

The man withdrew the knife from her neck and released her.

Sarra stumbled forward.

On an oath, Giric sheathed his blade as he ran to her and drew her against his chest. Her body trembled against his as he glared at each man, his gaze halting on Léod.

The bastard. Giric pressed a kiss on Sarra's brow. "Stay here." Anger raged within as he strode to the men's leader, a man he knew well. He and Léod had reived together since their sixth summers, and had both trained beneath his father's hand. Although as Giric was in line for a title, every so often he'd caught Léod watching him with envy. Over the years he'd ignored the man's resentment, the slights, and the snide comments.

Until now.

A pace away, he caught Léod's neck, pleased to see fear on his face. "If I ever find you within a league of Sarra, I will kill you." He shoved.

Léod stumbled back, sprawled onto the snow.

His heart pounding, Giric glared at Léod's men. "The same for the lot of you."

Their leader picked himself up and began to brush off the snow. Hatred burned in his eyes, but caution as well.

As much as Giric would like to beat Léod to a pulp, Sarra had experienced enough terror this day, nor could any actions change their fate.

'Twas done.

He curled his hand around the hilt of his dagger. "Out of my sight!"

Léod's lip curled with fury, but a glint of satisfaction lingered as well. He gestured to his men. "Let us go." They headed toward their mounts.

Fergus glanced to each of the men with utter confusion outlined on his face, then his gaze landed on Giric. "What in Hades is going on?"

His throat choked with emotion, Giric shook his head. "I will explain later. Right now I need to speak with Sarra inside, in private."

Fergus's eyes narrowed, then understanding dawned in his expression. "Aye."

Walking to where Sarra stood trembling, Giric lifted her in his arms and strode toward the hut. "Giric?"

At her rough whisper, he pressed a kiss on her cheek, fought for calm. "You are safe." Blast it, he shouldna have chanced staying here last night. Because of him, she'd almost died. Neither was her trauma done. Once she learned the truth of his past, she would never forgive him for this day's mayhem, nor would he ask her to.

He'd taken a risk.

Failed.

With a silent curse, Giric shoved open the door and carried Sarra inside.

Esa glanced up from a tub of water where she was scrubbing clothes, her face covered by sweat, and her skin flushed. When she caught sight of Sarra, she dropped the garb and the worn stick, and rushed over. "God's deeds! What happened to the lass? There is blood on her neck and she looks like she has seen a ghost!"

"Blood?" Sarra's fingers shook as they skimmed over the narrow line.

"She just had a bit of a run-in with Léod and his friends," Giric said, his voice rich with sarcasm as he damned himself. With care he set her down, then wiped the blood from the cut the knife had made on Sarra's neck and wished he could erase their confrontation or their marriage with such ease.

Esa grimaced. "I will be talking to Léod when I see him again, you can be sure of that. It matters little if he is nae fond of the English. Lady Sarra is a guest in our home." The anger in her eyes faded to motherly concern. "Come now, lass." She took Sarra's arm and with Giric's help, guided her to a chair at the table.

* * *

Tremors whipped through Sarra as she tried to slow her breaths. "I-I thought I was dead."

His eyes dark with regret, Giric knelt before her and drew her into his arms. "You are safe now."

She welcomed his strength as she fought the nightmare of when the fierce warrior had held the knife to her throat. On a shudder she closed her eyes. Oh, God. She would not think about that. Not now. If not for Giric . . .

"'Tis all right now," he whispered, his soft encouragement giving her an anchor in her torment. Another tremor swept through her. She clung to him as a sob built in her throat. He'd saved her life. How could she ever repay him?

Esa set a steaming mug on the table. "Drink this tea, lass, 'twill help calm your nerves."

Sarra fought back the tears as she stared at the fragrant brew, wanting naught but to remain in Giric's arms. Here she was safe.

The door opened and Fergus stepped inside. His worried glance rested on Sarra. "How are you, lass?"

She shivered from the rush of cold air he'd let inside. "B-better."

Fergus speared a glance at Giric then nodded to his wife. "Esa, I need your help outside."

"I will be there in a bit," Esa replied. "The lass needs—"

"Now."

Her husband's terse command had Esa's eyes narrowing, but she snatched her worn wool wrap and donned it. "I will be back in a mite," she said to Sarra, her gaze softening. She turned to Fergus; her expression promised they would discuss his terse manner once outside.

When the door closed behind them, Sarra sagged against Giric. His heartbeat pounded slow and steady. Long moments passed, each becoming entwined in the other, and she rested against him until her shudders abated and she felt naught but his warmth.

On a sigh he placed a kiss on her brow, and then held her before him.

At the anguish in his gaze, foreboding crawled through her. Questions she'd not thought to ask during the confrontation slammed to the fore. "Why did the men let me go?" The nerves she would rather hide edged her voice. At the distress on his face, she remembered his claim that she was his wife and her stunned amazement that the men had believed him. At his silence, she fought to keep calm. "Giric, the men left because they believed we were married did they not?"

He released a rough sigh. "They did."

Relief poured through her. "Thank God they were so foolish to believe such a tale. When the men heard—"

"'Twas no tale," he interrupted, his voice rough.

Panic swirling in her gut, she clutched his cloak. "We cannot be! There was no priest to witness and sanction our union, and I have signed naught agreeing to such."

Regret darkened his gaze. "I am sorry."

Her heart pounded. "'Tis nae true!" She tried to shove free, but he caught her shoulders. "Let me go."

"Sarra, the men released you, because now we *are* wed."

Hysterical laughter welled in her throat. "No!"

He tried to take her hand, but she stumbled back. "Sarra."

"We are not married! Why do you insist on this lie?"

Sadness flashed in his eyes, and then his gaze became empty. "In Scotland," he explained, his words cold, "when a couple declares they are married before witnesses, as we did moments ago, 'tis done."

Why would he continue with this nonsense? "'Tis a barbaric law that I have never heard of, nor will I participate in." She lifted her chin. "I am English and cannot be bound by the decree of a heathen country, and . . ." Her guardian's words during her youth came to mind, of his explaining the unique way that couples in Scotland could wed. By the rood, what Giric had explained, 'twas all true!

He moved toward her.

She took another step back. Sickened, she understood. "You planned this all along," Sarra charged, hurt that he could use her emotions with such callousness.

Blue eyes darkened. "What are you talking about?"

She scoffed. "As if you do not know? How could I have been so foolish, so trusting?" Trust. She clenched her hands, remembering his request. "You asked me to trust you when all along you planned this."

"What are you talking about?" he asked, his words ice.

"You knew the men who pursued us," she charged, her voice rising, "*and* you plotted with them right up until this moment to ensure my wealth would never fall into hands that would support John Balliol." Her breath fell out in sharp rasps. "Admit it. We were never in any danger. From the start you used me, played me to believe that you cared."

His eyes narrowed into dangerous slits. "Is that what you believe, that I would use you for my own political gain?"

She ignored the ache in her heart, the whisper from her conscience that assured her that he would never betray her. "You will not use my money to back Robert Bruce, the Competitor. Not a penny do you hear!"

Giric started toward her, his steps predatory.

She took a step back. "Do not touch me again, ever!"

"I do nae give a blasted damn about your money."

"Not as long as it falls in the right political hands? At least be honest in that." A sob caught in her throat. She'd wanted him, desired him, but every step of the way he'd never cared for her. His words, everything he'd done for her was all a lie.

And for that she could never forgive him.

Tears blurring her eyes, she bolted for the door, not caring where she went. At this moment, she wanted to be anywhere but trapped here with him.

Giric caught her before she made it halfway across the room.

She flew at him all nails and anger. "Release me!"

He backed her up and pinned her against the wall, his face taut, and his eyes raging. "You will hear me out."

Sarra twisted in his hold. "Let me go. Have you not done enough?" He held firm, his body snug against hers, his eyes hot, and at that moment, if she never saw him again, 'twould be fine with her. She glared at him, angry with herself that she could want him still. "I hate you."

He remained silent, watching.

"Did you hear me? I hate you!" A sob stumbled through her words, and she tried to discern his reaction, but he stared at her, his eyes void of emotion.

With a curse, he released her. "We must leave. Lord Sinclair awaits our arrival."

By the rood, in the chaos she'd forgotten her betrothed. As if he mattered now? "Go where? Surely 'tis unnecessary to continue on? I doubt I could explain our marriage to Lord Bretane or his son."

A muscle worked in his jaw. "You shall nae have to, I will."

She gave a cold laugh. "And I am supposed to believe that?"

"Though we are married, you are untouched," Giric explained with riotous calm. "Due to circumstance, I believe an annulment can be obtained. In the end, there should be naught but a delay in your marriage to Lord Sinclair."

Did he expect her to believe that he hadn't contrived their union and would give her up without a fight? What trick was he planning now?

Giric watched her, his eyes hard.

Thoughts to flee raced through her mind, but if she tried to run again he would catch her. As if she had a chance to escape in this rugged hill country.

Or survive.

She swallowed hard. At this moment, as her husband, he had every right to stop her.

She stilled.

What was she doing giving in? In the past she'd faced the challenges of running Rancourt Castle. Was this situation any different?

Granted, this wasn't as simple as bartering for a fair price of grain or working to diffuse a rift between her people, but the situation still required calm and deliberate thought. Like it or not, however temporarily, she was married. She would face their farcical union and its dissolution head-on.

Having regained a degree of control, she gave a curt nod. "We will travel to my guardian's." If all went well, they would acquire an annulment. After, she prayed that she could convince her guardian that it would not be necessary for her to marry his son, nor forsake all of her holdings and be exiled to a nunnery. If the time to choose a husband came, she wanted the decision to be hers and hers alone.

A muscle worked in his jaw. "Bundle the rest of your clothes and bring them to the stable. I shall be waiting." Snow slipped inside as he exited.

Shaking, Sarra stared at the door. *Please, God, let this be a horrid nightmare.* In the next moment she would open her eyes and wake up in her own bed. But as she scanned the interior of the aged hut, the truth stared back at her. Her nightmare had just begun.

The midmorning sun streaked into the stable as Giric stared at Fergus and Esa. "I should have explained everything to you both from the start. I am sorry I didna." He blew out a rough breath. "As I said, I wasna sure how to explain."

"Blast it, if you had told us about the dire state of Wolfhaven Castle," Fergus stated, "I and a few of the men would have ridden with you to procure—"

"Nay. I will nae reive again," Giric said, vehemence hard in his voice. "My father condoned that way of life, but I will nae. From now on, any coin I earn shall be through fair means."

Fergus eyed him for a long moment, and then his face creased into a smile. "You are fortunate, at least the lass cares for you."

Esa gave him a warm smile. "Aye, that she does. And 'tis a better beginning than most marriages. Though your life together didna start as you both would wish, with persistence and understanding, you will find a bond to each other that will last a lifetime."

However optimistic their advice, emptiness filled Giric's heart. Too easily he could envision a life spent with Sarra.

His chest squeezed tight and dismissed his thoughts. He wouldna think about what she made him feel. 'Twould make walking away from her more difficult in the end. "Sarra and I will obtain an annulment," he said with a forced calm.

Fergus arched a brow. "But you are taken with the lass as well. A blind man could see as much. Though you and Sarra were wed by Scottish custom, it willna be easy to acquire dissolution of the marriage."

A fact he was all too aware of, but from the day he became Earl of Terrick and keeper of Wolfhaven Castle and its people, what he cared for long since mattered. He had responsibilities. "I have given my word to deliver her to her betrothed."

Fergus scoffed. "'Tis foolish to give away what is rightfully yours."

"I need the gold paid to me for my escorting her to rebuild my home," Giric said, his throat tight. "Even if I hadna the responsibilities, I have given my word to Lord Bretane to deliver Lady Sarra to wed his son."

"Blast it, lad. From the looks of her fancy garb, she has plenty of gold," Fergus spat. "Regardless of your original intent, you are now her husband and entitled to her estate. You will nae be needing Lord Bretane's gold nor anyone else's."

He remained silent. Never would he want Sarra for her money, but his friend would never understand.

"If you are through discussing my financial status," Sarra said with cold disdain from behind them, "I would like to depart."

With a muttered curse, Giric faced her. Of all of the times for her to walk inside. He opened his mouth to explain, then stopped. Why even try? She'd accused him of marriage to claim her inheritance and with her anger fresh, she wouldna believe any different. 'Twas best if they left.

Fergus took in Sarra, his gaze shrewd. "Terrick is a good man, respected by his peers, and a man of his word. A lass couldna do better."

Sarra stiffened. "Thank you for the hospitality."

Esa stepped forward. "Do nae judge him too harshly. All is nae what it seems."

At Esa's subtle reference to his title, Giric gestured to Sarra. "Let us go." At this point, he doubted his being an earl would impress her, nor would he want it to. If she ever cared about him, he wanted her to respect the man, nae a title.

Once mounted, after a brief good-bye to his friends, Giric kicked his horse into a canter and headed east.

Throughout the day they rode in silence, stopping to water his mount and share a portion of the oatcakes Esa had given them along with a flask of wine. Hours later, with the sun edging toward the horizon, the weariness of their hard travel took its toll.

He scanned the knolls ahead, battered by clumps of brambles and edged with thick firs and pine layered within the snow, and searched for a place to make camp. With naught in sight, he guided his horse across the open field. When they reached the perimeter of the forest, almost halfway up the next steep incline, he pulled his mount to a halt.

Sarra shot him a cool glance.

Her mood hadna improved since they'd left, as if he expected otherwise? For the remainder of the journey she would tolerate him, little more. Giric dismounted. "We will camp here for the night."

Mouth tight, she surveyed their winter-fed surroundings. "Outside?"

"Aye." Let her be upset at their encampment. In her mind 'twas just another injustice added to an already overwhelming pile. "Put your hands on my shoulders."

"Is there not anywhere else we could go? A hut? Something?"

At the hit of nerves in her voice, he softened a degree. This entire mess wasna her fault. "I will make a shelter for us, and then build a fire."

With reserve, she placed her hands on his shoulders, and he lifted her down.

Once he'd decided the best place to build a windbreak, Giric laid the sack with the food stores along with the wine by her side. "Wait here while I begin a fire." He started to walk away.

"Is there something I could do to help?"

Surprised by her offer, he turned. Though angry, and righteously so, she refused to be waited on. Her damnable pride. 'Twould be easier if they ignored each other, but it appeared he wouldna even be offered that respite. "If you can gather dry wood, I will start a fire."

In silence she headed toward the trees.

Using a flint and his dagger, he had a small pile of tinder smoking posthaste. As he blew on the glowing embers within the shredded wood, Sarra returned with several finger-thick branches. Without comment, she departed, and moments later, she dragged out a small tree limb.

Pleased, he stood and gestured toward a fallen log he'd rolled over to use for a seat. "Break off the small branches and slowly feed them into the flames. When you have a solid bed of coals, add a few larger pieces. I will start on our shelter."

As he worked, shadows grew and the sky darkened to a burnished hue. From the labor of cutting green boughs, he'd removed his cape and now worked in his shirt. Sweat streaked down his back as he wove the last pine bough into the makeshift structure, then gave the frame a hard shake.

The windbreak stood firm.

He wiped his brow as he stepped back to survey his work. Though crude, 'twould hold. Pleased, he turned to find Sarra watching him, the anxiety in her face easy to read, but the hint of desire catching him off guard.

*   *   *

As Giric held her gaze, however much Sarra wanted, she couldn't turn away. While he'd constructed their temporary shelter, she'd busied herself, but could never quite rid her thoughts of the upcoming night. And watching him, his exposed skin sleek with sweat, his muscles outlined where his shirt clung to his honed frame, sent her imagination places she forbade it to go.

The reality of the situation doused her mind's wanderings. How could she think of him in such an intimate manner? Though he'd said they would acquire an annulment, they were but words. With nightfall, would he change his mind and seek his marital rights? She clenched her hands at her sides, irritated that she was unsure if her nerves were due to anger or desire.

"You will be hungry," Giric said, his voice shattering her thoughts. Warmth stroked her face as she absorbed every ripple of his muscles as he tugged on his cape. Embarrassed to find herself attracted to him after everything, she returned to the fire.

Seated on a stump before the flames, Sarra fought to ignore Giric as he sat on the opposite side of the blaze. She broke off a piece of the smoked venison, placed it into her mouth, and slowly chewed.

"It should be a good night to sleep," he said.

Sarra stilled. What did he mean by that?

He gestured toward the sky. "'Tis clear and the wind has quit blowing."

"'Twill be cold," she said, but she didn't miss the hint of stars beginning to shimmer in the darkening sky, or the calmness of the night. Layers of snow cloaked the branches of the pine. Elms, oaks, and silver birch arched toward the gloaming sky, and the fresh scent of the forest surrounded them. Any other time she would have appreciated the beauty of this eve, mayhap considered the setting romantic.

At this moment she wasn't sure of anything, especially Giric's intent.

As she slid her boot through the snow, a tumble of white spilled from its wake. Why wasn't anything easy when it came to him? From their initial meeting he'd disrupted her life. Their journey had added to the convoluted mix. With their wedding, their already strained relationship had taken another plunge.

He reached into the pack and retrieved another slab of jerky. "If the weather holds, we should reach our next stop soon."

In silence, she tore a small strip off her dried meat, but as she held it between her fingers, her appetite evaporated. With a sigh, Sarra set aside the food and stared at the fire.

Orange-blue flames sputtered and slowly consumed the dry wood. The flicker of ash burning hot swirled into the smoke, then blackened and became lost in the churn of gray.

Sadness stole over her. A loneliness she hadn't felt since her parents' death swept over her, but she understood the reason. 'Twas her wedding night. Over the years she'd harbored romantic notions of a man who loved her, cherished her with his every breath. Instead, she sat stranded in the wilderness with a Scot. A Scot she didn't particularly like.

Liar.

How could she like him? All he wanted was her inheritance. Or, would he indeed accept the measly offering that Lord Bretane would pay him upon her arrival? She squashed a wedge of snow under her boot.

"Lass, why do you nae tell me what is on your mind?"

With caution, Sarra looked up, surprised to find irritation in his gaze. In a perverse sort of manner she found comfort. At least it proved he was human.

And cared as well?

No, she was fooling herself if she allowed that thought to exist, remembering his all too eager vows of marriage. "I have naught to say to you."

"Nay?" He arched a brow, the teasing in his eyes leaving her on edge. "That I seriously doubt."

"Have you not done quite enough to ruin my life? Why can you not leave me alone? More preferable, why do you not leave?"

He frowned. "Regardless of my wishes, until we reach your guardian's, we are bound together."

"You have achieved everything you came for, so 'tis unnecessary to continue on with this ruse."

Anger flashed in his eyes. "Are we back to that again?"

She stood, disgusted with this entire situation. Hating him. Wanting him. "As if you would forget?"

He stood, the slow, predatory motion igniting tingles over her skin. She cast a glance behind her. Snow, trees, and the ragged hills greeted her.

Alone.

The nerves that'd built through the day shattered. Panic overrode logic and her mind spun out of control. With his strength and expertise with his blade, if he wanted to kill her and claim her inheritance for his political cause, he could. She tensed, if necessary, ready to fight for her life.

CHAPTER 12

With a curse, Giric walked away from Sarra. From the fear in her gaze, he knew what she was thinking. He'd never taken a woman against her will, nor would he begin now. Nae that he didna want her, or recognize the desire in her eyes. A man could lose himself in a lass like her. And at this moment, he was tempted to take, to find the passion he knew simmered beneath her cold façade—a passion he'd tasted nights before.

He stalked through the woods illuminated beneath the full moon. Saint's breath! Nay wonder she stared at him with panic, surely she all but read his lust-driven thoughts. 'Twould be the way with a maiden on her wedding night.

Their wedding night.

Blast it, why hadna he thought of that before? Regardless of his promise to bring her to her guardian's untouched, Sarra was waiting to see if he would keep his word.

Caught in the pale swath of moonlight ahead, a large, dead limb angled to the forest floor. Giric trudged through the deep snow to the stocky base, grabbed it, and jerked.

Wood groaned from his effort, but the limb held fast.

"Come on." He jerked harder and put his weight into it.

Wood snapped, but the limb gave only an inch.

'Twas a blasted conspiracy! The realization of what he was doing hit him. He released the branch and stared at it with disgust. Like his dealings with Sarra since they'd left Fergus's home, he was trying to wield the bough to his will. And like the wood being forced to move in an unnatural position, she resisted.

With a deep breath, he studied the angle of the limb. If he pushed it back, he would work with the natural break at the base of the limb. Moments later, dragging the thick branch through the snow, he headed toward camp.

As he stepped from the shield of trees, the shimmer of stars and moonlight lent a magical setting over the blanket of snow. Each curve and dip lingered in the shadows like an intriguing mystery, embracing Sarra as she sat quietly by the fire.

At his approach, she looked over, and then drew her cape tighter.

At her protective gesture, he kept his approach casual and banked his desires, wanting to put her at ease. Near the fire, he broke off several smaller branches, knelt, and fed them into the flames. After, he angled the larger branch over the pile of dried limbs.

Flickers of orange and blue crept higher and slipped through the crevices of the wood.

Though she pretended to ignore his actions, he caught her watching him. Each time their eyes met, hers narrowed with challenge. And he hoped he could win back a token of her trust.

As the heat from the blaze grew, he sat on the log opposite Sarra. Giric took in how moonlight slipped through the trees and shimmered across the sturdy land. On many occasions, he'd camped beneath the stars on a night just like this. At times, he, along with his father and their men, had been on the run and hadna taken the time to appreciate the setting. Then, there were other nights when he could sit back and absorb the beauty.

"When I was a lad," he started, and immersed himself in his memories, surprised to discover that he wanted to share a part of his past with Sarra, "my mother used to tell me stories of the wee folk. Whenever I camped beneath the stars, I would look for them." He noted her prim posture. "I do nae suppose that you have ever spent the night outside?"

Suspicious eyes slid toward him. "No."

That she'd answered made him smile. He exhaled as he studied the ebony backdrop that cradled the brilliant display of stars and the moon. "There is something magical about being out on a night like this." He paused and let the aura surround him, the quiet, serene peace that he could almost touch. "If you listen, you can hear the fairies dancing through the trees."

Sarra arched a skeptical brow. "I do not believe in fairies."

And why would she? Raised by servants, her nights were spent alone. The weaving of tales or the small gestures of love he'd taken for granted as a lad would be void from her life.

He could picture her as a child, huddled in the master chamber at night, engulfed in finery. Though well-mannered and stoic during the day, at night the little girl returned, the one filled with fears who missed her parents, the one who cried herself to sleep.

And for her, his heart wept. He wished that he could heal her past, but with the discord between them, the chance was slim. But for this night he would give her the gift of magic. If she chose to believe, that would be her decision.

"On a fine night like this," Giric began, "the sky awash with a million stars and the forest quiet, 'tis a favorite time for the fey to be about."

"The fey?"

"The fairies."

Sarra scanned the forest, cast in silky shadows, the layers of snow glittering with moonlight. Heat stroked her cheeks and she turned back to the fire. What was she doing looking for fairies? There was naught out there. But a part of her, the child who had wished desperately for even a bit of magic in the shadows of her life, had her again scouring the setting for the tiniest bit of proof.

"Most never see them, except for a shimmer of light made from the sprinkle of fairy dust," Giric continued, his voice rich and smooth with the quality of an experienced bard, luring her to listen, enchanting her to believe. "But if you catch one, you will see their tiny wings. If they look up and by chance you see their face, they are beautiful, as if painted by an angel."

She met his gaze, curious yet cautious. "And have you seen them?"

He shrugged, but beneath the moonlight, a wisp of humor danced in his eyes. "On occasion, though they tend to show themselves when mischief is about." He stretched out his legs and settled into a more comfortable position. His breath misted before him, curling then evaporating into the chilled air.

"Mischief?" With a frown, she glanced toward the forest caught in a dance of moonlight and shadows.

"Aye, they are known for their cunning, though often they ply their magic for good causes as well."

She scraped her teeth across her bottom lip, unsure what to make of these magical people he spoke of. "Where do these fairies live?" she asked, intrigued a rogue would believe in mythical creatures or any such lighthearted nonsense.

"Beneath the earth with heather above their homes," he replied. "If you look close as you travel around Scotland, you can see the hillocks. The Otherworld, the fairies' home, is ruled by their queen. A fair maiden she is. Many men have tried to catch her as she rides through the fog-enshrouded moors on her shimmering white steed, but she has blessed only a few with the golden apple."

"The golden apple?"

"Aye, 'tis the only way to enter the Otherworld. And, the apple is also to eat." He shot her a wink. "A man will be hungry on his journey."

A smile tugged at her lips. Hungry indeed. 'Twas rubbish. But soothed by his voice, lured by the picture his words painted, and with his teasing she couldn't help but find herself charmed. Though she doubted such creatures existed. They were naught more than stories to lull a child to bed.

But a fragment of her could envision the whisper-soft flutter of wings, red lips that would curve into an inviting smile, or the man smitten and giving chase to find the elusive beauty.

Sarra shoved aside the ludicrous thoughts. She was tired. 'Twas the only explanation of why she would try to imagine such foolishness. She lifted her gaze to find him watching her.

Laughter danced in Giric's eyes, but beneath, sincere concern lingered as well.

Her pulse jumped and she looked away, not wanting him to care, or to try to soothe her when everything in her life was in chaos. Why was he telling her about these magical people or try to comfort her and ease her mind? They were married. He need not play games to seduce her. But through her fears, she had to admit that as he'd told her of the fey, she noted naught but concern in his eyes.

Mayhap he was telling the truth. Once they reached her guardian's, they would send a request to the pope to petition for an annulment.

She struggled to understand Giric's intent, and in the end she found her attempts as elusive a mystery as the fairies he spoke of.

"Sarra?"

"'Tis late." She stood and turned toward their shelter, not wanting to face him now with a foolish part of her desiring a man who had proven by their marriage that he wasn't a person she could trust.

The shuffle of clothes sounded, then snow crunched as Giric walked up behind her.

She held her breath as his warm breath caressed her cheek, yet he made no move to touch her, and she wasn't sure if she should be happy or sad.

After a long moment he sighed. "Come." He strode past her and headed toward the makeshift lean-to. At the entry he halted.

Their gazes clashed.

"Are you coming?" She hesitated.

"I will nae touch you if that is what worries you."

Pooling her courage, she walked to the woven limbs, and then ducked inside. When he entered, her breath caught, but he merely leaned over and lifted a wool blanket.

He handed it to her. "Use this."

She clutched the coarse cover, her relief tangible. He would leave her here alone?

Giric knelt and spread out another blanket in the sleeping area. "Lie here," he said, and gestured to the left. He moved to the right and sat, his attention on removing his cloak.

Dread curled in the pit of her stomach. The shard of worry ignited into panic. She took a step back.

Giric looked up. Moonlight carved harsh angles against his face, leaving his expression ominous.

Gone was the man who had charmed her with stories of fairies, had lulled her with his rich burr. The fierce warrior before her was every bit her husband!

"Come here."

Fighting for calm, she shook her head and stumbled back into moonlight.

"Saint's breath."

He stood, and her heart jumped. He was going to take her now. "Do not touch me!"

Giric shot her a look of disguist. "I have given my pledge to bring you to your guardian innocent."

"I . . ." Confused, embarrassed that after his earlier assurance she'd believed the worst, she reentered the shelter and sat on the pallet.

"Our travel on the morrow will be rough. Get some sleep." He lay on his blanket. Though inches away, he kept his word and didn't touch her. After a while his breathing slowed in the deep rhythm of sleep.

Two days later, Sarra scanned the hills that were growing steeper and more treacherous with each passing hour, trying not to think of Giric. Though she'd assured him that she hated him, what he made her feel was far from cold.

She stared into the wilderness, thankful they would sleep with a roof over their heads this night.

In the distance, a crofter's hut, half-hidden in a shield of trees, came into view. Hope ignited. "There is a home."

Giric nodded. "We will see several more before we reach Kirkshyre Castle."

"Castle?" She glanced back unsettled by this news.

The mirth in his eyes made her heart jump. "Did I nae mention that we would be staying in a castle with my friends?"

"Friends?" she said with reluctance, and wondered what type of people she would meet.

"Aye," he replied.

They passed several more crofters' huts as they rode, the sturdy homes formidable against the blistering winter. And with each league, her nerves wrapped tighter.

A falcon's cry echoed over the ridge. A smith's hammer pounded in the distance. When they crested the hill, the land fell away to a rolling valley. On the opposite side, half-carved into the ledge of rock, a majestic castle arched toward the sky.

Giric drew his mount to a halt, smiled. "'Tis always a welcome site."

The light breeze toyed with the hood of her cloak as she took in the formidable stronghold. Sleek curves of granite melded with hewn boulders to craft a castle as impressive as it was impenetrable. With the castle forged into the edge of a cliff, the noble within could focus his defenses on the entrance. He would need but a handful of archers for those brave or foolish enough to attempt to scale the cliff.

"'Tis beautiful," she whispered.

"Aye, that it is," Giric replied.

"I had not expected to find anything so grand in the wilderness."

'Twas a far cry from their previous lodgings. 'Twould seem her escort was filled with surprises.

Giric guided them down the steep slope, then across the valley. The road to the castle wound up, another defense to slow an attacking force.

As they rounded the next bend, the entry to Kirkshyre Castle came into view. Guard towers positioned on either side of the gatehouse connected an expanse of quarried rock. She scanned the battlements, arrow slits, and crenellations which added another layer of defense. Whoever had designed this stronghold knew their craft.

A guard's call echoed in the distance. Then the rattle and scrape of chains sounded as the drawbridge began to lower.

On a shaky breath, Sarra glanced at Giric.

"'Twill be fine, lass."

Mayhap, but as she took in the murder holes above the gate where hot rocks, oil, or a slew of arrows could be released on an attacker, she had her doubts.

As they crossed the wooden drawbridge, the clatter of hooves shuddered through her frayed nerves. The shadows of the gatehouse enveloped them. Moments later, they rode into the sunlight illuminating the bailey.

The scents of simmering meat and the freshness of winter merged. A bearded man wielded his hammer to hot steel; the blacksmith she'd heard working as they'd crossed the valley. To her left the butcher was hanging a carcass of venison in front of his shop, while next door a cobbler stretched leather to dry. As did her own castle, this one thrived.

The clang of blades drew her attention. She glanced past the keep at another bailey, where pairs of men were engaged in practice.

"Terrick."

She looked toward the keep, stilled. A large, well-muscled man with whisky-colored hair strode down the steps. At his side she recognized Sir Colyne, the knight who'd traveled with them earlier.

Sarra scanned the entry for her maid, Alicia, but no one else exited the keep.

Giric reined in his steed, then dismounted. "You will be safe here."

Before she could reply, he lifted her from the saddle and set her before him.

Rubbing the back of his neck, Giric faced the men who were walking toward them.

As they neared, the taller of the two, a man she didn't recognize, shot Giric a smile. "It has been too long since you last visited."

"Aye, Gryfalcon," Giric replied. "As of late, there is much which needs my attention."

A solemn expression creased Gryfalcon's face. "I was sorry to learn of your father's death. He was a fine man."

Giric nodded, but she didn't miss the flicker of sorrow across his face. "My thanks."

"'Tis good to see you both safe." Colyne glanced toward Sarra and gave her a nod. "My lady."

"Sir Colyne. My maid Alicia?"

"She is in Archerbeck," he replied, "until she receives word from you."

Relief swept her. "My thanks."

The man Giric had called Gryfalcon glanced toward Sarra. Male appreciation filled his gaze. "'Twould seem my brother has already made the acquaintance of the fair maiden."

Giric stiffened at her side, and the momentary warmth in his eyes fled.

Tension wove through Sarra. How would he introduce her? She prayed he would not be foolish enough to claim they were wed; such would do naught but complicate matters.

As if sensing her distress, Giric laid his hand on her forearm and drew her to his side. His gaze solemn, he released a slow, regretful breath.

Why was he looking at her as if he was coming to a monumental decision? What in God's name was going on? He'd assured her that they would file for an annulment once they'd reached her guardian. Had he changed his mind?

His body tensed, and her nerves grew.

With a premonition of dread, she stilled.

"'Tis my honor," he said, his burr pronounced, "to present my wife, Lady Sarra Bellecote, Countess of Terrick."

CHAPTER 13

Giric silently cursed as Sarra's face paled and she mouthed, *Count-ess of Terrick.* Her eyes narrowed on him, but she remained silent. Too much a lady to create a scene in public, no doubt once they were alone she'd release her fury. Nor could he blame her.

As if his announcing their marriage wasna enough of a shock, she'd now learned of his nobility. En route to Kirkshyre Castle he'd planned on concealing the fact that she was his wife, which would invite no speculation of impropriety. Then, as they'd ridden through the gates, his mistakes over the years had stormed him.

And when he'd stood before Colyne and Gryfalcon, shaken by his lifetime of misdeeds, he realized that he couldna add another—and the fact of his and Sarra's marriage had tumbled out.

If only he held the wealth to back his nobility, he could consider making their marriage real.

What was he thinking? Even if he possessed the coin to rebuild Wolfhaven Castle and keep Sarra in the grandeur to which she was accustomed, once she learned of his past as a reiver she would despise him. Nor would her guardian be pleased with an oath broken, an issue he'd deal with later.

Surprise flickered on Gryfalcon's face, then his mouth creased into a wide grin. "You have married!" He gave Giric a hearty thump on his back. "A joyous occasion indeed. We shall celebrate your vows this night." He shot a mock scowl toward Colyne. "'Twould seem my brother neglected to pass on the good news."

Giric nodded, nae missing Colyne's jaw dropping before his friend concealed his shock. Once in private with his friends, he would explain the unexpected circumstance. "My lady, may I introduce Adam MacKerran, Earl of Gryfalcon."

"'Tis a pleasure, my lady." Gryfalcon gave a courtly bow, lifted her hand, and pressed a kiss on the back of it.

"A pleasure to meet you as well, my lord," she replied, her words smooth, but Giric heard the slight tremble.

"You have met Colyne," Giric said, anxious for the introduction to be over.

Colyne nodded to Sarra with a warm smile. "My congratulations, Lady Terrick."

"Th-thank you."

Enough! Giric drew her to his side. "Our travel has been difficult. If you could please show us to a chamber, I shall allow my wife to rest."

"Of course. Lady Sarra must be fatigued." A pleased smile on his face, Gryfalcon led them inside, his brother at his side.

Several women worked in the great hall setting up trencher tables for the upcoming meal. At the hearth, a lad tended a rack of lamb spitted over the flames, its rich fragrance filling the room.

A group of knights engaged in a heated discussion near the stairs called to Gryfalcon as they passed, and he acknowledged them with a hearty return. Paces later, they entered the turret and started up.

At the second floor Colyne paused. "I will await you in the solar."

Giric nodded and continued up the stone steps behind the earl.

On the third floor, Gryfalcon opened the door to a sprawling chamber near the stairs.

On edge, Giric ushered Sarra inside, halted. A canopy of red velvet draped a large bed centered against the back wall. To the right, a small table held an earthen bowl, two goblets, and a bottle of wine.

"When you have rested, please join us for the evening meal." Gryfalcon smiled. "You know your way around."

"My thanks," Giric replied. "I will be down shortly."

With a nod, the noble exited and pulled the door shut.

The clang of men practicing in the bailey echoed into the silence. "Sarra—"

She rounded on him. "An earl!"

Guilt swept him. He would be truthful with her, as much as he could. "Aye."

She clenched her hands into fists at her sides. "Was it not enough that you tricked me into this farce of a marriage? Now I find that you have withheld that you are nobility?"

"I never meant this to happen," he said, irritated that he had allowed his emotions to sway logic. As if with the mayhem of late he
was logical? Since their impromptu marriage, his entire life had
turned upside down.

Her mouth tight, Sarra watched her husband prowl the chamber,
his eyes dark with secrets, his body taut like a wolf ready to spring.
She crossed her arms over her chest. "Why did you not tell me?"

He paused and his eyes met hers. Hard. Angry. Frustrated.

"Or is the truth too much to ask?"

The tension on his face crumbled. With a sigh, Giric rubbed the
back of his neck. "Nay, 'tis fair."

His soft admission caught her off guard. "Explain."

"Remember I told you about the attacks on Ravenmoor Castle
after 'twas seized by the English?"

She nodded, his retelling of his father's death a gruesome image
seared in her mind.

A muscle worked in his jaw. "Due to the retaliatory assaults on
Wolfhaven Castle, my home has fallen into a ravaged state. Our food
stores are low and the land barren."

Regret streaked his face even as pride echoed in his heart-torn
reply. Neither had it been easy for him to admit his impoverished
state. His desperate need for gold had humbled him into accepting
the mundane task of escorting her for coin.

If naught else during their time together, she'd learned that Giric
was a proud man. So, he'd posed as a knight and had intended keeping his title hidden from her.

The story of Sir Galahad came to mind. How many men would
have made such a sacrifice for their people?

Few indeed.

Questions of Giric's true intent for their marriage resurfaced. Had
he indeed wed her to save her life? The chamber pulsed with unspent
energy as she took in the dignified man before her, a man loyal to his
friends and those he loved. A man who'd risked his life on numerous
occasions to protect her. Would he plot against her for a political
cause? Desperation guided many a man down fallen paths.

Unsure of what to believe, she crossed to the window.

Quiet steps moved up behind her.

"You never planned our marriage to support Sir Bruce or for your own gain, did you?" she asked, needing to hear him confirm his earlier claim.

"I did nae." The regret in his soft burr made her heart ache. "If I could have avoided it, I would have."

She swallowed the lump rising in her throat. "Thank you for that."

"I have nae earned your thanks," he said, his voice rough with self-condemnation. "I should have never risked remaining overnight in Fergus's home."

Sarra turned and searched his face, found only remorse. "You did what you thought was best."

His mouth thinned. "It doesna forgive our marriage."

She was unsure what to say, or how to handle this humble lord. 'Twould be easier if he were the arrogant man she'd initially faced, the man who irritated her at every turn. That man she could dismiss.

His eyes darkened, and a flicker of desire ignited within. He stepped away, the emotion shielded. "You should know that Colyne is titled as well. He is the Earl of Strathcliff, and his home, Taigh Castle, is in the Highlands."

Disappointment lanced through her at yet another deception. "Why did you reveal that we were married?"

He gave a long, slow exhale. "I was tired of lies."

Silence fell between them.

He cleared his throat. "I know you are weary from travel. With Alicia nae here to serve you, I will have a maid sent to help you." Giric strode from the room, tugged the door closed behind him with a soft click.

Time seemed to pass in slow motion. The maid arrived; though young, she helped her with a deft hand, issuing orders to four lads who after her bath, pulled the tub from her room.

As they departed, Sarra closed the door, feeling very alone. She should be weary, exhausted from their hard travel, but she couldn't sleep.

The crackle of the fire echoed in the chamber as she stared at the large bed.

Man and wife.

If a true union, this night they would share this bed in the most intimate of ways. His kisses promised a passion she'd never dreamed, his touch ignited emotions that left her aching, except this night as any other in their future, could never be.

With a sad sigh, Sarra walked to the bed and ran her fingers across the finely woven cover. Due to circumstance, it wasn't proper that they would share this room. Neither would she shame Giric before his peers. They would remain here together but apart.

Thick blankets lay stacked atop the large chest in the corner. Giric would sleep on the floor. A reasonable solution.

A wave of tiredness swept over her, and she pulled back the comforter. Slipping into the softness, she drew up the finely crafted covers, and gave in to sleep.

Giric shut the door to the solar behind him. Muted sunlight cast the room in a dismal light. Rushes lay scattered on the floor, and a woven wool tapestry reflecting a Celtic battle adorned the far wall.

He glanced to where heavy cushioned oak chairs were arranged in a semicircle. Colyne and his brother Gryfalcon both stood.

Confusion etched Colyne's brow as he stepped forward. "A sword's wrath, you were to escort the lass, nae wed her."

"I blasted know what I was hired to do," Giric muttered. He crossed to the table where several bottles of wine sat, poured a goblet, downed the first cup, and then refilled a second. "'Twould seem since we last saw Léod, he has embroiled himself within the political cause and become a supporter for Robert Bruce, the Competitor."

"If I know him," Colyne said with disgust, "his actions have naught to do with politics but for his own gain."

"Aye. Léod's loyalty extends nay further than his own pockets," Giric agreed. "'Twould seem that Sarra's betrothed, Lord Sinclair, is a staunch supporter of John Balliol, and Léod is determined to ensure that none of her wealth reaches Balliol's pockets." He took a swallow of wine, swirled it on his tongue, and then swallowed. "Sarra and I stayed overnight with friends en route. While I was in the stable, Léod and his men cornered her."

Understanding dawned in Colyne's eyes. "And only by claiming that Sarra was your wife were you able to save her life."

"Aye," Giric replied.

Gryfalcon frowned. "Did the lass understand the Scottish custom when she agreed?"

Giric shook his head. "Nay."

"A sword's wrath!" Colyne thrummed his fingers over the hilt of his blade. "The bastard Léod knew what he was about. With her married to you, her betrothed can nay longer touch her inheritance."

"Speaking of which," Gryfalcon said, "how will you explain your marriage to her betrothed? With your arrival, I take it you are continuing to her guardian's?"

"Aye, once there, we will petition for an annulment." The thought of letting Sarra go weighed heavy on Giric's heart.

Gryfalcon refilled his goblet. "Annulments are nae easily given."

A fact Giric well knew, but he had to try. What would he do if the pope refused to annul their marriage? Blast it! He shoved the thought aside. He had enough to worry about. "Due to circumstance, I believe an annulment will be granted."

The earl sipped his wine. "'Tis within her guardian's rights to refuse to pay you for your escort until after the annulment is achieved. If I can be of help to your home and people, let me know."

"Your generosity is appreciated," Giric said, "but I will rebuild Wolfhaven Castle by my own hand. I will neither accept charity nor reive." He caught the glance that passed between the brothers. He didna expect them to like his decision, but for him to respect himself as a man, 'twas what he must do.

"'Twould seem there is little more to be done," Gryfalcon said.

"For the moment." Giric drained his cup. "Before I departed, I was informed that the pass is blocked. I would like to remain here until it is open."

Gryfalcon nodded. "You are always welcome."

"My thanks." Giric glanced at Colyne. "I am in desperate need of sword practice, if you are up to it?"

The glint of challenge sparked in his friend's eyes. "You need nae ask twice."

Looking forward to venting his frustration in a spar, Giric headed toward the door, Colyne at his side.

A short while later after each had donned their armor, they walked in companionable silence. As they exited the keep, a whirl of snow slapped at them, but Giric ignored the chill. Practice would take his mind off the upcoming confrontation with Lord Bretane and his son, Lord Sinclair.

"About the extra guard," Colyne said. "If you would like, I will travel with you to meet with her guardian."

"That willna be necessary." Giric tugged on his padded coif, pulled the mail hood into place. "Since my marriage to Sarra, with Léod's ability to gossip and half of Scotland knowing by now, she is nay longer a political threat."

Colyne cast a sidelong glance. "What is wrong then?"

"Naught."

Colyne grunted. "I have known you since we were lads. There is more than confronting Sarra's guardian or his son that has you on edge. Have you told Sarra that you were a reiver?"

His mouth tightened. "Nay. She doesna know, nor will she. I . . ." He muttered a curse. "Her parents were murdered by reivers."

Colyne's eyes widened. "A sword's wrath!"

"Now you understand why I willna have her finding out about my past."

Colyne nodded. "Indeed."

They reached the upper bailey where several knights sparred while another man worked on his horse with the quintain.

Frustrated by the situation, Giric withdrew his sword. He took it through a succession of several slow maneuvers to stretch out his muscles, and then moved into a readied stance.

Opposite him, Colyne followed suit. A moment later, he raised his blade chest high, a slow, calculating smile in his eyes. "Last time we sparred, I trounced you."

With a smile, Giric began to circle Colyne. "Your mind was frozen in the blizzard. As I remember, you begged for me to spare your life."

"Ha!"

Giric swung his sword in a tight arch, deflected Colyne's thrust.

His friend lunged, then sidestepped Giric's weapon at the last second.

Giric laughed, exhilarated, feeling better than he had in days. He swung. Their blades met. Steel shuddered through the air then scraped apart.

Skirting around him, Colyne kept out of Giric's reach, darting in for a quick strike, and then jumping back in a tactical retreat.

However deft with the blade, Giric knew Colyne too well and lured him closer with an over-wide swing.

Colyne took the bait and gave a solid thrust.

Prepared for his friend's maneuver, Giric drove his blade forward. Their swords locked, trembled, backed by sheer muscle. "You should have learned that move by now."

With a grunt, Colyne shoved Giric away. "At least I didna fall in love with my charge."

Giric froze. "I did nae—"

With a laugh, his friend shoved aside Giric's weapon then lifted the tip to touch his chest. "My match! I canna believe that you fell for that old trick."

"Nor I." With a muttered curse, Giric sheathed his sword. He didna love the lass. He cared for Sarra deeply, nay more.

But as he fell into step beside his friend as they headed to the keep, doubts lingered.

CHAPTER 14

Three days later, Giric glanced past Gryfalcon and Colyne to where a young maiden carrying a torch led the large procession. At Wolfhaven Castle, Candlemas would be celebrated as well, a time of rebirth, a time to welcome the coming spring to the lands, and to purify the fields for a hearty crop.

Sunlight sifted through the thinning gray clouds, exposing hints of blue as thick, icy flakes, fluttered like fairies' wings to the earth. From the clearing skies, the promise of spring seemed a distinct reality.

Giric took in Sarra as she walked at his side scanning the snow-blanketed fields with interest.

"The day will be a fine one." She looked over. "And according to the proverb, bodes ill for our travel."

"Mayhap," Giric said, aware of the belief that if Candlemas fell on a fair day, winter would maintain its hold on the land for a while longer. "But the day's warmth will melt the snow in the pass. Another few days of fair weather, and we shall be able to resume our journey."

She nodded and looked away, but nae before he saw a hint of quiet yearning, a desire growing within him as well.

Since his spar with Colyne, his friend's claim that he loved Sarra, though said in jest, haunted him. Each night after he and Sarra had retired, true to his promise, he'd lain on the pallet near the hearth and left her untouched, but he couldna quell the feelings the lass inspired.

Did he love her? He covertly studied Sarra, nae wanting the need for her that grew with each passing day. But as the sun's rays poured across the land to prism through the snow like a million crystals and caress her face, he was forced to admit the truth.

Saint's breath!

Pain lanced his heart as he stared at the vibrant blue sky opening before him. How fitting to realize that he was in love on a day of re-birth and purification. If she were any other woman, if it were any other time, he would revel in this omen. With Sarra promised to an-other, he could embrace naught.

That reality didna sever his longing for her, or stop his noting her every action throughout the day. Her quiet smile this morning when she'd helped craft the ceremonial wheel of rushes and straw for the door to the keep. The way her eyes had clouded with emotion when she'd held a newborn child. Or, without her realizing it, the way she fit into his life with such ease. As they completed a circle around the field, the maiden leading the procession began to sing, her voice soft and pure. She halted.

Giric, along with the others, followed suit.

The maiden knelt. On the snow-glazed earth she laid bread, milk, and oats before her. A wash of brilliant sunlight enfolded the woman as if caught in a spell.

In silence she rose, turned to the crowd, and lifted her arms high. "We have sent our offering to the goddess Brigid for a blessed sea-son. Let our soil be rich and our harvest bountiful."

Cheers rippled through the crowd, then murmurs of excitement tangled with talk of the upcoming festivities. With warm smiles, the crowd began making their way back to the keep.

With solemn steps, Giric walked alongside Sarra. In a few days they would resume their travel, and he would hand Sarra over to an-other man, never to see her again.

As they entered the lower bailey, a horse's scream ripped through the air.

"Catch him," a man's deep voice yelled.

Near the stables, a squire seized the reins of a young stallion.

With an angry snort, the horse bared his teeth.

"I told you to keep a tight hold on him," a stocky man chastised, striding toward the lad. The man Giric deduced to be the squire's knight shook his head with disgust.

Before the knight could reach the lad, the horse reared, hauling the boy into the air. The stallion landed hard and bolted, dragging the lad straight toward the crowd.

People dressed in brightly colored garb scattered as the infuriated steed closed.

Bedamned! Giric pulled Sarra from the horse's path.

A shrill scream pierced the air. The horse, as if realizing the squire still held the reins, whirled toward him and charged.

"Stay here!" Giric bolted toward the horse, caught sight of Gryfalcon and Colyne racing toward the stallion as well.

Squeals of fury melded with the squire's screams as the horse attacked.

Gryfalcon, Colyne, and the squire's knight caught hold of the steed's bridle. Together they dragged the stallion back while Giric knelt beside the lad.

Blood splattered the snow-drenched earth where the squire lay unmoving. With a seasoned eye Giric took in the nasty gash across his forehead, the cuts through his tunic, and the unnatural angle of his right leg—broken. He pressed a piece of the shredded tunic against the lad's brow to staunch the flow of blood.

Sarra knelt at his side. "Let me help."

Upset she'd followed, Giric noted the strain in her eyes and the paleness of her face. "Get back."

Her chin lifted and she laid her hand near his on the compress. "I am not leaving."

People gathered around them, but Giric watched Sarra. Through her shock at witnessing the mauling was determination. "Keep the compress tight on the head wound," Giric finally said, unsure if he was more irritated or surprised by her action. A fool could see the cost of her decision.

The last thing he'd expected was for her to aid a Scot, but from the concern in her eyes, she truly cared. Though she may nae have realized it, she'd taken the first steps in accepting his people.

Which made him love her more.

Humbled, Giric peeled back the layers of torn tunic to check for other serious wounds. During his and Sarra's time together, he'd noted her shift in feelings. When she mentioned Scots, or looked upon those within Kirkshyre Castle, no longer did fear or disdain exist in her eyes.

He wished that somehow Sarra could find the same forgiveness for reivers, but with her painful memories, 'twas a wish.

"Move back," an older woman's voice called. The crowd separated, and a gray-haired woman, still wearing her gown embroidered with designs to celebrate Candlemas, waded through the throng, a basket of herbs in her hand. She knelt opposite Giric, her experienced eyes already searching the lad's battered body.

"His leg is broken," Giric said as he peeled away a swath of the squire's shredded trews and exposed the disfigured joint, the skin turning an ugly mix of yellow and purple. "There is a nasty gash on his forehead that will need sewing, but only a few cuts and scrapes on his chest."

"He is lucky to be alive," Gryfalcon said, moving to the perimeter, the lad's knight on his heels.

"Aye," Giric agreed.

"My squire wasna paying attention to his duties and the horse got away from him," the knight explained.

Giric nodded. Until gelded, stallions must be handled with extreme caution. "Next time your squire will nae be remiss."

"Nor will he be receiving punishment," Gryfalcon said. "The cuts and bruises he bears will more than enough teach him a valuable lesson."

The knight nodded. "I agree, my lord."

The squire gave a low moan.

After securing a splint on the boy's leg, the healer stood. "He needs to be carried to the keep where I can tend to him."

"I will take my squire inside." The knight lifted the lad.

Sarra rose alongside the knight, keeping pressure on the boy's brow.

"I will take that, my lady," the healer said, and moved up to her side.

"I can help you," Sarra replied. "I have treated many men in the past."

The elder woman hesitated, and then gestured to the knight. "Let us go then."

With Sarra holding the compress on the squire, the knight hurried toward the keep, and Giric followed.

Once inside a small chamber, the healer ordered two men to hold the lad down, while another pulled his leg until his bones fell into place. The healer quickly bound the limb in a snug wrap.

Sarra helped cleanse the cuts and sew stitches in the larger gashes.

When the healer began to stow her herbs into her basket, Giric laid his hand on Sarra's shoulder. "You have aided the lad all that you can," he said, taking in the smear of blood on her cape and a small line streaked across her cheek.

"I had to help him," she said, shock woven through her voice. "He could have died."

A knot clenched in Giric's gut and he understood. For a moment, she'd seen herself in the boy's terror; a child helpless to circumstance. Though the settings were different, for that moment she'd identified with the squire and reached out to help.

Moved by her selfless action, Giric drew her against him.

On a shuddering sigh, she laid her head on his chest, her warm breath fanning against his neck.

And he foolishly wished that they were man and wife in every way and that he could take her to their chamber, hold her until her tremors stopped, and kiss away her fears. Then they would make love, slow and sweet.

Concern darkened Gryfalcon's eyes as they met Giric's. "Is Lady Sarra well?"

"She is tired. I will take her to our chamber to rest."

"My lady," Gryfalcon said, "my thanks for your assistance, 'tis appreciated."

She looked toward him, her body trembling. "Thanks are unnecessary. Had you been within my castle, you would have offered the same."

The earl held her gaze, his eyes solemn. "I will nae forget your kindness, my lady." Gryfalcon looked at Giric. "Take good care of her."

He nodded. Concerned by the paleness of her face, Giric ushered Sarra from the room and toward their chamber. "I will call for a bath and—"

"Wait." She halted beside a window, laid her hand against the sill. "I would like to go outside for a breath of air."

At the weariness in her voice, he hesitated. Tending to the squire and battling her own emotions had exhausted her, but he understood her need to rid her senses of the stench of blood and to find a measure of peace. "After you change, and then only for a short while."

Too tired to argue, Sarra allowed Giric to lead her to their chamber. After a maid had helped her into another gown, he led her from the keep. They exited the castle and headed toward the field where they'd walked with the procession a short time before.

Her emotions unsteady, she glanced over. "Where are we going?"

"There is something I want to show you."

As they continued on, a stand of oaks arched before them like a gateway to the snow-laden forest beyond. The absence of wind enhanced the pristine setting, and sunlight warmed her face. As they entered the shadows of the forest, a raven chirped upon a barren branch, then flew off with a flutter. From far away a falcon screamed, and ahead, animal tracks dotted the forest floor.

Her breath misted before her, her each step muted by the layer of snow as she scanned the woods. "Is it much farther?"

"Nay." He took her hand, and she let him, allowing the rush of emotions to fill her. After witnessing the stallion's attack on the squire and his near death, she savored the taste of life.

The faint rush of water reached her first, then the rumble of distant thunder. "A waterfall?"

He smiled, a playful, charming gesture that made her heart skip. "If I told you it wouldna be a surprise."

Warmth rushed through her at his teasing, seconds before panic swept through her. She shouldn't be out here with him alone. Not when her resistance toward him was low, not when she fought her growing feelings toward him with every passing day, and not when she wanted to believe that at this moment they could be friends.

To remain with him, to succumb to the ease which he made her feel, and to allow them to grow closer would only make their parting more difficult in the end.

They stepped past a cluster of boulders, and snow-capped rocks jutted upward before them like a white wall.

Giric smiled. "Close your eyes."

On edge, Sarra halted. "I do not think this is a good idea."

"You are nae afraid to be alone with me are you?"

He watched her with a teasing look, making her statement sound absurd. Since their marriage he'd been naught but a gentleman. The truth be told, her doubts rose from her own desire for him. She lowered her lids. When he laid his hand over her eyes, she started. "You do not trust me to keep them shut?"

His warm laugh slid through her like a fine wine. "You would peek."

She pushed his hands away. "I would not." A smile curved her lips, feeling foolish, but also wonderfully unencumbered. "Mayhap I would have looked a small bit."

A smug grin slid over his face. "I knew it."

"You are so sure of yourself."

"In most things." He caressed the side of her face with his thumb, and his expression grew solemn. "With you I am nae so sure."

She swallowed hard. When they'd first met she'd loathed the sight of him, waited for the day when he would ride from her life. Now, in the coolness of the forest and with her body trembling at his touch, hatred toward him was the furthest thought in her mind.

"Close your eyes again and follow me."

Without hesitation, she did.

He gently guided her forward.

The rush of water grew to a roar. Cool moisture filled the air, and excitement thrummed through her. "Are we there?" By the rood, but she sounded like an eager child. For this moment, lost to sensation, giddy with happiness, and caught in the whirlpool of emotion, what did it matter?

"Almost." After several more steps, he gave her hand a soft squeeze. "Halt."

"Can I look now?"

He released her hand. "Aye."

Sarra opened her eyes. Water thundered over a high cliff to a pool of the deepest blue. Huge icicles framed the magnificent cascade of water, the force of the downpour casting a layer of mist shimmering over the basin.

In awe of the sheer beauty before her, she gasped. "Thank you for sharing this," she said, unsure if words could truly express her appreciation for such a wondrous gift.

His eyes searched hers with a desperate tenderness.

When she thought he would draw her to him, her body trembling with anticipation for his touch, he took her hand instead.

"There is more."

"More?" she asked, trying not to show her disappointment.

"Aye." He led her along the steep ledge rimming the gorge.

She glanced down the ice-slicked rocks to where the water pounded far below. "Should we walk so close to the edge?"

A smile touched his mouth. "'Tis the only way to get where we are going."

The land dipped then curved toward a stand of firs. After pushing the heavy boughs away, a cave stood before them.

Confused, she glanced over. "You wanted to show me a cave?"

"I want you to see something inside," Giric said with irresistible charm.

"Oh."

He led her inside. In the murky light, several smaller tunnels branched out before her, the rush of water beyond but a muted roar.

"Where do these tunnels lead?"

In the dimness she caught the twinkle in his eyes. "It depends on what you are trying to find."

At the desire roughening his burr, prickles of sensation wove through her. And in that moment, however wrong, she wanted him more than anything else in her life. "And what am I trying to find?" she asked, her words breathless.

"A question for you to answer," he whispered, his burr thick. Giric guided her toward the tunnel the farthest to the left.

Blackness swallowed them, but he continued along the twists and turns with familiar ease along the underground passageway.

"Have you never been given a surprise?"

She hesitated. "No."

"I am sorry for that," he said, his voice as tender as sincere. "Then this will be my surprise to you."

Her breathing grew unsteady. She trembled in his hold.

He paused and after a long moment continued on.

What had she expected, that he would kiss her? Yes, foolish thoughts she had no rights thinking.

With each step, the thunder of the waterfall grew. As they rounded the next bend, a large cavern unfolded before them.

Sunlight streamed through the rush of water, bursting into a riot of color. Enchanted, she walked into the prismed light, paused several feet before the falls, the mist cold against her face. "'Tis wondrous."

"As are you." Giric kissed her, soft, slow, and with a hint of desperation.

Wanting him, Sarra gave in to the emotions, drowned in his taste. At this moment, however wrong, she needed him as much as he needed her.

When he skimmed his mouth along her jaw, she moaned with the tenderness of it. "Giric . . ." But his fingers were already working their magic, sliding through her hair, as his mouth took, teased until need ignited into a scorching flame.

The roar of the water dimmed, the cool shimmers of mist against her skin lay forgotten. When he drew her against him until their bodies merged as one, she ached for more.

On a shudder, he caught her face in his hands, his own unsteady. "God forgive me, I want you."

CHAPTER 15

A myriad of emotions flickered in Sarra's eyes—desire, innocence—but Giric focused on one, utterly amazed: love. Never having expected her to look at him with such tenderness, the need that thrummed him seconds before churned into a riotous demand.

Reasons he'd erected why their marriage wouldna work fell away. Bedamned her guardian and bedamned his son Lord Sinclair. To Hades with his own meager means. What they had here, now, would bind them forever. Although she'd nae spoken the words, she loved him. It shone in her eyes as bright as the midday sun, and was proven in the gentleness of her every touch. Together they could overcome any obstacles life chose to wield.

Giric lost himself in the taste of her lips, basked in the rightness of this moment.

On a moan she pressed herself against him demanding, giving, her innocent response seducing him until his body ached for her.

Though he'd made love before, never had anyone moved him like Sarra. How could he have ever doubted his feelings toward her? She was everything he could ever want in a woman and more.

And she was his.

Would always be.

Forever.

Overwhelmed by emotion, his hands trembled as they slid beneath her cape until they met skin.

She drew back, her eyes dark, tangled with nerves and desire. "Giric, I . . ."

He brushed his mouth over hers in a tender kiss, understanding her shyness, but tasting her passion. So he moved with slow strokes until her hesitancy fell away, her hands skimmed over his shoulders, and her lips moved against his with an urgent demand.

In moments his garb as well as hers lay discarded in a tangled heap, save for his woolen cloak, which he laid on the ground.

She stood before him, her nipples taut in the cool air, and the questions in her eyes those of an innocent.

Giric interlaced his fingers with hers. "Trust me. In this. In our life together." He brought her hands to his lips. Turning one hand over palm up, he kissed the sensitive center.

A blush stained her cheeks, and she started to look away.

"Nay," he said, "never be ashamed when you are with me."

"But I . . . I do not know how to . . ."

"Follow your heart." He drew her into a tender kiss, stunned at how his body fit perfectly against hers. "You are beautiful."

Her eyes searched his as if afraid to accept his words as truth.

And at that moment, he would do whatever it took to make her believe.

He grazed kisses over her face as he cupped her breast. A tremor shuddered over her skin, and he slid his thumb across her taut nub. "I am going to make love to you." He pressed soft kisses against the slender column of her throat, and reveled in the feel.

On a soft moan, she arched her neck giving him better access. "I want you, too," she said in a rough whisper.

Emotions stormed his every coherent thought as Giric laid her upon his woolen cloak. Her slender form, accented by firm, round breasts, the wedge of downy hair that lured him to look, invited him to taste.

Emboldened by his sensual perusal, Sarra slid her fingers across the ripple of muscle over his chest.

He tensed beneath her touch.

Nervous, she glanced up. "I did something wrong?"

His face twisted in a half-pleasure, half-pained expression, Giric shook his head. "Nay, lass, you are doing everything right."

She hesitated.

"I enjoy your touch, immensely so."

With a steadying breath, she continued, enjoying the feel of his skin, the hard silk of honed muscle along the flat of his stomach. As she moved lower, took in his impressive size, she stilled. Nerves edged through her, and she lifted her eyes to his.

"Everything will be all right," he whispered, his eyes darkening.

And she believed him. She released a slow breath, ashamed at her ignorance when she wanted to show him how much she . . . By the rood, she loved him!

The anguish of trying to sort out her feelings toward him all made sense. The turmoil she'd struggled over as they'd traveled was due to what her heart already knew.

Overwhelmed with emotion, when Giric lowered his mouth to hers, she tumbled into the kiss. He laid siege to her mouth in a devastating plunder. As his hands stroked her breast, a coil of heat ignited and she arched against him. "Giric," she moaned.

His eyes hot with passion held hers as he slid his tongue over the tip of her breast.

Flames burst hot inside, the warmth wonderfully destroying.

Hunger in his eyes, he brought an icicle to her nipple and traced the cold length over her sensitive flesh.

A tremor rippled through her, then the heat of his mouth replaced the icy tingle and she gasped with delight.

Water rushed several feet away, the cool mist tingling against her flesh as he used the wand of ice to trace a slow curve along the flat of her stomach, his tongue following with excruciating slowness. Then his fingers brushed against her most private place.

Sensation stormed her, and she arched against his touch.

His eyes flicked to meet hers, hot with desire. "I want to taste you."

At the explicit request, a tremor ran through her. She felt exposed, but wonderfully so. Never had she imagined making love could be so incredible, but wrapped in his intimate embrace, she wanted everything and more.

With their gazes bound, he dipped his head and tasted her in the most erotic caress.

Heat poured through her with a potent force. The world tilted, and before she could grasp a fragment of sanity, his finger slid inside her moist heat.

And she was lost, caught in an unearthly ride filled with unspoken promises, of blistering heat, and mind-spinning pleasure.

Then his finger began to move in rhythm to his tongue.

And she shattered.

The world spun around her, sweet like honey, warm like summer heat. As she floated back, dazed from the pleasure of his lovemaking, his hands held her while his tongue continued its sweet torment.

She gasped as again she was spinning up. On a ragged cry, she again plunged over the edge.

Giric moved beside her and held her until her tremors subsided.

Embraced by a soft warmth of her release, on a sigh she laid her cheek against his neck. "I never knew it could be so wonderful."

A tender smile curved his mouth, and the love in his eyes almost brought her to tears. "There is so much more I want to show you."

"More?" Sarra blushed remembering the intimacy of his actions, but her body tingled at his sensual promise.

"Much more." Giric outlined her finger with his tongue then swirled it along the crevice.

Heat slid through her. Before she could regain control, he drew her finger into his mouth and began to suck.

Sarra shuddered, the familiar desire thrumming through her veins straight to her core.

"There is so much more." As if to further prove his claim, one at a time, he drew each finger into his mouth for the same, thorough caress.

Pulse racing, she tried to catch her breath, but his other hand slid to caress her breast, then moved to cup her moist heat. He slid his finger inside her while his mouth suckled and his eyes watched, and she could only whimper from the pleasure of it.

Giric continued to stroke Sarra, loving watching her every shiver, how her body tightened around him, and how with his each stroke, she now arched against him.

Need to claim her stormed him. With her body trembling from her release, confident he'd prepared her for their joining, he pressed kisses along the soft curve of her neck as he eased inside her slick folds. As he nudged her barrier, he stilled.

Her tight sheath closed around him and her body began to shudder. "Giric!"

His fragile control shattered and he drove deep, then stilled, witnessing the surprise in her eyes and the pain. "I am sorry." His body raging to take her, he held, honored to be her first lover, vowing no man would ever touch the woman who belonged to him. He brushed a damp tendril from her cheek. "I promise from now on you will only feel pleasure."

The hurt in her eyes of moments before faded to trust.. "I love you."

"Sarra I . . ." Humbled by her words, and however much he wanted to whisper the same, fear tore through him. With gentle strokes, he began to move within her; though he hadna spoken the words, he would show her.

As he increased the pace, her nails clung to his back. "I—"

He drove deep.

On a moan, she threw her head back.

Her moist rush engulfed him, and his body began to quake. Blast it, there was so much more to show her. And he would, he promised himself, if it took forever. "Sarra," he breathed as he spilled into her, her cries of release matching his own. Enwrapped within the rush of emotions pouring through him, he drew her against his chest, amazed how this one woman had reached his soul.

"You love me?" he asked, his throat tight, needing to hear the words.

With her heart in her eyes, she nodded. "Yes. I never thought that I could . . ." A blush spread up her cheeks.

Joy filled him. "Love knows no bounds. You have my heart and so much more." Sarra watched him, her eyes filled with hope.

His happiness of moments before faded. And why would she nae? They'd made love and she'd shared her feelings. Now, she waited to hear his declaration in return.

Except she didna know that he was a reiver.

She shivered.

"You must be cold." Giric gathered her clothes. The time to speak of his past would come soon enough. They would have this one night. On the morrow he would tell her, and he prayed that she would understand.

Confusion touched her face. "A bit."

"Once we have dressed, there is something I would like to show you."

She lifted a questioning brow, her confused look lost to one of curiosity. "If 'tis anything like this, we shall be a while."

Warmth filled him at her teasing, and then he grew somber. "Naught could be as special to me as you." He claimed her mouth, pouring his love for her into his kiss. On an unsteady breath, he drew back. "From this moment we are man and wife. I vow that no one will ever break what we have, the love we feel for each other."

Eyes raw with hope searched his. "But what of—"

He pressed his finger against her lips. "We will have this day. On the morrow we will discuss the future. *Our future.*" Her skin tingled from the growing cold, and goose bumps dotted her flesh. "Let us hurry before you freeze."

"It did not feel so cold a moment ago," Sarra said, yanking on her dress, the warm glow of their lovemaking glistening in her eyes.

However tempted he was to strip her naked and make love with her again, her body needed time to rest. After Giric secured her cape, he took her hand.

Curious eyes met his. "Where are we going?"

"To show you what I brought you here to see in the first place." He led her to the edge of the cavern wall where water spilled past with a thunderous rage.

Sunlight slipped between the edge of the cave and the wall of water to entwine in a spectacular prism. Encased within the mist of colors along the floor's border grew green stalks that arched toward the sun, each stem tipped with a slender-petaled white flower, the inner leaves tipped with a swath of green.

Sarra crouched, cupped a crisp bloom, and lifted it to her nose. She smiled.

"Snowdrops." He knelt beside her. "Because the waterfall protects the ledge, these flowers bloom here up to a month earlier than the surrounding forest."

She inhaled the flower's scent one last time then released it. Her eyes misted with tears as she pressed her lips against his. "Thank you." When she drew back, a smile curved her mouth, one that shot straight to his heart. "I would never have guessed you to be a man who would be aware of when snowdrops bloom."

"I care about many things great and small." He stroked his fingers over her cheek, afraid he might be caught in a wondrous dream and suddenly wake up. But the silkiness of her flesh was real, and he sent up a silent prayer for the precious gift of her love. "You know little about me."

A shadow of doubt crossed her eyes. As quick, it vanished. "True, but in the years ahead I will discover what it seems I originally dismissed."

The cold, skeptical woman he'd first met came to mind. "Perhaps you will nae like all that you find?"

She angled her chin with the familiar defiance he adored. "For too long I have lived bound by my past," Sarra said, her eyes growing reminiscent. "During our travels, you have shown me that I was wrong to condemn the Scots for the actions of a few. 'Twould seem that I chastised many people who hold the same values as I do without ever giving them a chance." She exhaled. "I am ashamed that for years I have allowed hatred to rule my life. Not all Scots live the brutal lifestyle of the reivers. But now, because of you, I can move forward."

The regret in his gut grew twofold. He should tell her about his past, but doubts slid through him, and he remained silent. He would tell her on the morrow. 'Twould be soon enough.

Shaking off his somber mood, he stood, forced a tender smile. "'Tis time we return."

She joined him, her eyes bright. "I am looking forward to the evening's festivities."

Sarra started to turn, and he caught her hand. "Wait here." Giric walked to where the flowers bloomed. He picked one, returned, and handed her the snowdrop. "To remember this moment."

A tear slid down her cheek as she lifted the flower to her nose, and inhaled the fragrant scent. "As if I could ever forget?"

Nor would he. After one last kiss, Giric led her from the chamber. Though the oncoming night held promises of passion, what of tomorrow? Could his telling her of his past destroy their newfound love?

"Saint's breath, I know what I am about." Giric glared at Colyne at his side as he walked down the steps toward the great room, the festivities below a growing buzz. "I didna plan on falling in love with Sarra, but I have."

"What will you tell her guardian?"

A question he'd pondered a thousand times. "The truth. 'Tis all I have. Nor do I expect her betrothed to understand. God help me, if I stood in his place, I wouldna."

With their union consummated, there would be repercussions for his defiance. He'd given his vow, but he was damned if he regretted the binding of their marriage. Sarra was worth any wrath he incurred.

"You could send a message and return to Wolfhaven Castle. If you want, I will deliver it."

Giric shook his head, however tempting the thought. "I have never run from my troubles, and I am nae starting now."

"Then have Sarra remain here. There is nae reason for her to continue," Colyne said. "Once your business with her guardian is through, she can rejoin you on your trip home. My brother would ensure her safety during her stay. In addition, I could travel with you to Dunkirk Castle."

The worry haunting Giric over the past few days faded. Why hadna he thought of that before? Without Sarra there when he broke the news to Lord Bretane, regardless of what happened to him, she would be safe. "You are right. Gryfalcon informed me earlier this morning that hunters have reported that the pass is open. Tomorrow, you and I will leave at first light."

Candlelight spilled throughout the great hall as they entered, the air rich with the scent of wax along with a hint of the yuletide greens scattered throughout the room, and the robust smell of roast venison consumed the hour before.

Sarra sat on the dais beside Gryfalcon where he'd left her a short while before. A smile played on her face as she listened to the bard who told their bold tales with relish, and entertained the crowd of gentry and peasants alike who filled the keep.

Pleased, Giric walked up, leaned over, and kissed her. "You are enjoying yourself?"

Eyes warm with desire lifted to his. "Immensely. He is a wonderful storyteller."

Heat smoldered in her sultry voice, and anticipation of the night to come wove through him like warmed wine.

A flush slid up her cheeks at his overt perusal, and she lowered her lashes.

Lured, he leaned forward, kissed the soft curve of her jaw. "You look sleepy."

"Sleepy?" Sarra frowned as if confused. "I am not . . ." Her eyes lingered on his, and her blush deepened.

The roar of the crowd pulled Giric from the moment. He glanced at Gryfalcon, Colyne, and several other men seated nearby, thankful they appeared engrossed in the storyteller's tale of a fairy outwitted by a mortal. He'd heard the story many times before. Then he re-membered the end. Blast it. "Sarra, let us go."

"I wish to hear the last of the tale," she said with a smile.

"I—"

"Though from the Otherworld," the bard boomed, "she had never matched wits with a reiver."

The crowd cheered, but Sarra's expression paled.

Giric silently cursed. What did he expect? She'd found forgive-ness for the Scots, but nae the reiver. "Sarra?" He laid his hand over hers; it felt like ice.

"I am fine." A feeble attempt at a smile wilted on her face. "I am sorry. When I heard the bard . . . I was not prepared."

"I know." Her reaction was a glaring reminder of how much stood between them. "You are overtired." Frustrated, he helped her to her feet. Her acceptance of his past would come. Time was the only cure. Tomorrow, after this night of making love, they would begin the heal-ing. And he prayed she'd find forgiveness for the choices he'd made.

Gryfalcon glanced from Giric to Sarra, rose. "You are retiring?"

"Aye," Giric replied.

One of the earl's brows lifted as he glanced toward Giric.

After their discussion, he understood Gryfalcon's concern about keeping his past from Sarra. There was plenty to go around. With a nod, he led his wife to their chamber, pleased to find the hearth ablaze, and the snowdrop he'd given her earlier within a delicate, slim-necked clay container.

As he closed the door behind them, Sarra turned. She gave a shaky exhale. "About below, I am sorry. I overreacted."

"Letting go of your past is nae going to be easy." And he had demons of his own to release as well. He drew her into his arms. "But I will be there for you. Always. Never forget that."

Tears glistened in her eyes. "I love you so much."

Heart aching, he brushed a kiss on her lips.

"Giric, now that we are married, with my inheritance I can help you rebuild your castle."

He stilled, his pride taking a direct blow. "I do nae need your help."

She angled her jaw. "I have plenty of gold."

"Nay." He released her, angry she offered, irritated that she held the funds and could. He'd set out to rebuild his self-worth, to become a man he could respect. He didna need a woman's hand smoothing his way. "Is that why you think I bedded you?" His ire shot up a notch. "Do you think I give a damn about your money?"

Temper rising, Sarra glared at Giric. 'Twas like him to put his back up when offered help. "'Tis because I know you do not care about my money that I want to help."

His nostrils flared. "Keep it."

Stubborn pride. There was no other explanation. "Without the gold from delivering me to my betrothed, what will you do now to re-build Wolfhaven Castle?"

Ice blue eyes narrowed. "That is my business." He strode to the hearth.

She waited a beat, tried to keep her temper in check. Both of them spewing angry words would make the situation worse. "As your wife, 'tis mine as well."

His shoulders stiffened. "I do nae wish to discuss it," he stated, his voice tempered, but an edge of steel in his words.

The fragile hold on her temper unleashed. "How dare you dismiss me! If you did not want me to be a part of your life, you should have left me untouched."

He whirled, his expression haggard with love and need, but beneath, regret.

Nerves slid through her. "What is wrong?"

"I tried," he answered, his voice raw with frustration.

Panic tore through her. Was she wrong and he didn't love her? Fighting for calm, she took a steadying breath. "Tried what?"

"To keep away from you." He exhaled a long sigh. "This, us, was never supposed to happen."

The room spun around her. Panic took shape, gripped her soul. "We were never supposed to happen? Hours ago we made love, sealed our marriage. Now you tell me," she accused, her voice rising, "'twas never supposed to happen?"

He started toward her.

Furious, she held out her hand. "Answer me."

"Sarra."

Her body vibrated with anger. "What is going on?"

Silence.

"Damn you, I deserve to know!" But she was afraid, petrified that he would leave her. After losing her parents, she'd spent her entire life not daring to trust, to love, but over these past few days, she'd taken the ultimate risk; she had allowed him into her heart. "Giric?" Her voice shook, and she cursed herself for that. But she would not grovel for his affection. If necessary she would go forward on her own, a life she'd lived until he'd arrived at Rancourt Castle. But the pain of losing him would leave her devastated.

"Sarra, I . . . never wanted to love you."

Her shoulders drooped and a hysterical laugh welled in her throat. He'd held back on declaring his feelings toward her because of his pride. "Do you think your lack of money matters to me?"

A muscle worked in his jaw. "I have a clan that depends on me, a castle in sad disrepair, and—"

"A wife who loves you."

"And shouldna."

At the vehemence of his words a chill raced through her. "Why?"

Again a haunted look shadowed his face. "Because in the end I will hurt you."

That he could be so vulnerable moved her. Her throat tight with emotions, and she shook her head. "I do not believe you ever could."

Darkness clouded his eyes. "If you were smart, you would walk away from me."

She loved him, but neither would she grovel. "Is that what you want?"

Ice blue eyes darkened, then he hauled her against him, his kiss dangerous in its intensity. "Damn you. I want you with my every breath."

Her heart exploded as he swept her into his arms, his mouth ravaging hers. He laid her on the bed, and his greedy hands stripped away her garb, touching, seducing every part of her. Candlelight flickered over her naked body as he caressed her with erotic precision until her body shuddered with need.

With a fierce growl, he discarded his garb, positioned himself over her, his look fierce with need. "I love you, never will I stop." Then he drove deep.

As she spun into a glorious climax, he followed, and she silently swore that whatever lay before them, together they would overcome.

* * *

A soft thrum fractured Giric's sleep. With a grimace, he reached for his dagger on the nearby table as he scanned the room for signs of danger. Embers glowed in the hearth, wind battered against the shutters, a soft gray light hinted that the sun rose in the east. At his side Sarra lay curled against him, her golden hair framing her face, his leg draped intimately over hers, and her breasts exposed where the blanket had slid to her waist.

With a groan he sheathed the dagger, then ran his fingers through her hair, amazed at the depth that he loved her. His mind shifted to more base thoughts and his body hardened at the wonderfully wicked ways he could awaken Sarra from her slumber.

A knock sounded on the door.

He scowled at the entry; which had caused him to awaken. Leaning over, he gave Sarra a soft kiss. Her warm scent tempting him, he edged lower and drew her nipple into his mouth, rewarded for his effort as she gave a soft groan.

Saint's breath! With reluctance he stood.

She wrinkled her brow and her hand moved to where he'd lain.

Moved she sought him in her sleep, with regret he tugged on his trews, crossed the chamber, and quietly opened the door.

Colyne stood outside, his expression grim.

Blast it, what had happened? With a glance to ensure Sarra still slept, he slipped into the corridor. "What is wrong?"

"Lord Maxwell is in the hall below."

"Why?" Giric asked, well familiar with Maxwell and his dislike for him. Once during his reiving days, in an act of rebellion, he and his men had stolen Maxwell's prize bull and feasted well for the next week. An act Maxwell had never forgiven him for.

"He stated that you murdered their blacksmith, and he is here to arrest you."

Giric grunted. "'Tis a blasted lie. I have been nowhere near their village. If any, 'twas the bastard's hand behind the killing."

"My thought exactly," Colyne agreed. "Maxwell said that their blacksmith was murdered five days ago. After questioning, several members of his clan stated 'twas your hand that took his life."

"Coerced, you mean," he spat.

"Indeed," Colyne agreed. "Gryfalcon explained that during this time you were en route to Lady Sarra's guardian and nowhere near Maxwell's home, but he claims the witnesses are adamant 'twas you."

Giric's mind churned for an explanation. "Why would anyone want to frame me for a murder I didna commit? It doesna make sense." The crime occurred after his impromptu marriage to Sarra—a union Léod had ensured. "Léod!"

Colyne's eyes narrowed.

"Who claims that I murdered the man?" Giric asked, already putting together the motley band in his mind.

"Maxwell mentioned Blar and Ranald as two of the witnesses."

"Both Léod's men." Why? Hadna the bastard thrown his life off-kilter enough? 'Twas a miracle Sarra had forgiven him, and a blessing that somewhere in the upheaval she had fallen in love.

"What could he hope to gain?" Colyne asked.

"I am nae sure, but nay doubt Léod is behind this."

"Aye, on that I agree," Colyne said.

Giric rubbed his jaw. "Léod wanted Sarra dead, but her marriage to me accomplished the same end. It took away the chance that Balliol would receive any of her inheritance."

"It doesna make sense . . ." Disgust pierced his friend's eyes. "What does Léod want more than anything?"

Saint's breath. "Money." He stepped to the window, stared at the flurries swirling against the gray of dawn. "Without meaning to, he believes through Sarra, I have been gifted with a fortune."

"And jealous, Léod means to see you dead so he can wed Sarra." Colyne grimaced. "Ever since your run-in with him while you were reiving, he has awaited an opportunity to seek revenge. He wants a hanging, and ensuring that you have been identified by supposed witnesses, he believes he will."

A muscle worked in Giric's jaw, aware his status as a noble forced Maxwell to formally present the charges against him before his peers. "'Tis a mess. I do nae have the luxury of time to sort this out. I need to meet with Lord Bretane, find a means to earn gold, and somehow to tell Sarra about my past as a reiver."

"Aye," his friend agreed. "'Tis best if you and I slip out as fast as possible. We will deal with any explanations later."

Giric nodded. With everything happening now, explaining to Sarra of his reiving days would have to wait. She would be upset enough to learn that he planned for her to remain here. "I need to talk with Sarra. I will meet you in the stables shortly."

"I shall be waiting. Whatever happens, Sarra will be safe."

"My thanks." The upcoming encounter with Lord Bretane guaranteed naught, including his life.

On a soft scrape, Colyne headed down the hallway. Giric watched his friend depart, and wished there was more time to spend with Sarra, to build upon the fragile bonds of their love. His mind raced to find the words to explain his leaving, but at every turn stumbled. Blast it. He'd faced death many times over, so why did the upcoming confrontation with one woman leave him at such a loss?

Because he loved her.

With the weight of the next few moments on his mind, he turned toward the partially opened door, stilled. Sarra stood within the entry, her features pale, and her eyes wide with horror.

CHAPTER 16

At Sarra's horrified stare, Giric's gut gave a sickening lurch. "A reiver!"

He'd wanted her to find out about his being a reiver, but nae like this. Giric moved toward her. She stepped back, the revulsion in her eyes cutting him to the quick. "Stay away from me."

"I need to explain."

Her eyes flashed. "How dare you withhold that fact from me! Did you believe it would not matter? Did you think I was so in love with you that I could overlook such?"

"Nay." He shook his head disgusted with himself, ashamed he hadna told her the truth from the start. She deserved that and more. And she was right. There wasna a good enough explanation. "I was wrong."

"Wrong?" Sarra swiped away her tears, furious he'd betrayed her trust. And for that she could never forgive him. Numb, she walked to the bed and began to gather her clothes, scrambling for a scrap of composure. "I am leaving. I do not expect or want you to accompany me." She jerked on her chemise.

At his quiet steps behind her, she squeezed the dress she'd picked until the fabric wrinkled in her grip. The bed they'd lain in, had made love countless times in, blurred before her. He deserved no tears.

She steeled herself against her emotions. They'd cost her enough and she refused to lose anymore. If nothing else, she would leave here with her pride. She shook out the dress and pulled it over her head, keeping her back to Giric and her thoughts focused on what she needed to do over the next few hours to leave.

Without him.

Her heart ached at the thought, and every nuance cried its outrage. But pride had her refusing to relent.

"You are staying here," Giric stated, an edge of pain in his voice.

She whirled, disconcerted that he stood inches away, close enough that if she chose, she could touch him. "You will not tell me where I will go or stay." Sarra stepped back, needing the distance. After pulling on her hose she reached for her boots and glared up at Giric. "I will speak with Gryfalcon about a proper escort. I will not be needing you again. Ever."

Hurt flashed in his eyes a second before the anger. "You are remaining here," he said, his each word edged with ice. "I have already made arrangements."

She narrowed her gaze. "You have no right!"

"I have every right. You are my wife."

And she hated that he would use his position to control her. "An oversight I will tend to at the first opportunity."

He caught her shoulders. "Oversight?"

She tried to push free.

Giric hauled her against him. On a curse, he caught her mouth, his anger and passion pouring out in his kiss.

She tried to ignore the way he made her feel, but her body betrayed her as his hands moved over her, igniting flames throughout her until she ached with need. With a shudder, she moaned.

He released her shoulders and cupped her face, his eyes fierce, the love she wanted blazing hot. "Tell me now that you do nae give a damn."

How dare he use sex against her! "Take your hands off me." Her cool words belied the roiling heat inside.

His lips thinned. "Nae until you admit the truth."

"As if you know the meaning of the word." He winced at her attack, but at the moment, pity wasn't in her arsenal to offer. "How dare you ask for the truth when you have lied to me from the start."

The anger in his face crumbled to frustration. "What do you want from me? I was wrong. I should have told you of my past as a reiver from the first, but now 'tis too late." His hold gentled, and his expression softened until 'twas as if she could see straight to his soul. "I wish I could go back, but I canna."

At the rawness of his words, she hardened her heart. "'Tis too late."

"I am nae letting you go."

She tried to jerk free, but he held. Anger bubbled to a dangerous level. "You tricked me into this marriage. Seduced me into bed. Lied to me about your past as a reiver. Anything we have ever built in our relationship is bound by deceit and lies. So tell me, is there truly anything to hold?"

She knew she was being unfair. Though he'd tricked her into marriage, he'd done so to save her life. And she'd wanted him in her bed, his seduction had sweetened their joining. But that he'd hidden his past when he'd known of her childhood trauma and her feelings toward reivers 'twas unacceptable. Exhausted, Sarra steadied herself. The time for discussion had passed. She knew what she had to do. "I am going to finish packing, then I will speak with Gryfalcon. Do not try to stop me, you will fail."

He hesitated, and she thought he would refuse. A part of her wanted him to demand that they would remain together and work through the rough times ahead.

"You will go, but I am going with you. 'Twill be safer that way."

"Safer?"

"You didna overhear our entire conversation in the hallway, did you?"

Dread filled her. What could she have possibly missed? Regret darkened his eyes. "I am wanted for murder."

Horror flickered in Sarra's eyes. "You murdered a man?"

Her instant belief of his guilt hurt. She hadna hesitated to believe the worst. "Finish getting dressed. We will leave once you are ready." Giric immediately regretted his temper. Blast it, her parents had been killed by reivers. Now she found out the man she'd pledged her life to, confessed her love to, was a reiver as well and on top of that, he was wanted for murder. What did he expect, her to welcome him with open arms?

At the moment he wasna sure, but he needed to put some distance between them and try to sort everything out. He strode to the door, jerked it open.

"Giric?"

At the tremor in her voice, he forced his face into an unemotional mask, turned.

Her eyes searched his, the shattered look devastating him further. "Did you murder the man?"

He remained silent. "Would you believe me if I told you nay?"

"I . . ." For the briefest of moments, tenderness stole into her gaze. Then as quick it evaporated. Her face ashen, she began to methodically pick up her few remaining garments.

His heart ached as he watched her. Hours ago they'd lain entangled within each other's arms, their future before them, love shared in their hearts. Though he still loved her, it wasna enough. He could try to explain, but with her trust in him shattered, at this moment she would never believe him. "I will be waiting outside when you are ready."

Giric stepped into the corridor, closed the door. If their relationship was to survive, the next step would be hers. He loved her, but he had his pride. He would nae beg.

A burning ball of brilliant color, the sun slid lower on the horizon to paint the landscape in a wash of gold, purple, and red. A raven called from the distance, its cry echoing in the forest.

Sarra inhaled the fresh scent of snow and wood and basked in the beauty of the day. 'Twas one of those mornings that tempted you to dream. The scrape of hooves through snow had her glancing toward Giric who rode next to her palfrey. She sobered. This day was far from a dream, but a testament of the divisions that stood between them.

After a short discussion with Gryfalcon, they'd slipped from the castle through a secret exit, and had now ridden for two days. She'd remembered Colyne's insistence to travel with them or to provide several men as an escort. In the end Giric had refused both options and held fast that only he and Sarra would finish their journey to her guardian's.

So they traveled alone.

Except for the few spoken words necessary for polite requests, he had remained silent, which was fine by her. She ignored the steady ache that tugged at her heart since she'd asked him if he'd murdered the man.

Giric was a reiver.

She knew his type all too well, had watched their horrific butchery firsthand. They took without thought, killed when needed, and departed without caring one whit about the lives shattered in their wake.

Tightness wove through her chest. If anything, his withdrawal had given her time to think, to try to put everything in proper perspective. Though they'd made love, the finalization of their marriage was far from complete. As she'd witnessed many times during her life, money held power. And she was a very influential woman, her inheritance ensured that. Even with their marriage consummated, with enough monetary incentive, she should be able to sway the right people and dissolve this farce of a union.

The comfort that she stood a chance at buying back her freedom eluded Sarra. Her heart squeezed, understanding the reason too well. When a child, the sparkle and beauty of the finest cloth, the intricate toys her parents gifted her with had enchanted her. But with their deaths, she'd learned that however powerful, money couldn't buy back their lives.

From that moment she'd despised her wealth with her every breath, only to be chained to the stigma it created, and suffocated with the responsibility her position demanded. Oh she'd used her coin for her people, wore the confidence it gave her like an ironclad cloak that most never saw through.

Except Giric.

Tears burned her eyes as she scanned the rim of the canyon now bathed in gold and a hint of purple. When she'd thought herself strong, capable of carving her own path in life, he had entered and unveiled the lonely woman within and had shattered her well-planned illusion.

Like a foul joke, the one man who had dared to tear down her emotional barrier was the one man she could never accept into her life.

Giric drew to a halt. "We have arrived at Dunkirk Castle."

Trepidation shot through her. In the past, her guardian's fairness had been a trait she admired, but times had changed, he had changed. His writ held proof of that.

And what of his son, Lord Sinclair? The foul-tempered child who seemed to thrive on misbegotten deeds flickered through her mind. Had the priest been correct? Had Drostan grown to be a man she could admire?

She frowned. Memories of Lord Bretane's son held little warmth. Even if she wished to marry, she doubted he would be the man she would choose to wed. At the moment, she'd had enough of marriage to last her a lifetime.

And how would her guardian react to the news of her union? Would he release her estate and funds into her possession as she'd originally hoped, or, enraged by her impromptu wedding, refuse to relinquish her inheritance and follow through on his threat to send her to the abbey? If so, what of her people?

Sarra tightened her fingers around the reins. She must remain calm, rational. She was overreacting. Since the arrival of the marriage decree, her guardian's actions bespoke an arrogant man, a man who cared not of her feelings. He'd summoned her to wed, given her an ultimatum that left no room to doubt his intent.

And what of Giric? How would he play into the upcoming confrontation? Or, would he hold any part at all?

She hated these doubts. Since her parents' death she'd kept her emotions under tight control. But from the first moment Giric had walked into her life, she'd been thrown into total emotional chaos.

"'Tis nae too late to turn back," he said, his voice quiet. "You can remain at Gryfalcon's while I meet with your guardian."

"I do not run from my battles." *Even if that means you.* She kicked her mare forward.

With a curse, he caught her mount's halter. "Then why with the first problem that arises in our marriage are you ready to dismiss what exists between us?"

She glared at him.

"What is wrong?" he asked, his burr edged with a dangerous air. "Afraid to answer?"

"I am not afraid of you." But she was. As much as she wanted to hate him, to expel him from her life, she still loved him. And, if he chose, he could tear her to emotional shreds, which she could never allow.

Giric's expression darkened, the emotions swirling through his ice blue eyes volatile. He started to speak, but a dog's low and frantic barking severed his reply. He released her mount and glanced toward the edge of the trees.

A hart bound from the woods, a mastiff on its heels.

The pounding of hooves echoed nearby. A moment later, a rider trailed by several men galloped into the clearing. With deft accuracy, the lead rider nocked an arrow in his bow, aimed, and released.

The arrow landed in the hart's chest. It stumbled, regained its legs, then staggered forward and collapsed.

The lead rider halted before his fallen prey. Nocking another arrow, he took careful aim, plunged it straight into the animal's heart. He backed his horse away, then waved to the men behind him to recover his kill.

Two men rode to the downed animal, dismounted, and began the task of gutting the stag.

With a nod, the lead rider turned in their direction, paused. He called out an order, and then galloped toward them, several men flanking his side.

"Looks like the welcoming party," Giric said, his voice tight.

She didn't recognize the dark-haired man in the lead, nor those who rode at his side, but the fact that they wore Lord Bretane's colors eased her mind.

Giric's hand curled on the hilt of his sword, and he moved his mount before her.

The lead rider halted several feet away. "You are on Dunkirk land. State your business."

"I am escorting Lady Sarra Bellecote from Rancourt Castle," Giric replied. "Lord Bretane is expecting us."

The man glanced toward her. Interest flared, then warmth. "Lady Sarra?"

She nodded, surprised by the man's smooth, cultured voice in this rugged setting. "Yes."

A smile curved his lips, and hazel eyes lit with approval. "My father and I have been expecting you." He paused. "You do nae recognize me? I am nae surprised. It has been many years since we played as children. All that counts is that you are here now."

"Drostan?" Sarra asked with a frown.

Sarra's familiar use of Lord Sinclair's name wound Giric's tense nerves tighter, and did not ease the flare of jealousy. The man before them sat his horse as if seasoned by long hours in the saddle. Confidence oozed in his every move. And Lord Sinclair was her intended betrothed.

That she'd been infuriated to travel to this marriage should have left him pleased. From the appreciation in her eyes as she gazed upon Lord Sinclair, had that changed?

The baron nodded. "You humble me, my lady, to remember me after all of these years."

A blush stained her cheeks. "I admit that I did not recognize you at first."

"'Tis of no consequence." The bells of None tolled. Lord Sinclair cleared his throat. "I am remiss in my welcome. Let us ride to Dunkirk Castle. You must be tired after your journey." He glanced at Giric with a dismissive look, and then nodded to the closest knight. "Take charge of the men."

"Aye, my lord." Lord Sinclair's man cantered to where they were finishing cleaning the hart.

"Lord Sinclair," Giric said.

The lord turned. His eyes watched him, cautious yet sure.

"There is a serious matter that we need to discuss." He glanced at Sarra, concerned at her presence. What had stirred that thought? He studied Lord Bretane's son finding naught untoward. If anything, the easy confidence of the baron should have made him relax.

"We can talk once Sarra is settled within the keep," Lord Sinclair said.

Giric took in their destination. The castle gleamed with an almost golden quarried rock. Guards could be seen through the battlements and once they'd ridden closer, he noted that the fortress was in an excellent state of repair.

Shame filled him as he realized the reason for his reluctance. He couldna begin to offer Sarra the wealth Lord Sinclair's father held, or the fortune his son would one day inherit. Peat fires and smoked meat were a far cry from the elegant dinners, wax candles, and array of perfectly spiced meals promised by such magnificence.

They rode across the drawbridge, then beneath the quarried stone of the gatehouse, a noble herald to peasant or king. As they cantered into the courtyard and headed for the stables, a squire rushed over to take Lord Sinclair's mount.

Jaw tight, Giric dismounted, handed his reins to another lad, then started over to assist Sarra.

Lord Sinclair cut Giric off.

She was his wife! Giric opened his mouth to speak as Sarra glanced toward him, her eyes cold with disgust. A look that said it all.

Nae more than moments within her guardian's castle and she'd chosen. Like bloody Hades!

Giric shot her a cool glance, strode past Lord Sinclair, his fists clenched, ready to tear the lord apart if he tried to stop him. He wouldna let Sarra go. If necessary, he would haul her to the Highlands and remain secluded until they worked their differences out. She said that she hated him, but in his arms, she'd acted anything but cold.

Giric clasped his hands around her waist. Their eyes clashed. He narrowed his gaze in challenge and lifted her to the ground in one easy sweep.

"Sir Terrick," Lord Sinclair said, his voice hard. "I will see to my betrothed."

Giric drilled Sarra with a hard glare. "Tell him."

"Lord Sinclair," she said, her soft tone in direct conflict with the fire shooting from her eyes. "Please, let us go inside."

"Is there a problem?" the baron demanded as he glanced from one to the other.

"No," Sarra replied, her eyes daring Giric to say otherwise.

Had he expected differently? Giric caught her arm and strode toward the keep.

"We will need to speak in private," Sarra continued, nerves edging her voice. "There are issues that must be discussed."

Saint's breath! Was that what their marriage was, an issue?

Lord Sinclair gave Sarra a cool nod. "As you wish." They entered the keep and walked through the great hall toward the stairs. "Olifard, bring food to the solar," he said to a woman helping break down the trencher tables. He led them up the curved steps. At the second level he entered the corridor, and headed toward the last room.

Inside, a fire danced in the hearth. Tapestries painted in bold reds and blues entwined with delicate bands of gold adorned the walls. On the floors more mundane but well-made rugs graced the stone. Sunlight poured through stained glass windows crafted with intricate designs to prism into the room with spectacular grace.

The woman Sinclair had spoken with below entered bearing a tray laden with breads, cheese, and a bottle of wine. She set them on the table.

"That will be all," Lord Sinclair said. "See that we are nae disturbed."

"Aye, my lord." She departed.

As the door clicked shut, he turned to Sarra. "Please, have a seat."

Sarra glanced toward Giric, the anger in his eyes tangible. "I will stand."

Drostan arched a brow. "As you wish." He walked to the table and poured them each a goblet of wine. He handed the first one to Sarra. "I regret to inform you that my father is ill and willna be able to join us."

"Oh." She frowned, the man she remembered robust and always wearing a smile. "How long has he been sick?"

"Regrettably, for the past few months," Drostan replied. "The doctor isna sure what is wrong. Unfortunately, his condition has grown worse."

Was that why he'd made arrangements for her to wed his son? "I must see him at once."

"We will both go," Giric stated, his voice ice.

With her attitude toward him, she'd expected his anger, deserved it. Since she'd learned of his past, she'd purposely begun to emotionally step back, needed to for her own sanity.

Though she'd prepared for the hurt of mentally walking away from him, she'd not realized the depth. Damn him. Why couldn't he have told her the truth from the start? Then she wouldn't be harboring this gut-wrenching pain. "We will see your father," she amended. "We will speak there. The sooner the better."

"I am afraid that isna possible. He is asleep now," the baron explained. "I have asked his servant to notify me when he is awake. I shall take you to his chamber then."

Uneasiness seeped through her. "'Tis urgent that we see him."

Drostan swirled the wine in his goblet. "Be forewarned, he may nae recognize you. Whatever illness has a hold of him is slowly claiming his mind."

Panic chewed at the edge of her composure. Her guardian had to recognize her. How else could she convince him that she couldn't marry his son or that she should retain her inheritance and run her own life. "I need to talk with him about the writ he sent me."

"And we will remain as long as necessary to take care of the matter," Giric stated.

Lord Sinclair arched a brow toward Giric. "Lady Sarra is nae leaving," he said with a confident dismissal. He turned to her, his eyes warming. "We are to be wed."

Sarra cleared her throat. "I—I need to speak with your father before we discuss this topic further."

Drostan's hand tightened on his cup, and then he set the goblet aside. "Anything that needs to be said to my father, especially as it appears it concerns me, you will inform me of now."

At the coldness of his words, ice slid through her veins. "I would rather wait until—"

"Nay," Giric said, his tone holding no apology. "He needs to know the truth. Lady Sarra is my wife."

CHAPTER 17

At Giric's claim that they'd wed, Drostan's face darkened in outrage.

By the rood! "Giric married me to save my life." Sarra shot Giric a cold glare. How dare he blurt the news of their disastrous marriage as if staking his claim instead of a humble explanation? As if there was ever anything humble about him. He was a man who knew his strengths as well as his weaknesses, and he wasn't afraid to stand up for what he believed in. She hesitated, stunned.

Did he believe in her?

Did he mean what he'd said before? Was he willing to fight for her?

Shaken, Sarra inhaled. Giric embodied everything she despised. She refused to allow herself to again become a victim to his charms. Hadn't he hurt her enough? Once she'd believed in him. And for that he'd betrayed her.

"Explain!" Drostan demanded.

"We were attacked," Sarra replied before Giric could make the situation worse. "The men wanted me dead. If not for Giric's intervention, they would have succeeded."

Doubt flashed in Sinclair's eyes. "Indeed?"

"A band of men who support Robert Bruce, the Competitor, learned of your father's betrothal of Lady Sarra to you," Giric explained, his voice thick with cynicism. "They decided they were nae interested in her wealth being added to back John Balliol's bid to become king."

Irritation flashed in Sinclair's eyes. "'Tis absurd."

"Is it?" Giric challenged. "'Tis no secret where your or your father's loyalties lie—with a weak-willed man who could never hold his own against England's king."

"Stop it, both of you," Sarra ordered, irritated with the two of them for delving into politics at this precarious time. "The issue is of my marriage. The rogues had me cornered. Giric's claim that I was his wife and my confirmation of the fact saved my life."

The baron's stance relaxed. "I see. A marriage of convenience." He gave a slight nod to Giric. " 'Twould seem that I owe you my thanks. I will ensure that you are paid the amount arranged, and then you are free to go." His expression grew tender as he turned to Sarra. "Thank God you are safe. I will send a missive to the bishop posthaste to explain the dire situation. Considering the circumstances and with his intervention, I have confidence that the pope will grant an annulment."

"I agree," Sarra replied, determined to take hold of the situation.

Sarra's ability to dismiss him from her life with apparent ease severed the last of Giric's control. "She is my wife in every way," he stated, aware he possibly could have signed his death warrant, but at this moment he didna give a bloody damn. He loved Sarra and was determined to make their marriage work.

Sarra blanched.

Red darkened the baron's cheeks in a brutal slash. "Is it true?"

She gave a shaky nod.

Lord Sinclair's hand curled around the hilt of his blade. "Did he take you by force?"

"No!" she gasped.

He withdrew his sword, his gaze slamming to Giric. "Be nae afraid to tell me the truth. I will nae let this scoundrel touch you again."

Scoundrel? With a curse, Giric withdrew his sword, relishing the taste of battle. " 'Twas her choice." *Attack, you bastard.* 'Twould expel the anger coiling through him like a blade's edge.

"Choice? That I doubt!" Sinclair scoffed as he stepped forward, blade raised. "You will nae seduce my intended and live to tell of it."

Flashing both men a warning glare, Sarra stepped between them, her gaze pausing on Sinclair. "I will discuss the matter of my marriage with your father. You will do naught until I have spoken with him."

"When my father is coherent he will meet with you," the baron said through gritted teeth. "I assure you, he will nae tolerate this farce of your marriage, and neither will I."

"At this moment," Sarra said with cold precision, "what my marriage is or is not is none of your concern. Now, will you please have someone escort me to my chamber."

Tension filled the room. For a moment Giric thought Lord Sinclair would refuse.

A moment later, mouth tight, the lord led them out. Several doors down he halted and opened a door. "Your chamber, my lady."

"I will be staying with her," Giric stated before the baron could dictate otherwise and strode inside. They'd already established their dislike for each other. He refused to act like the polite guest now.

Sarra gave a frustrated exhale. "Giric, I—"

"What time do we sup?" he asked, the baron's face growing redder and bringing Giric immense pleasure.

"I assure you," Lord Sinclair seethed. "This will be sorted out." He turned to leave.

"Lord Sinclair," Giric called.

He whirled, his jaw taut.

"My full title is Giric Armstrong, Earl of Terrick, Lord of Wolfhaven Castle. You will address me as my title demands."

Hazel eyes narrowed. "Lord Terrick," Sinclair all but hissed. With a curt nod, he strode away.

Satisfied, Giric shut the door.

Sarra rounded on him. "What do you think you are doing!"

"Telling the truth! Mayhap I should have lied? Is that what you expected? Now that you know that I am a reiver, everything I say is suspect, is it nae?"

Silence.

"Is it nae?"

"You know what I mean. You could have had the gold you sought even after our forced marriage, then you could have left."

He arched a brow. "Mayhap my goals have changed."

"Yes," she said with ominous conviction. "Mayhap you have raised your stakes."

Unease coiled tight through him. "What do you mean by that?"

Sarra folded her arms across her chest. "Mayhap you have decided that you want more than the amount initially offered to escort me. But I tell you now, you will receive naught more than agreed." She angled her chin. "We have no more to discuss. I am sure Lord

Sinclair will ensure you are properly quartered. On the morrow you can depart with the gold promised."

Saint's breath! "When I leave, you are going with me," he all but shouted. *Good going, Terrick. You will win the lass with that charm.* It wasna like she hadna pushed him at every step and shoved his good intent into the cesspit.

"The job you were hired to do is over. You are no longer a part of my life."

Blast it! "Is that what you want, me to leave?"

"Yes."

Her fierce reply echoed in the silence. He would have turned then if nae for the shiver that touched her skin, the hint of desperation in her eyes.

Giric stepped toward her.

She backed away. "Leave me alone."

And if he did, he'd be nay better than the rest. Since her parents' murder, everyone had left her alone. Throughout her life she'd fought her own battles because there'd been no one else to stand up for her. At every turn she'd been let down.

Now, she expected nothing.

Though she said that she hated him, if he left right now, he would hate himself more.

"I love you, Sarra. I am nae going to walk away."

Her eyes shifted as if seeking an avenue of escape, and then they focused on him. "Do not."

At her trembling words he halted. "What?"

"I hate you, can you not understand that! I want you out of my life."

But from the tears sliding down her cheeks, he understood too well. He'd broken her heart. "I love you," he repeated, aware she needed more than the reaffirmation, but time to forgive. Time that he would ensure they had.

She interlaced her hands in a protective gesture. "You do not know what love is."

He drew a steadying breath. "I know that I have made mistakes, that I have hurt you, and for that I am sorry. But as much as you wish otherwise, I love you and always will."

"Do not do this. This. Us." Sarra waved her hand in a dismissive gesture. " 'Tis destined to fail. There is too much that separates us."

Temper had him stepping forward and catching her chin. "So I just walk away and make it easy on you. Is that it?"

She tried to pull free, but he held firm. "Do not play the martyr. 'Tis for your own good."

"I think you are afraid to take a chance on us."

Her eyes blazed. "There is no *us*. You assured that when you kept secrets from me."

Giric glanced at her lips, the warm taste of her already sliding through him. "Mayhap I should test your claim?"

"No—"

He severed her refusal with his mouth, determined to prove what she would deny. Frustrated with their situation, angry that she would dare disavow her love because of her fears and her inability to trust, incited him further.

She stiffened under him, but he knew her body too well, was aware of how to touch her. And to convince her to let him be a part of her life, however less than fair, he would use every advantage.

He angled his mouth to gain better access as he grazed his thumb over her nipple.

She shuddered against him. On a whimpered curse, she returned his kiss, her hands desperate on his clothes, fumbling to push them aside.

Giric needed no further invitation. As his fingers deftly removed her garments, he seduced her with his mouth, taking, tasting until she grew frantic in his arms. He grazed his lips over the angle of her chin, and then nipped along the soft flesh of her throat.

"I should not be doing this," she whispered as her hands tossed his shirt on the floor. "'Tis a mistake."

"Then we will make it together. I love you and I am never letting you go."

Her eyes searched his, the doubts, fear, easy to read. "I am so afraid. For so many years I have hated the reivers. I do not know if I can overcome my feelings. What if I can't? What then?"

"So do we walk away from us because you are unsure? Will your past dictate your future?" He caressed her cheek. "I willna lie, loving someone is never easy. But I am willing to chance a future with you, aware that after everything, you may hold back a part of yourself from me forever."

Another tear slid down her cheek.

"Back at the falls you said you loved me. Do you still feel the same?"

Sarra stiffened.

She was remembering his betrayal. "Nay, we willna talk about that now. Trust takes time, that we have." He drew her into a gentle kiss, skimmed his fingers along her neck in a soft caress. She trembled against him, but he kept his movements gentle, nonthreatening. She needed to trust him in every way, otherwise their marriage would fail. When she was ready, had accepted his past, she would say the words he longed to hear.

It'd always been easy for him to love, but for her it was a new journey. He wouldna press her further, but he wouldna allow her to withdraw either. Though her past still haunted her, by discussing it, she'd taken an important step toward letting it go.

He scraped his teeth along the velvety column of her neck. "I want to make love with you."

"Giric, I do not know if we should."

"Then do nae think. I love you with all of my heart. Nay," he said when she opened her mouth to speak. "I am nae asking for promises. Nae now. For this moment, that we have each other is enough."

"There is still so much left to discuss. What about my guardian? Until he awakens—"

Giric silenced her protest with a kiss. "It will all work out," he whispered against her mouth and reveled in her taste. He just hadna figured out exactly how, but he would. Hope spiraled through him. "Just feel."

He tilted her mouth to his then traced his tongue over the vibrant warmth. When her body melted against him and she returned his kiss, his heart burst with love. As his fingers skimmed over her naked flesh, caressed, savored, his entire body shuddered with need. Giric reined in his own desires and focused on her.

He seduced her with deliberate slowness, her remaining clothes, as his, quickly pooling at their feet. With tenderness, he placed soft kisses along her shoulder, then slid down to nuzzle the soft underside of her breast.

Sarra's pulse began to race beneath his touch.

Humbled, he skimmed his mouth along the flat of her stomach, breathing in her scent.

"Giric."

Her throaty moan had him looking up to find her watching him. A flush graced her skin, and her gray eyes were dark with pleasure.

She reached for him.

Unable to resist he lifted her into his arms and carried her to the bed. He laid her upon the thick covering, and then lowered his body intimately over hers. As they tumbled into the kiss, he sheathed himself in her tight warmth and began to move in a slow, steady rhythm. He quickened his pace until her movements became frantic, and her body arched to meet his every thrust.

Sarra's cries of release fueled his own. The world tilted around him until it was only him, only her. On a final thrust he poured into her, then lay beside her and drew her into his arms.

Her face glowed as she watched him. The love she hadna spoken shimmered in her eyes, but he saw the doubts. And prayed that one day she would accept his past. He gave her a tender smile and pushed a swath of hair away from her cheek. "I will love you always."

Tears welled in her eyes, and one dropped onto his skin.

He wiped it away, and she gave him a wilted smile. "All will be well." And he prayed 'twas truth.

The soft silence of the night greeted Sarra as she opened her eyes. A solid, warm body lay next to hers. Giric. The hours they'd made love, his reaffirmation that he loved her, of how he'd touched her as no one had before sifted through her mind.

Unease swept her. Was she fooling herself? With her past pitted against his, would a future with Giric stand a chance? But what if she risked it all? Believed in him? Did she dare? If she turned away what then?

She studied Giric as he lay beside her, his face softened in sleep, his breaths quiet and steady. Her heart tightened, and the emptiness of a life without him held its own answer. If her choice was a mistake, then she made it with her eyes wide open. Nervous but another part sure, she curled up next to him and gave in to the warmth of sleep.

A firm knock sounded at the door, and Sarra opened her eyes heavy with sleep. Her thoughts of last night came to mind. Though nervous at her decision, her heart overrode any doubts. It felt so right to wake up beside Giric, to know that he would be hers forever.

"Who is it?" Giric called, his arm possessively around her.

"Lord Sinclair sent me to inform you that his father is awake," a youthful voice called. "I am to escort you and your wife to Lord Bretane's chamber."

Giric's mumbled curse had her smiling.

"You think 'tis funny do you?"

His arched brow offered her anything but a threat, and her smile grew.

He wedged his hardness against her slick warmth. "Mayhap you willna be laughing once I make love to you?"

Her body ached for him. "I guess we will have to find out." Had she said that? Yes, and it felt good, wondrously so.

The knock sounded again.

With a muttered curse, Giric stepped from the bed and jerked on his trews. "One moment," he all but snarled to whoever waited outside their chamber.

At her chuckle he skewered her with his gaze, the intensity of love there making Sarra catch her breath.

A roguish light streaked in his eyes. The tunic he'd picked up and began to don, he tugged off and tossed it to the floor.

Sarra scrambled back unused to this free-spirited teasing, but finding excitement as well. "Giric, I—"

He caught the edge of the blanket and hauled it from the bed with her in tow.

On a squeal, she grabbed for the other side of the mattress. Giric gave a final pull, and she flopped unceremoniously on the floor ensnared within the heap of linen.

His rich laughter filled the room.

"You think this is funny?" she charged as she lay sprawled before him naked, laughter welling in her throat. Never had anyone dared to treat her so, but never had anyone loved her without reserve.

Giric scooped her into his arms. "I will never walk away from a challenge. Especially from you."

"Lord Terrick?" the voice called from the other side of the door.

He gave an exasperated sigh. "Hurry up and dress if we must leave."

Moments later, the squire nodded when Giric opened the door. "If you will follow me." He started down the corridor.

"My lady wife."

Sarra laid her hand on Giric's forearm and they followed the lad. Tapestries portraying battles with ancient Picts and druids adorned the walls. Sarra took in each work of art, each masterpiece painstakingly woven.

Fleeting memories of walking these same halls as a child came to mind and she smiled. Then, she'd held her father's hand. Her smile faded. 'Twas on their return trip from that visit when the reivers had attacked.

Their steps echoed in the turret as they headed up the stairs, and the flicker of torches shuddered along the walls with a morose sputter. Air, cold with the edge of winter, chilled her face.

With a shiver, Sarra glanced into the darkness broken only by shards of yellowed light. When they entered the well-lit hallway, she sighed with relief. Odd that she should feel this way when she was about to speak with her guardian.

The lad led them toward a chamber at the end of the corridor. As they neared, the guard at the entry gave a soft knock on the door, leaned inside, and said something that she couldn't hear.

Moments later Drostan emerged, sadness in his gaze. "I caution you, my father is very ill. I had hoped that he would be more lucid today." He shrugged. "Some days are better than others. Be prepared. He may nae recognize you."

She nodded, prayed her guardian would. With the undercurrents between Drostan and Giric, she needed to convince Lord Bretane to release her inheritance to her, and then they could leave.

The guard opened the door and stepped aside.

"After you," Lord Sinclair said.

The stench of sickness hit her first. Her stomach roiled as she forced herself to take another step inside. The cheery fire and warmly decorated room did little to dissolve the dismal air within. Giric's hand gently squeezed her own, and she glanced at him, thankful for his presence.

A hacking cough from a large bed draped with blue velvet drew her attention. Ensconced within the folds of the thick bed covers lay a man, his eyes haggard, his face taut and withered.

Stunned, she halted. This couldn't be Lord Bretane, the man who'd lifted her high with a wide smile and turned her in a circle as a child, the same man who'd snuck her sweets. That man had towered over her, his sturdy frame muscled and honed from battle, his eyes alight with the glint of humor.

"Father?"

Drostan's quiet question confirmed her worst fears. She swallowed hard. From her guardian's struggle for each breath, that he still lived was a miracle.

CHAPTER 18

Sadness etched Drostan's face as he walked to his father lying in the bed. "You have visitors."

Lord Bretane remained still. Then his bony hand clutched the bed covers, and his fingers trembled as he turned. Blue eyes hazed with confusion stared at her. Shaggy gray brows scrunched together in a frown, then his eyes flared with delight. "Aeschine?"

The baron laid his hand upon his father's shoulder. "Nay, 'tis Lady Sarra. Remember you sent her a writ several weeks ago requesting our marriage?"

Lord Bretane's face twisted into a grimace. "Lady Sarra?" His low-spoken words spilled out in confusion. "I know of nay Lady Sarra." He scanned the room as if expectant. "Where is Aeschine?"

"Mother died five years ago," his son answered in a bland tone as if the question was commonplace.

Face pale, Lord Bretane deflated into the layers of sheets. "She is dead?"

"Aye." Drostan gave his father's shoulder a gentle squeeze. "Go back to sleep. The herbs you swallowed earlier will soon begin to help relieve your pain."

"I will find Aeschine when I awaken," his father muttered, his eyes slowly drifting shut.

"We will return after you have rested," Lord Sinclair said, but his father never turned to look, nor give any sign that he'd heard. With a quiet sigh, Drostan walked toward them. "I am sorry. He has been like this ever since his fever several weeks ago."

Sarra gave a shaky nod. So caught up in her own indignation to be summoned to wed, she'd never considered the possibility that her guardian had acted without his faculties in order. It explained everything.

"We will talk further outside." Lord Sinclair exited the chamber.

Sarra and Giric followed. The guard closed the door behind them as they walked down the corridor. When they reached an alcove, Drostan turned.

The overwhelming sadness on his face touched her deeply. She understood his pain, had experienced the same regret. Though his father still lived, in many ways he'd already lost him. "I am sorry."

"My thanks." Drostan stared at the handcrafted glass where the sun dusted the land within its golden glow. After a long moment, he faced Giric. "I want to apologize for my behavior earlier. I admit that your marriage caught me off guard." He gave Sarra a wistful smile. "I never deluded myself into thinking that you would love me, but I was looking forward to spending my time at home with someone I cared for. I remembered you as a child, so carefree and loving." He toyed with the edge of his cuff. "I allowed my imagination to override reality."

Though surprised by his admission, Sarra remained silent.

"I willna say that I am pleased by your marriage," he continued, "but life is too short to hold grudges or to linger on regrets." Lord Sinclair dropped his hand to his side. "My father was wrong to decide who you should marry. Whatever is stealing his senses must have begun months before I realized it. I didna agree with his decision to our betrothal without your consent, and I willna force you to abide by his decree now."

She glanced at Giric. Surprise flickered in his eyes, but suspicion as well.

"If you love Lord Terrick and he makes you happy," Drostan continued, "when my father is lucid, I will explain the dissolution of his request for our marriage."

Moved by his kindness, shame filled Sarra at the horrible thoughts she'd harbored toward him when she'd first received the writ. 'Twould seem that in her chapel before the journey, Father Ormand had spoken the truth. Drostan had grown into a strong and good man. Handsome and caring, he would make a woman a fine husband when he wed.

Her concerns of the self-centered lad she'd remembered with an attraction toward wicked acts no longer existed. Hadn't the shift in her feelings toward the Scots given credence to how much one person could change?

And Lord Bretane. Who wouldn't be on edge having to watch their father die a slow, painful death? In light of Drostan's struggles, he was generous to offer to speak with his father to relinquish his writ.

"You said he does become lucid?" Sarra asked.

"Aye," Lord Sinclair replied. "On rare moments. Though, over the last few days, those are fleeting."

Her curiosity piqued, she still wished to know her guardian's reason for requesting the marriage, if in fact he'd done so while he was lucid. Then there was the issue of her inheritance to settle.

"When he is of sound mind," Sarra said, "I wish to speak with him privately. There are other concerns that I need to address."

Interest flickered in Drostan's eyes. "Of course. Then you will be remaining here for the time being?"

"Yes, until I have spoken with your father."

In support of Sarra's decision to remain until she'd spoken with Lord Bretane, Giric laced his fingers through hers.

Sinclair grimaced at their entwined fingers.

Giric kept hold of her hand. As if he cared that the baron was present.

Her face flushed, Sarra tried to pull her hand from Giric's as if embarrassed.

He held tight. They were wed, had joined in the most intimate of ways. Though she'd refrained from showing outward signs of love throughout her life, he refused to allow her to withdraw from him in any manner. He would show her that love was as natural as each breath.

After a long moment, Sinclair nodded. "If that is your wish, then I will take care of the writ."

"Thank you," Giric said to her guardian's son, nae giving a damn if he approved of their marriage or nae. She'd chosen him.

A flash of anger whipped through the baron's expression, and then it was gone. "'Tis the least I can do. Lady Sarra has had to endure tremendous difficulties during her journey here, unnecessarily so. Lord Terrick, I will see that you receive the gold that you were promised. Though during your travels you became married, your actions were done to protect Lady Sarra. As for the consummation of the marriage, that discretion is hers."

Giric gave a curt nod. He would have thought a man with such insight would have supported Robert Bruce, the Competitor, the obvious candidate to become Scotland's next king over John Balliol. Nor would he ponder the matter further. That he'd released Sarra from the writ more than made up for his ill-chosen personal preference for their country's sovereign.

"During your stay, you are welcome to move freely within my home," Sinclair offered. "Now I must leave. There is business that I must attend to. I will send a page to notify you when we sup."

Sarra's body relaxed. "Thank you."

The baron nodded to Giric. "While here, if you choose to spar, I would enjoy a round."

However coated with sincerity, Giric didna miss the subtle challenge in Sinclair's offer. "I would seek a bout with you as well," he replied, intrigued by a man who could step away from a woman like Sarra without a fight. "I shall look forward to our match." Sinclair departed.

After he'd left, Sara turned. "Do you think 'twas wise to accept when he is clearly upset?"

Her question caught Giric by surprise, and he smiled at the concern in her eyes. "You are nae worried about me are you?"

"I—"

He gave a soft chuckle. "'Tis only a spar."

Her expression relaxed. "'Tis."

As she stared at him, he grew somber, wanting her with every breath, but more so needing her vow of love. When she found the courage to again give it, he would cherish it always. "Let us nae talk of spars." He drew her into his arms, and she tensed. "What is it?"

"I . . ." Her expression became tense, urgent. "I believe that your deeds of the past, however illicit, were to aid your people, not derived for personal pleasure. Neither did you kill my parents. Nor do I think that you are now a murderer." She swallowed hard. "Still, I do not know if I can accept your past."

Humbled by her forgiveness, he shook his head. "If I could change my past, I would."

"But then you would not be the man you have grown to be, would you?"

He'd never considered that, but it didna lessen the mistakes of his past or the shame. She'd managed to accept him when he hadna done the same for himself. There was so much he needed to tell her, so much that he wanted to share. Here, where anyone could walk upon them, wasna a place that he could speak freely.

Giric kissed the curve of her jaw. "If we stay here longer, I might do something I will regret—in public."

A blush stained her cheeks, but excitement filled his eyes.

On a soft groan he lifted her in his arms and strode toward their chamber, doubting they would make it to dinner this night.

"Are you sure you want to wait longer?" Giric asked Sarra as they headed toward her guardian's chamber. "We have remained here over a fortnight and with your each visit Lord Bretane doesna recognize you."

A pensive frown wrinkled in her brow. "Drostan said that for moments he becomes lucid, and I pray we will stumble upon such a time soon."

"There is much both of us need to tend to back at our homes," Giric said. "If he doesna regain cognizance, you may have to speak with his son about your concerns."

Worried eyes turned to him. "I would rather not."

He nodded, understanding her apprehension. Since their arrival and after the initial confrontation, Sinclair had treated them with the utmost respect, but Giric hadna missed the displeasure that lurked in his eyes. "We will stay another sennight, then you need to speak to his son." He didna add that by that time, due to his continued failing health, her guardian could be dead.

Since their arrival, with each passing day, Lord Bretane grew worse. His eyes had sunken into his frame, his skin had grown pale as death, and his ramblings were now commonplace, centered on conversations with his dead wife.

After watching his own father die in the cramped confines of the dungeon, Giric understood Sinclair's anguish. Though no bars restrained the baron, he lived in his own personal strife. In a way, 'twas worse.

Resignation sifted through Sarra's expression. "A sennight. Then we will depart."

Relief swept him that she'd accepted the reality of the situation. "I am sorry that your guardian is so ill."

"'Tis so unlike him," she said, her voice soft with memories. "He was always so strong and healthy."

At Lord Bretane's chamber, Sarra paused. "I will go in alone." She gave him a brave smile, but he noted the despair beneath.

"Sarra, I—"

"Please. I must do this."

He understood her pride, the need to see this through. "As you wish. I am going to practice arms. When I am finished, I will return."

"My thanks." With a steadying breath, she walked inside.

He didna want to leave her alone in that dismal atmosphere, but in the past weeks they'd shared with each other, Sarra knew that if she needed him, all she had to do was ask and he would be there.

Trying to shake off his frustration, he strode down the hall, flexed the stiffness from his arms, looking forward to the upcoming bout. Sword practice would help clear his mind.

A short while later after donning his armor, Giric headed toward where men sparred in the upper bailey. Through the flakes of drifting snow, he scanned the paired men who wielded their swords in mock battle, some knights, others a combination of knight and squire.

Two knights fought near the closest tower with fierce abandon. The tallest of the two cursed as his opponent's blade slashed dangerously close. Then the man side-stepped, turned, and attacked.

His opponent lifted his weapon. Their swords clashed.

Giric studied the pair as they sparred, impressed by the skill of both. Either would be a worthy opponent.

With a growl, the tallest man shoved his sparring partner back. As fast, the men engaged, their curses as quick as the clash of steel. They merged and broke away once again. The tallest man glanced toward him and signaled for the other to stop.

He removed his helm; Sinclair. The baron murmured to his opponent who nodded and left. "Are you up for a match?" Drostan asked as he walked toward Giric, the sheen of sweat beading his brow in direct conflict with the excitement surging through his gaze.

"I have the unfair advantage of nae having sparred, I will select another man." However much he wished to trounce Sinclair in a match, 'twould be done when both were rested.

"I had just begun to warm up when you arrived." Sinclair moved his sword through a series of difficult maneuvers with ease. "What do you say that we play for stakes?"

"Stakes?"

Sinclair smiled. "If you have something to lose, it makes the battle all the more appealing does it nae?"

Unease wove through Giric. Did he speak of Sarra? "And what would you suggest as a prize?"

"Your dagger."

He relaxed a degree. "And if I win?"

"Then you win mine of course." Sinclair withdrew his dagger. The emeralds embedded in the ornate handle shimmered in the sun. He sheathed the weapon. "So, Lord Terrick, are you game?"

If the man was fool enough to risk such an expensive dagger, then yes, he would happily relieve him of it. "With pleasure." Giric donned his helm and withdrew his sword. He took it through a series of movements to loosen his muscles, the rush of adrenaline that came with the upcoming challenge welcome. He stepped back and positioned his legs slightly apart, his blade held waist high. "Ready."

Sinclair secured his helm, then angled his blade and began to circle Giric.

Giric followed his lead and kept him a safe distance. They maneuvered around each other for several minutes, and he assessed his opponent as he knew he was being weighed.

When the sun again shone in his face and momentarily blinded him, Sinclair attacked.

Anticipating his opponent's tactic, Giric repelled his swing. He dodged the next strike then lunged. Steel screamed as their swords clashed. Their hilts merged. Sweat streamed down Giric's face, his hand trembling from the contest of force. Metal scraped with a foul hiss as he shoved the baron away, then charged.

With a nimble twist, Sinclair stepped to the right and escaped his drive. Barely. In response, Drostan lifted his blade, swung.

Rotating, Giric thrust his weapon to ward off the blow.

Again their blades locked.

Strain creased Sinclair's brow, but the fervor of battle glittered bright in his eyes. "A good match," he said between breaths. Like a madman he shoved him back then charged, his blade aimed straight at Giric's heart.

"Saint's breath!" Giric dove. Snow crunched beneath him as he landed hard. He rolled to his side, his opponent's following swing missing his shoulder by a hand's width. With a curse he sprang to his feet finding Sinclair already raising his sword for his next attack.

If 'twas a fight the bastard wanted, by God he'd teach him a lesson. 'Twould seem the baron's ire at his marriage to Sarra would be unfurled here. Sinclair would learn that no man would take what was his.

Their blades rang out with a bitter scrape. Sweat melded with anger. Giric worked his sword, each swing fueled with determination. When his opponent began to weaken, with an impassioned cry he attacked.

Caught off guard by his charge, Sinclair swung his weapon in a defensive blow.

Anticipating his move, Giric shifted to the side and slammed his blade to work with Sinclair's desperate swing. With brute force, he angled both blades into the air.

Inches apart, their swords locked, he glared at Sinclair. With the twist of his wrist he could throw his adversary's blade to the ground. "Concede," Giric hissed.

Sinclair's eyes narrowed.

"Lord Terrick," a guard called from the main gate. "A runner has arrived who says that he must speak with you immediately!"

"'Twould seem you have been given a reprieve," Giric spat. They both knew he'd won. He shoved him back.

Fury burned in Sinclair's eyes as he caught his footing. He sheathed his blade. "A pity our match is to be interrupted, but know this, 'tis far from through."

"Aye, that it is nae." Giric secured his sword, shoved back his mail hood and padded coif. "When I return, we will finish."

"That we will," the baron replied, "but as your host, I would be remiss nae to accompany you."

Giric remained silent. That bastard likely wanted to eavesdrop. More than ready for the day he and Sarra would ride away from Dunkirk Castle, he headed toward the rider waiting in the courtyard.

As he neared, he recognized Sir Neyll, one of his knights who'd ridden with him when they'd left to escort Sarra. Fear tore through him. He wouldna be here unless something was wrong!

Sinclair glanced over. "You know him?"

"'Tis one of my men."

"You are expecting news?"

"Nay." And that was what worried Giric the most.

As he closed, Sir Neyll dismounted. He handed his mount to the stable hand and walked to meet Giric, his stride purposeful, his expression grief stricken. "Lord Sinclair," Sir Neyll said with a respectful nod, and then his gaze shifted to Giric. "I come bearing urgent news."

His mind laden with worry, Giric nodded to their host. "I would like to speak with my man in private," he said, refusing to share information that could be personal with their host.

"Of course." Sinclair started toward the practice field.

Giric led Sir Neyll to the solar. Once inside, he shut the door and turned. "What is wrong?" The regret flashing on his friend's face shot fear through his heart.

"'Tis your sister."

Panic swept him. "What about Elizabet?"

"I am sorry."

"Blast it, tell me!"

"News arrived that while out hunting, she fell from her horse."

Nay! "Is she alive?" he demanded. "Tell me if she is blasted alive!"

"Barely."

"Will she live?" He couldna help the desperation clawing through his voice. After their mother's death, he'd raised his sister when his father had shunned her.

"No one is sure. Her husband requests your presence immediately."

Giric nodded. "We will leave posthaste. Meet at the stable."

"Aye."

As his man departed, Giric hurried to find Sinclair. Any details of the release of her guardian's control could be dealt with by courier. As he exited the keep, Sinclair was starting up the steps.

The baron scanned his face with cool interest. "I pray naught is wrong?"

"An urgent matter needs my attention," Giric stated. "Sarra and I are leaving at once." He headed inside, and his host followed.

"Is your destination far?"

"Four days. Three if we ride hard." Giric took the tower steps two at a time.

"You canna push Sarra like that," Drostan said as he kept pace.

Giric halted and whirled. "She is my wife—"

"She has barely recovered from your journey here," the baron said, his words rich with concern. "She is a lady and unused to such harsh travel. What if she leaves with you and due to her already weakened state, becomes ill? Will you take that risk?"

The baron's angry, vicious attack during their spar a short while before weighed in Giric's mind. "She will travel with me." Lord Sinclair may have stated his acceptance to their marriage, but he had his own ideas as to the lord's pleasure of his and Sarra's union. Or rather, displeasure. Though the travel would be difficult, she'd proven that if necessary, she could keep pace.

Red slashed Lord Sinclair's cheeks. "'Tis foolhardy to subject her to such adversity. She is—"

"Departing with me posthaste."

"You are foolishly putting her life at risk."

"The decision is nae yours to make." Giric strode to her guardian's chamber, entered.

Sarra started, then rose. "I have only . . ." Concern darkened her eyes as she glanced from one man to the other. "What is wrong?"

He wanted to hold her, to tell her of his fears for his sister. "I must speak with you." He shot the baron a cool glance. "Alone."

Irritation flashed in Sinclair's eyes. "If you need further assistance, I will be below."

"My thanks," Giric replied.

Their host departed.

Sarra frowned at the baron's terse manner, and then faced Giric. "What is wrong?"

"I just received news that several days ago, my sister was thrown from a horse." He shook his head, his throat thick with emotion. "They do nae know if Elizabet will live."

"Oh God!" Sarra hugged him. "I am so sorry," she said, her words rough with emotion.

Her compassion left him humbled. The haughty woman he'd first met at Rancourt Castle would have shunned him, dismissed his plight, and walked away without a second glance. Now, she gave of herself without question. He threaded his fingers through her hair. "We must leave immediately."

She pulled back, her eyes rimmed with tears. "I want to go with you, but I need to stay and speak with Lord Bretane."

"I refuse to allow you to remain."

"Why?"

She may as well know the truth. "I do nae trust Sinclair."

"Giric, however much I want to go with you, if I leave now, I may never have the opportunity to speak with my guardian again." She laid her hand over his. "We agreed to leave in a sennight. Give me that. I am safe here. Drostan would never harm me. And alone, no doubt you will travel faster."

Saint's breath.

"Until our marriage, I have handled matters on my own. I will be fine now." She gave him a trembling smile. "Go, your sister needs you. Whatever happens, I will follow within a sennight with appropriate guard."

"Sarra—"

"Please, Giric."

He released a rough sigh. Mayhap he was being overprotective. Nor would she be alone. The castle was filled with people. Servants who served Sinclair, his mind added. Blast it.

"Giric?"

Bedamned! He didna like the thought of her remaining here without his protection, but she deserved his trust. "Stay then, but I still do nae like it."

Her eyes softened. "I know, but I will be fine, truly."

"Come." With her at his side, he strode down the hall. At this point, each moment could make the difference if he saw Elizabet alive. Blast it. He didna want to think about that. He'd already lost his father. Was fate so cruel it would take his sister as well?

"I will be fine," Sarra assured him.

He halted and drew her into a heated kiss. "I love you, Sarra. Never forget that."

Tears shimmered in her eyes. But her returning words of love never came.

Time, he assured himself.

At their chamber, he collected the few items he would need then headed to the stables.

They met Sinclair as he exited the keep. He glanced at Sarra, and then lifted his brow. "She is nae going?"

"We have decided that she will remain—for a sennight," Giric replied.

"I will ensure Sarra's safety while she remains and provide a proper guard when she travels," the baron said. "You have my word."

Giric stared at him hard. "See that you do."

Sinclair's eyes narrowed on him, the dislike clear, but another emotion, satisfaction, stirred there as well.

Fear for Sarra overwhelmed his senses. "Sarra, 'tis nae too late for you to accompany me. We will return after I have taken care of everything at home."

She shook her head. "Giric, we have already discussed this."

They had, but here, with Sinclair paces away and his warrior instinct shouting its warning, he didna feel comfortable leaving her in the bastard's care. Or was his dislike for Sinclair warping his normally keen senses? Blast this entire situation. If only Lord Bretane had been cognizant, her remaining here wouldna be an issue.

"You are worrying for naught," Sarra said, pulling him from his musing.

Giric leveled a look on Sinclair that assured the lord if she wasna kept safe, he would pay for it with his life. "Mayhap I am. Come." He took Sarra's hand and they walked to the stables.

Thankfully Neyll sat astride his horse, and a lad held Giric's steed as well as Sarra's, readied for their departure.

"Lad, the lady will nae be needing her mount." Giric turned to Sarra one last time. "Take care. My heart will be with you, always." He gave her one last hard kiss, and then mounted. With his heart filled with love, his mind raw with terror for Elizabet, he kicked his steed into a gallop.

The clatter of hooves over the drawbridge gave way to a muted strum on a blanket of snow. They galloped on the cart trail that sliced across the open field then entered the shadow of the forest.

Overhead, angry gray clouds began to spew thick, fat flakes that promised to make a difficult trip more dangerous.

An icy burst of wind hurled the falling snow into a blustery cloud and for a second blinding him. Giric slowed his mount to a canter, nae taking a chance of injuring him. He glanced to where his friend rode at his side. "Looks like a storm is blowing in."

"It does." Sir Neyll tugged his cloak tighter. "'Twill slow us."

"Aye." Time they didna have to waste. The whirling snow that had blocked their view moments before settled. Able to see, Giric urged his mount faster.

They crested the next hill and over the treetops, naught but hills and forest spread out before them. The rugged beauty, isolation he normally appreciated, now became his enemy.

Sir Neyll fell behind.

Giric glanced back, found his friend pulling up. He slowed. "What is wrong?"

"My horse seems a bit lame." Sir Neyll waved him forward. "I will catch up to you."

Giric hesitated.

"Go on with you now."

Torn to leave his friend, in the end he acceded. If Sir Neyll's mount proved lame, he could always lead his horse back to Dunkirk Castle. "Take care." Giric kicked his mount forward.

Without warning, pain ripped into his back. He fell forward and grasped a handful of his horse's mane. His steed shifted, and he almost lost his grip. The world hazed around him as he tried to keep consciousness against the pain. His grip on the reins loosened and his horse slowed to a stop.

Warmth seeped down his back. Confused, he reached behind him; his fingers nudged the shaft of an arrow.

Had Sir Neyll been shot as well?

Pain shooting through his back, he turned, expecting to find his friend splayed on the ground, an arrow embedded in his chest. In stunned disbelief, he watched as Sir Neyll lowered his bow.

What in God's name?

Grayness hazed his vision. Though he tried to remain in the saddle, his body refused to cooperate. On a groan Giric slammed onto the ground, somewhere in the anguish thankful for the blanket of snow to cushion his fall. A hysterical lunacy swept him. If he didna bleed to death, he'd freeze.

Either way he was dead.

Hoofbeats sounded, and then paused at his side.

With immense effort, Giric stared at a man he'd once claimed as friend. Too late, he remembered how Sir Neyll had addressed Lord Sinclair with proper respect and address.

Sir Neyll glanced to where blood spilled from Giric's wound into the snow. Satisfaction creased his face.

"My sister?" Giric demanded. "She was never in any danger was she?"

"Nay."

"Sinclair?" he said, damning his knight's betrayal.

"You will nae be a threat to him any longer."

"Why? We have known each other all our lives."

Sir Neyll spat by his side. "You are an earl, and I have naught but a horse and a pair of worthless spurs. With the gold I am being paid to see you dead, I will have more than you would ever have paid me." He galloped toward Dunkirk Castle.

Sarra!

Giric struggled to kneel, and the world hazed around him. He had to warn Sarra! Wind whipped around him as he shoved to his feet. Pain screamed through his body and he began to tremble. He collapsed. Sprawled within the snow, he felt a sense of doom crash over him.

He was going to die.

What would Sarra do when she learned of his death? God's teeth. She didna deserve this.

Another blast of pain ripped through him. The lure to slide into unconsciousness, away from the agony raging through his entire body, grew. He struggled to remain awake.

Flakes of snow swirled with a hypnotic bliss, the fragmented clusters twirling like fairy wings as they tumbled in haphazard angles to the ground. The wind increased with a low moan. A snowdrift began to form on his left side.

From somewhere in the distance he heard the strains of music, pure and sweet. A smile creased his. A fairy's song. He'd heard it before, but never so lovely. The tender serenade lulled him, engulfed him in its warmth.

A hand touched his brow.

Giric looked up into emerald eyes. The pixie smiled down at him, her wings fluttering as she seemed to take him in. With calm sureness, she laid her hand against his eyelids and drew them shut.

Sleep now. You will be safe. 'Tis the gift I give thee.

The words drifted to him from faraway. He tried to open his eyes, but his lids refused.

Then he realized it was the fairy's voice. He sighed, understanding her gift. This time when the shroud of blackness threatened, he surrendered to its merciful bliss.

CHAPTER 19

The door to Dunkirk Castle's keep slammed open, and a man staggered inside. Blood streamed from a gash in his forehead, and he clutched the shaft of a broken arrow. On a broken gasp, he stumbled forward and crumpled to the floor.

"Sir Neyll!" Sarra jumped from her seat on the dais. Heart pounding, she ran to him, glancing toward the door, expecting Giric to enter.

Empty.

"Fetch the healer," a man near the back yelled.

As Sarra reached Sir Neyll, a hand caught her shoulder. She turned.

"I will take care of this," Drostan said, his face grim. "Please."

"I need to find out where Giric is."

Sir Neyll groaned. Blood dribbled from his mouth, and he shifted, favoring his left arm. "We were attacked."

She pulled free of Drostan's hold and knelt by his side. "Attacked?" The man's head lolled to the side and he moaned.

"Where is Giric?" she all but shrieked.

Men gathered around her, the room a buzz of activity, the scents of spiced fish and sauce rich in the air.

When the man's eyes began to roll back, she clutched his wrist. "Where is he!"

"De—" Sir Neyll coughed. Fresh rivulets of crimson oozed from his mouth. "He-he is dead. I brought back his horse ou—" He began to cough again, each bout wracking his body. "Outside."

"No!" She jumped to her feet. "He is lying! Tell me where he is!"

Deep lines wedged Drostan's brow as he caught her arm. "You are distressed. Let me take you to your chamber so that you rest and calm down."

Calm down? How could she be calm when Giric lay somewhere dead? It had to be a mistake! She pulled free and rushed outside, halted at the top step.

Paces away, Giric's mount stood alongside Sir Neyll's. Blood streaked both saddles.

A shiver tore through her, then another. Her body began to shake.

Hands, soft but firm, settled on her shoulders. "Come inside," Drostan urged, his voice rough with regret.

"I must find—"

"Sarra." Sinclair turned her to face him. "You are overwrought. The snowstorm has just begun and 'tis too dangerous to risk allowing you to join the search. I will send men out immediately. If he is alive, my guard will find him."

As much as she wanted to go, with the hazardous weather, no room remained for error. And with her emotionally exhausted, too easily she could make a mistake. She nodded, and she prayed that they found him alive.

"You shouldna be outside," Sinclair said as he strode toward her on the wall walk. "The storm is growing worse."

"How is Sir Neyll?" she asked, praying that he was wrong and Giric lived.

"The healer is still with him, but his wounds are severe."

The thud of hooves sounded in the distance.

Hope ignited as she shielded her eyes from the thick, fat flakes and stared into the swirl of white.

Two riders came into view, three, and then the fourth man he'd sent out; all riding alone.

Nausea rose in her throat, and she began to shake.

"Sarra." Drostan caught her hand as she started toward the turret that led to the courtyard. "Go inside. I will speak with my men."

"I must know for sure."

Worried eyes held hers. "Then I will accompany you. Whatever news they bring, I willna have you face it alone."

Thankful for his support, she hurried down the steps. They reached the courtyard as his men cantered into the bailey.

A moment later, the knights halted before them.

The lead rider glanced toward Lord Sinclair, then toward Sarra, his expression grim. "My regrets, my lady."

His somber words shattered in Sarra's mind. She gasped for a breath, then another. "Where is he?" she asked, her voice raw with tears.

"About a league away, my lady." He shook his head. "I had intended to bring his body back, but by the time we arrived, wolves had found him."

At the gruesome image in her mind, she almost wretched. "Oh, God!" The air became thick, hard to breathe. Her vision began to haze. From far away, someone called her name, but she didn't respond, couldn't. Hands caught her, and she crumpled into the blackness.

A cool cloth pressed against her brow and a pounding thrummed in her head as Sarra slowly regained consciousness.

"Sarra?"

Drostan's gentle voice reached into the misty void.

She fought against it, unsure why.

Someone removed the cloth. Water trickled nearby, and then the refreshing cloth was again laid against her brow. With difficulty, she opened her eyes. The chamber swam into view, but her memories remained in a fog.

"She is awake," Sinclair said. "I will take care of her now."

Confused, Sarra took in the lines of concern on Drostan's brow as he sat beside her.

"Yes, my lord," a woman replied. "See that she has plenty of rest." A plump elderly woman plucked a wicker basket from the floor.

"I will," he replied.

After one last worried glance toward her, the elder departed, her footsteps scraping into the silence. The door closed behind her with a soft snap.

Uneasy to be alone in the bedchamber with Sinclair, Sarra met his gaze. His actions were inappropriate. Giric would be . . . Everything came rushing back.

Sir Neyll's injuries.

His claim of Giric's death.

Drostan's knight's confirmation.

Grief overwhelmed her and she looked away.

"Sarra," the baron said.

"Leave me." She wanted to be alone in her misery. Couldn't he understand that?

He withdrew the moist cloth. "I am sorry."

Silence filled the room.

A ragged breath fell from her lips, then another. The pain, hurt, too immense. Sarra fought to control her emotions. Once she was alone, then she could fall apart. "How is Sir Neyll?" she forced out, her voice breaking at the last.

"I am sorry. He died shortly after I carried you to your chamber. His injuries were extensive. Naught could be done."

A hot ball of grief swelled in her throat. Would no one be spared from this tragedy? God in heaven, who would do this? Then she remembered overhearing Colyne and Giric's conversation at Kirkshyre Castle. Giric was wanted for murder. Had the man called Maxwell tracked him down and delivered his own brand of justice?

She closed her eyes, wishing back the hours when Giric had held her in his arms, his last words of love.

"I promised your husband when he left that I would take care of you." Face dredged with concern, Drostan shifted in his chair. "At the moment you are overwrought, but 'tis important that you know that you are welcome to remain in my home, however long you wish. If you need me, anytime, day or night, I am here for you."

Sarra nodded, unable to reply, wanting to be left alone.

He leaned forward and laid his hand on her shoulder. "Please rest."

She remained silent, her eyes burning with unshed tears.

On a sigh Sinclair stood. "There is water by your bed if you are thirsty. I will order a tray of food sent to you in a bit."

Not caring, she didn't respond.

"I will check in on you later." He departed. Silence filled the room.

Thick.

Cloying.

Firelight danced in the hearth. Embers popped. A spark tumbled into the ashes, the warm, red glow stark against the faded gray. "Why?" Her rough whisper echoed into the silence. Last night they'd made love until exhausted, and then they'd fallen asleep in each other's arms. Now Giric would never touch her or whisper words of love to her again.

Pain streaked through her soul. Unable to face the present, she closed her eyes. How long she lay there, she wasn't sure, but sometime in the mangled void, when only coals glowed in the hearth and the sunlight on the panes ebbed, did she finally succumb to exhaustion and slept.

Heat strangled him. Giric tried to twist away from the flames, but they crept forward to scald, to char his skin until he couldna stand the pain. "Nay!" He jerked back. Strong arms pinned his shoulders.

"Settle down, lad," a woman's voice urged.

"The flames," he gasped. "Must get away." He fought to free himself, but firm hands kept his shoulders still while another pair secured his legs.

"The fever is a bad one," the woman said, her voice filtering through Giric's ravaged haze.

A male grunt from near his head sounded in answer. "He is lucky to be alive."

Alive? The prickle of hay on his back pierced him like a thousand needles, heat scorched his body and eroded his thoughts with caustic accuracy. He fought their hold, but they held tight. In the next moment, iciness washed over him to extinguish the heat. His teeth chattered as he began to tremble.

"Looks as though his fever is breaking," the woman said. "Hold him while I fetch a cup of water."

A woman's face swam before Giric. Her pale beauty stunning, her smile when given brilliant. Then he recognized her.

Sarra.

Giric smiled. The memories of the past few weeks rolled through him, the attack, their escape, their fated marriage, and eventually her love.

Pain jerked him to his senses along with memories of Sir Neyll, who'd tried to murder him, a man he'd known since a lad. And a traitor, loyal to Sinclair.

The baron's name curled in his mind like rotting fish. With Sarra refusing an annulment, furious, he'd plotted to end Giric's life. But the plan had failed. The bastard would pay for his treachery with his life!

What of Sarra? Had Sinclair murdered her for her wealth? Or, would he play the grieving friend, help her through the loss of her husband, with his intent to gain her bed? Like blasted Hades!

Giric tried to rise.

The woman tsked, but firm hands held him down. "There is nay Sarra here." She wiped the cool cloth across his brow.

"He canna understand you," the man said, his voice gruff.

"I know. He has been calling out her name since he fell into a fever. Looks as though he is beginning to settle. Thank the Lord. If he keeps fighting us, he will reopen the stitches I put in him three days ago."

Shivering, Giric blinked open his eyes. Muted colors blended in his hazed vision. "Th—Thirsty."

A woman's slender shadowed form came into view. "You are back with us are you?"

"Ay-Aye," he rasped.

She released her hold, and then laid another blanket over him.

A man held a leather pouch against his lips.

Giric drank several sips, thankful for the cool slide of water against the rawness of his throat. When he started to drink more, the stranger moved the pouch back.

"Nae too much at once," he cautioned.

"So—So cold," he whispered, the new blanket offering but a token of warmth.

"Aye, you have had a fever for three days now." The woman sat back. "We had begun to fear that you wouldna come out. My name is Mary and this is my husband, Iames."

Giric shivered. "I have been here three days?"

She nodded.

Saint's breath! If Sarra still lived . . . Nay. He had to believe that she was alive. What had Sinclair told her? He couldna lay here wondering. Giric pushed through the pain and focused on the room, on the woman by the bed. He glanced to where the man stood at his side.

"I am the Earl of Terrick. I need your help. My wife must be informed that I'm alive and that she's in danger."

"Your wife?" Understanding dawned on the woman's face. "That would be Sarra?"

Giric nodded, taking in the shabby clothes worn by both, then his bleak surroundings. "Where am I?" He turned his head to see more, and a throbbing at his temple began in earnest. "'Tis nae much of a shelter," the woman explained, "but 'tis the best we could do under the circumstances." She gave the man a warm smile. "We were traveling north when we came across you sprawled in the snow. At first we thought you were dead."

They had saved his life. "My thanks, but I need to send word immediately to my wife that I am alive."

The man shook his head. "Impossible."

Panic swept him. "If you have an extra horse, 'tis enough. I shall ensure that your mount is returned along with a bit of gold." Giric tried to rise.

The woman caught his shoulders. "You are too sick to be going anywhere, my lord. After we took out the arrow, I had to sew several stitches that are still healing." She grimaced. "As for the horse, we have one, but he is well past his prime."

"We made a travois to bring you here," the man added.

That they'd brought him here and tended to him was a blessing in itself. Many would have left a stranger to die.

"We were lucky to have stumbled upon this abandoned crofter's hut," the woman explained, her gaze locking with her husband's. She scowled her disapproval.

Giric focused on his predicament. A day's ride north with the horse dragging a makeshift travois; they'd nae traveled far. On a sturdy mount, he could make the ride in half a day. But where would he find a dependable steed in the middle of the wilderness? "My thanks for the care you have given me." He would figure out his dilemma. The last thing he wished was to sound ungrateful.

The woman held the cup to his mouth, nodded for him to take another drink.

When he tried to hold the crafted wood, a wave of tiredness swept him and his fingers grew clumsy. He let his hand fall back to his side.

She frowned. "You will be needing several more days' rest, my lord, before you should be on your feet, much less travel." Mary stood. "We will remain with you until you are fit to walk, then we must go."

"My thanks." He swallowed several sips of water and took the opportunity to scan his surroundings. Besides the straw piled across the room where his hosts had slept, his makeshift bed was the only other piece of furniture in the hut. They'd gone out of their way to help him when it was obvious that their own means were meager at best.

Regardless of the woman's advice, as soon as he could make it to his feet, he was heading out.

With a heavy heart, Sarra walked through the courtyard of Dunkirk Castle. Sunlight glittered across the land, the wind carrying a hint of warmth. A child's laugh had her glancing toward the well where children played while their mothers laundered clothes. Two knights walked past, their faces moist with a sheen of sweat from their practice.

Sarra's heart ached as she watched men in mock battle in the upper bailey where days ago Giric had sparred as well.

She stumbled on her next step, halted as tears burned her eyes. Why did he have to die?

The bells from the church rang.

A desperate longing pierced her as she studied the ornate structure that represented a God she'd turned away from so long ago. In a daze she stumbled toward the church. A muffled groan echoed as she shoved open the thick, handcrafted wood.

The scent of candle wax entwined with a hint of frankincense and myrrh greeted her as she entered. Sarra pushed the door shut. Slowly, her eyes adjusted to the dimly lit interior.

Two benches sat before an altar adorned with candles, behind which hung a cross, curtained by a swath of rich burgundy velvet.

Pressure tightened around her heart as she stepped forward. Before the cross she knelt. Years had passed since she'd prayed. But here, now, 'twas all she had left.

With her body trembling, she purged her soul into the silence. Seconds gave way to minutes, then the passage of time became a blur. A trickle at first, a sense of warmth filled her, easing the sense of hopelessness.

And in the silence, with the candles flickering like shimmers of hope, she realized that she'd been wrong to banish God from her life. For a while he'd given her Giric, who'd taught her how to love and how to forgive her past. How could she have ever doubted Him?

Tears rolled down her cheeks as she stood, stared at the cross, but a new strength filled her. Though she must go on alone, she had tasted love. She would persevere, for Giric's sake as well as hers.

The door scraped open.

Sunlight framed Drostan as he stood within the entry. With a frown, he closed the door and shadows engulfed him. Within the candlelight, slowly he came into view. "Sarra?"

The concern in his voice touched her. Since Giric's death he'd remained steadfast by her side. "I am fine. But, I have come to the decision. 'Tis time that I return home."

And with her declaration, she realized that she'd delayed attending to her original motive to travel here, her inheritance. That purpose had not altered, but her reasons to claim it had. Not only would she live her life as she chose, but she would use her wealth to rebuild Giric's home. Though she'd never met his people, through marrying him they'd become a part of her.

Sinclair walked over. "You have nae spoken with my father."

An image of the wilted man who lay abed each day only to grow weaker filled her mind. "With his failing health, I fear such an opportunity may never arise."

"Aye. 'Tis difficult watching him deteriorate each day knowing that . . ." He cleared his throat. "'Tis only a matter of time before I will handle his matters. If you wish, we can discuss your inheritance so you may leave."

"The last thing I wish is to cause you further difficulty at this troubling time."

He gestured toward the back pew. "My father would wish to see you happy. Please, let us sit."

Before, she would have refused to remain within the church, but now, with the sense of warmth filling her, Sarra sat.

Drostan settled next to her. His back straight, his hands clasped as if in prayer, he stared at the cross a moment before facing her. "Over the past few days I went through my father's accounts with the steward," he stated, his words grief-torn. "I have refrained from stepping in, but I must face the facts and assume my responsibilities."

"I understand." And she did, along with empathizing with his grief.

"Over the next week, I will settle matters concerning your estate. From my review, there is little reason why you should nae be given your inheritance or freedom to choose the life you wish."

She laid her hand on his, gave a gentle squeeze. "My thanks. I know this is difficult." He set his free hand over hers, catching Sarra off guard. Though uneasy, she didn't pull away. He needed comfort as well, and if this moment helped give him strength, 'twas asking little.

"There is an issue that I feel is my duty to broach." In the flicker of candlelight, his eyes searched hers with a sad but almost urgent appeal. "While I believe you should receive your inheritance, the issue of your protection is one of great concern."

"My protection?" She made to withdraw her hand. For a second his grip tightened, then he let go.

"I understand your wish to live your own life," he explained, "but the next few months willna be easy for you. You are grieving. Only time will allow you to heal, but a rich heiress alone will be a target for unscrupulous lords who seek naught but your wealth."

"I have managed my life alone quite well," she replied, but she couldn't erase the thoughts of the numerous unpleasant suitors who'd shown up to woo her in the past. Then it had been a matter of sending them to her guardian whom she trusted to turn them away. With Lord Bretane out of her life and her wealth in her hands, she must handle every aspect of her life, including those who would try to take what was hers.

"Sarra?"

She cleared her throat. "I will deal with what I must."

A wan smile touched his face. "Of that I have no doubt. You are a strong, beautiful woman. Any man would be proud to have you as his wife."

Uncomfortable with his praise, Sarra stood. "I must be going."

"A moment more. Please," he added when she hesitated.

She nodded.

"I understand that this is nae an opportune time, but I feel that I must raise another issue."

A tingle trickled down her spine. "And what is that?"

"To ask for your hand in marriage."

CHAPTER 20

Sarra's empathy of moments ago faded. "How dare you offer marriage when my husband has been dead less than a fortnight!"

He rose. "You are mistaking my intent."

Trembling with anger, she stepped back, the pew between them not far enough. "I understand your intent."

"Listen, please," he continued, with a soft plea. "My interest is in your well-being. I want none of your inheritance, I swear it. I want naught but to see you safe."

The urge to flee swelled inside her, but another part cautioned her to listen. She narrowed her eyes. "Why would you care for my safety?"

"That you have to ask disheartens me greatly, but in your distressed state, your doubt is understandable." He paused. "Our marriage would be in name only. It offers you nae only the protection of my name, but 'twould sever the necessity of your dealings with those who seek your wealth. You need time to heal. 'Tis what I offer."

Cynical doubts rose before she could stop them. "And I would live here?"

"'Twould be of your choosing. If you decide to return to Rancourt Castle to live out your days, then so be it. We have known each other since childhood, and you are someone I care for deeply. I offer you the protection of my name for your own peace of mind."

As stunned as she was repulsed by his offer, Sarra remained silent. Mayhap she wasn't being fair, but her heart, still tormented over the loss of Giric, refused to consider his suggestion.

With a sad sigh, he shook his head. "I have overwhelmed you. 'Tis nae my wish. I could think of nay better way to bring up this delicate matter." He walked past her, opened the door. Golden rays of the sun highlighted his handsome face, exposed how his gaze rested humbly on hers. "I do nae expect your answer now, but please consider my offer. I will wait a sennight. After that if you decide you wish to remain unwed and deal with the issues of suitors and such, so be it. But if after a sennight you decide to marry me in name only, you are free to live the life you choose."

"Why?" she said before she could stop herself.

He turned. "Because I love you. Though I know you love Giric and always shall, I would be honored to have you as my wife, even if only in name." He walked into the sunlight, closed the door.

In the muted darkness, she shivered. He loved her? She'd not suspected the depth of his feelings. Regardless, she couldn't marry him. The idea was ludicrous. But the thought of the freedom to live her life without men vying for her attention offered its own appeal.

Giric chewed thoughtfully on the oatcake, and then swallowed. "You will be departing tomorrow then?"

Iames nodded. "As you are able to walk, 'tis time we go. We will leave you a bit of food."

"Your hospitality and delay of your travel is more than I have a right to ask." Giric broke off a bit more of the flat biscuit. "I owe you my life."

The woman's eyes softened. "You owe us naught. 'Tis the way of our people to care for our own."

"With the fight for the Scottish throne, some seem to have forgotten that," Iames grunted. "Brother has turned against brother. 'Tis a shame to see our country being torn apart when we need to stand together."

Saddened by the fact, Giric nodded. He finished the oatcake. At the moment he could do little to change the misshapen state of their country. Once he'd brought Sarra home, then he could join Scotland's political fight to name their next king. "If you ever travel to the western lowlands, you are always welcome at Wolfhaven Castle."

Iames stood and extended his hand.

Giric rose and accepted it, his shake firm. "A safe journey to you both."

"You as well." The couple walked to their pallet. Straw rustled and firelight captured them as they lay on their makeshift bed.

Guilt coursed through Giric as he moved to his pallet. He'd vowed to never again reive. Yet, in a few hours he would, and this time his actions would be worse. Nae only would he take this couple's only horse, but he would steal from the people who had saved his life.

Their quiet murmurs filtered through the small hut.

Shame, deep and dark, rolled through him. What type of man was he? He closed his eyes seeking to understand why his decision had come down to this, hating what he must do, unable to find another choice.

With each passing day his fear for Sarra's life grew. This morning when he'd arisen, his unease had grown to a foreboding that had consumed him with an almost suffocating force. Whatever ill was about, he must reach Dunkirk Castle.

Giric waited for Iames and Mary to fall asleep. Their quiet whispers, their laughter, left him with an empty ache.

After the fire in the hearth was naught but embers and the hovel silent, Giric carefully dressed. The note he'd written earlier trembled in his hand. With deep regret, he placed it by their pallet, thankful that during his brief acquaintance he'd discovered Iames could read. The apology within could never explain his wrongful action, nor his promise to return their horse.

With care he exited the hut, closed the door, then hurried to where their mount stood tethered, a torn wool blanket draped over him. He caught the horse's halter, and then glanced skyward. Through the thick cloak of mist, the shimmer of stars could be seen.

A full moon.

A reiver's moon.

Shame filled him. In the past few weeks his life had come full circle. The times he'd ridden with his father to plunder came to mind. He'd vowed never again to take, yet here he stood ready to break his oath.

Or did he?

Looking back he realized that his father and their men had only taken from those who could afford to lose their stock. By the same token, when a needy family was on the verge of starvation, his father had replenished their food stores from his own larder.

Now he stood ready to reive a horse, but was he, like his father, truly stealing? What he was doing was improper in a sense, but his decision was made to save Sarra's life. The churn of turmoil fell away as he realized the truth. At times in each person's life they are forced to choose. Their decision may nae be the right one, but for the moment 'twas the best choice.

This was such a time.

He drew in a ragged breath, Sarra's words of the good in him echoing in his mind. 'Twould seem that she had understood what only now did he see. And with the acceptance of his past came a freedom he'd nae felt in a very long time.

Giric swung upon the steed. After one final glance toward the hovel where Iames and Mary slept, he kicked the horse into the night.

The call of a hawk drew Sarra's attention. Through the window she watched the raptor ride the currents over the treetops toward the setting sun. She thought of Sir Galahad. It seemed like forever since she'd left her home. Never could she have imagined how in a few weeks her life could change so irrevocably.

The shifting of covers had her glancing toward where her guardian slept. Another day had almost passed. The few times he'd awakened, he'd rambled to his dead wife. At some point before she departed, Sarra hoped that he would become alert.

Frustrated, she sat in a chair and took in the gaunt man, who even in sleep appeared one step away from death. His each breath rattled from his chest as if a victory.

Did the question she'd ridden here to pose to Lord Bretane matter? Drostan had vowed to sign over her inheritance at the end of this week, and then she could leave and live her life how she chose. With her freedom would come the suitors seeking her wealth.

Sarra traced the delicate embroidery along the cuff of her sleeve. Should she consider Drostan's offer of marriage? 'Twould give her what she sought, plus protect her from unwanted advances.

Still, she found it odd that he wasn't married. A handsome lord who would inherit his father's fortunes would lure many a woman to vie for his attention. He said he loved her, but was he obsessed by her to such a degree that he would shun others and wait for her? Obsessed? A strange word to use. However much he professed his feelings, doubts lingered that he cared for her as he claimed. The child she'd known had loved no one but himself. Yes, as an adult, Drostan seemed different, but she'd witnessed his momentary lack of control, the anger that slipped out before he'd reined it in.

By the rood, she must make a decision as to her future. Mayhap she was being foolish to doubt his sincerity? Anxious, she stood. At the window she watched the last red-orange rays of the sun waver in the sky.

Another day gone.

Unbidden tears misted her eyes. Damn Giric! He should be here by her side holding her, whispering words of love. She hated the empty life ahead of her, or the thought of bearing the name of another. At a rough cough she turned.

Her guardian coughed again, and his body jerked from the effort. Wanting to ease his pain, Sarra filled a cup with water. "Here, drink this."

His eyes flickered open. For a moment he stared at her. His brows lifted with surprise, and then a smile, warm and tender, creased his face. "Sarra?"

Memories of her childhood swamped her, his laugh mixing with hers as he twirled her around. "Yes," she said, breathless. "Please, take a sip."

A feeble hand curled around the mug. "My-my thanks."

"You are very sick. I did not think . . ." Tears burned her eyes. "Thank God I have a chance to see you."

He took a sip, pushed the cup away, and then laid back. He frowned. "How did you know that I was ill?"

"I did not know until I arrived." With a steadying breath, she spent the next several minutes explaining how she'd received his writ to marry Drostan, her journey to Dunkirk Castle, her aversion to Giric, the man he'd hired as an escort, then her impromptu marriage.

Warmth filled her guardian's eyes. "So you have found love. 'Tis an occasion to celebrate."

Like an arrow to her heart, grief sliced through her and she stood. "What is wrong?"

A fresh wave of despair rolled through her. "He—He's dead." The room swayed. She caught the edge of the bed to steady herself.

"Dead?" Though his body trembled from the effort, Lord Bretane sat up.

He held his arms out, and she moved into his comforting embrace. "A messenger arrived with tragic news that needed my husband's immediate attention a few days past," she sobbed against his shoulder. "He departed, but a short distance from the castle he was attacked and killed." With a sniff she sat back. "The man who rode with him returned, but died hours later."

Lord Bretane studied her. "By the grace of God 'tis tragic."

She sniffed. "I do not know what to do. All my life I have always known, but now . . ." Sarra wiped her eyes. "I am sorry to break down like this."

"After what you have been through, you have naught to be sorry for." A frown marred his brow. "I never sent you a writ to marry my son."

She stilled. "But . . ."

He exhaled. "Lass, why would I do such a thing? Though you were never told, I promised your father that when the time came to choose your husband, the choice would be yours and yours alone. I would never go against my word."

The discomfort that had gnawed at her over the last few weeks burgeoned into full-fledged concern.

Her guardian fell into a bout of coughing, and Sarra held his shoulders as his body shuddered. A moment later he quieted. She handed him more water. "Here." She held the water to his mouth. "Take it easy now."

After several slow sips, his fragile body trembling, he pushed the goblet away. "My th-thanks."

However much she wanted to know more, she wouldn't risk answers at the cost of his life. She prayed that after a few hours' rest he would be strong enough to continue. "I should be going," Sarra said, wishing anything but. She started to rise but his fragile hand caught hers.

Concern darkened his gaze. "Tell me all you know of the origin of the writ."

Sarra settled back in the chair, and drew a steadying breath. "You have been ill. I should not—"

"I will know now," he said, a flicker of his old fire surging through his voice.

She nodded. "Over a fortnight past, a small entourage of Scots arrived at my home bearing a writ supposedly from you." She struggled to keep the growing fear from her words. "It stated your wish that I should marry your son."

He searched her face with distress. "I have never written a message of this sort or authorized the penning of such."

Confusion flooded her. "If you did not send the writ, then who did?"

Drostan stepped inside the chamber. With a quiet, lethal move, he shut the door. His face twisted in macabre pity as it rested on her. "A shame that my father regained cognizance in your presence."

Furious, she stood. "How dare you—"

Lord Bretane fell into a fit of coughing.

Sarra helped him until he settled. She glared at Drostan, the vile taste of treachery seeping through her. "You planned this. What did you hope to gain?"

He gave a cold laugh. "Why, everything."

And she understood. "You manipulated me and your father, for money to aid in your political cause." Disgust poured through her as she took in the bedridden man who lingered on the edge of death. Aghast, she leveled her gaze on Drostan. "Your father is not sick is he, but poisoned!"

Without warning Drostan stalked over, caught her wrist in a brutal grip. "The pathetic old man will die within a fortnight."

Fear slammed through her and she tried to jerk free.

His fingers tightened.

"Damn you! What about Giric?" she demanded, wanting to retch at the horrific truth. "You had him murdered!"

Cold eyes narrowed. "Careful what you accuse me of."

The anger, devastation, and pain that had ravaged her since Giric's death exploded. Sarra attacked with a wild fury, her nails raking across his face.

Drostan screamed and stumbled back. Lines of blood drizzled from the wounds as he glared at her. "For that you will die!"

Cold fear whipped through her, but the dangerous lunacy in his eyes almost brought her to her knees.

He was insane.

He would kill her without remorse, would justify her death with the ease with which he'd poisoned his own father.

Drostan lunged toward her.

With her guardian unconscious, she bolted from the chamber.

CHAPTER 21

Giric's body threatened to collapse as he crested the last rise, but he refused to quit.

Dunkirk Castle, illuminated by the full moon, slid into view.

With a kick to his steed's flanks, he guided the mount down the hillside where but a short while before he and Sarra had ridden as man and wife. In the cascade of silvery light, he arrived at the entrance. His body ached as he secured the horse in the shadows. "You will be returned, lad," he whispered as he rubbed his withers.

Now to get inside. With Sinclair behind his attack, no doubt if he was recognized, he would be slain on sight.

A shout from the guard tower had him looking up.

"I tell you I saw a horse and rider," a man called out to another.

"I do nae see anything but snow and trees," another man replied.

Giric stiffened.

"I am going to check," the first man said.

"Freeze if you want to."

The other man grumbled, and then silence fell into the night.

This late, they wouldna open the drawbridge. Confident of where the man would exit, Giric hurried to the side entry. As the guard opened the door, Giric subdued and muffled the man. Exhaustion weighing heavy on him, he hurried inside. Little time remained to find Sarra before they discovered the unconscious guard and raised the alarm.

The courtyard, illuminated by torchlight, unfolded before him. People milled about, each occupied with their evening routine. He slipped into the stables, donned a cloak, and then strode to the keep as if he belonged.

Inside the great hall, women were breaking down trencher tables used during the evening meal.

He covertly glanced around but found nay sign of Sarra. Mayhap she was in their chamber? Once in the turret, Giric took the steps two at a time, then ran down the corridor to their room.

Empty.

Her scent lingered assuring him she'd been here a short while before. Blast it, where was she?

Her guardian!

He rushed from the room, his body screaming with his every step. When he reached the third floor, a hacking cough echoed down the corridor. Lord Bretane's door stood wide open without a guard. Saint's breath!

Giric ran into the room.

Lord Bretane looked up, his face beaded with sweat, heavy lines of distress clouding his features, and coughs wracking his thin frame.

"Where is Sarra?"

Though weak, fire flickered in her guardian's eyes. "Who are you?"

"Lord Terrick," he replied, damning each passing second. "I am looking for Lady Sarra, my wife!"

"Sarra?"

"Yes," he said, desperation edging his voice. "Where is she?"

"My son—" He coughed, but waved Giric off when he reached for the cup of water. "My son has her. I am sorry, I didna know of his twisted intent."

Panic swept him. "Do you have any idea of where they are?"

"I passed out moments ago while they were arguing. When I came to, they were gone. The lass is in trouble. Please, save her."

Giric nodded, and then bolted from the chamber, ignoring the warm sticky wetness of his blood against the back of his shirt. Where had Sinclair taken her?

He ran down the corridor and started down the turret, halted as he recalled the normal activities he'd seen downstairs moments before. Turning, he rushed up the steps. As he exited onto the wall walk, moonlight crafted a myriad of shadows over the hewn stone. He scoured the walkway for any trace of Sarra or Drostan.

Naught.

Where are you! He half-ran along the smoothed stone pathway, the flash of moonlight through the arrow loops flickering upon him with a steady beat. Several guards stood at their posts on the southern end of the castle nae edged by the cliff, but naught untoward came into view.

He started to turn back.

Sarra's muffled scream echoed from near the mews.

On a curse, he bolted toward the sound. As he closed he saw Drostan pin her against the stone. Giric unsheathed his sword with a vicious slide. "Sinclair!"

The young heir turned, fury carving his face. "You are supposed to be dead!"

Sarra twisted in his hold. "Giric! He tried to have you murdered!"

Drostan jerked her head back, pressed a dagger to her neck. "Quiet!"

"Let her go." Giric stepped closer. "Your fight is with me. Are you going to be satisfied killing an unarmed woman like a coward?"

The baron tilted his head. Moonlight streaked across his expression in a pale wash, leaving his eyes odd black hollows in his face. "We do have an unfinished battle."

"We do," Giric agreed, shaken by the twisted calm of the noble's voice. Saint's breath, he was insane!

Sinclair shoved Sarra away, and she stumbled to the side.

She made to rise, but Giric gestured her to stay. "I am the one you want," he challenged, needing the baron to keep his entire focus on him. Once they were engaged in battle, Sarra could escape.

Steel hissed as Sinclair withdrew his sword. "It seems we will finish our match after all. Only this time, the stakes are raised." He glanced to where Sarra stood, her face ashen in the moonlight. "Victor takes all." He attacked.

His blade nicked Giric before he could move aside. With his muscles screaming, Giric fought, but after several minutes, weakened from exhaustion and hard travel, he began to falter.

Their swords locked.

The gleam of victory shimmered in Sinclair's eyes. He shoved their hilts an inch before Giric's face. "Admit defeat. Mayhap I will let you live."

"What of Sir Neyll?" he spat, furious at his friend's betrayal.

"Greed buys many a man." Blades scraped as the noble shoved him back.

Giric evaded the swing and began to circle him. He had to keep him talking so that he could catch a breath. "And after he thought he had killed me, you murdered him."

"*Murder* is such a harsh word," Drostan spat, moving to block Giric's next step. "I prefer to use the term *dismissed.*"

"Bastard!" Giric lunged, pleased by the flash of disbelief in the baron's eyes. With his strength fading fast, if he didna overpower Sinclair now, he'd nae have another chance.

The baron swung. Missed.

Giric's blade met flesh.

On a curse Drostan whirled, slashed his sword.

Pain knifed through him as steel severed flesh. Giric dropped to his knees. A wave of dizziness swept him as the baron's hazy outline barreled toward him. Gasping for breath, he wavered, and then caught himself against the cool stone wall as a plan formed in his mind.

Stars danced in the pristine sky as death hung like a cloying mist in the air and footsteps slapped louder.

Sinclair closed.

Two steps closer.

With a fierce cry, Drostan angled his blade for a lethal thrust, his body poised, his legs in motion.

Another step closer.

At the last second Giric ducked.

The noble's blade swooshed over his head.

With a cry, Giric lunged up, the motion propelling the lord through the air.

Sinclair slammed against the flat of the crenellation and rolled. He caught the edge of chiseled stone as his body tumbled over. The full moon painted the baron in a pathetic light as he swung over the side, struggled to hold on. "Sarra. Help me."

"Stay back," Giric ordered as she ran to the ledge. As much as he should let the bastard die, he couldna. He clamped his hand over Sinclair's. He would let his peers decide this man's fate.

"Pull me up!" the baron screamed, "I canna hold on much longer!"

Pain shot up Giric's arm.

He slid an inch.

Saint's breath! "Sarra, I—"

Sinclair's fingers slipped from his hold, and his scream echoed throughout the night.

A dull thud.

The whisper of wind filled the night.

His chest heaving, Giric turned.

Sarra ran into his arms, her tears warm against his neck, and her sobs muffled against his skin. "I am sorry," he said. "'Tis nae the way I wished this to end."

"Drostan's treachery brought on his death, not you." She choked down a sob. "I thought you were . . ." She shook her head. "No, I will not let this chance escape me. I was wrong not to tell you before, but I will be telling you now. I never stopped loving you."

He caught her chin with his hand, the tenderness in her gaze everything he could ever ask for. "Truly?"

She nodded, tears in her gaze. "You have taught me to judge people for themselves, not by the acts of a few. And more important, you taught me how to love."

His heart swelled at her admission, and then he sobered. Though he'd struggled to earn gold to rebuild his home, he realized that he could never force her to live in a country that held tragic memories of her youth.

"If you wish to live in England, I will adjust."

Surprise flickered in her eyes. "You would live in England for me?"

His heart ached at the thought of living anywhere other than Scotland, but for her he would forsake everything. "Aye. I will appoint my steward to oversee Wolfhaven Castle. I love you, and I am never leaving you again."

She sniffed. "But what if I do not want to live in England?"

"What?"

A smile, filled with love, bloomed on her face. "Let me say that I have lost my heart to a reiver, and that I could never live anywhere but in Scotland with you."

Stunned, he stared at her in disbelief. "You wish to live in Scotland?"

With tears in her eyes she nodded. "Aye, I do at that. Take me home, Giric."

His heart full, he drew her into a fierce embrace and claimed her lips. With her in his arms, his life was complete.

And in the shadows, he could have sworn he saw the flicker of a fairy's wings.

Keep reading for
An excerpt from the
Next in the Oath Trilogy
AN OATH SWORN
Available December 2015
And be sure to read
AN OATH TAKEN
Available Now

CHAPTER 1

Scotland 1295

The rumbles of hooves filled the air as the contingent of knights closed.

Lady Marie Alesia Serouge ran faster. Dropping to her knees, she shoved aside the tangle of brush and started to scramble beneath. Stilled.

Fragments of moonlight exposed the outline of a large, muscular male form.

The man turned. His face, savaged by shadows, focused on her. Even in the feeble light, his gaze burned into hers with ferocious intent.

Twigs caught in her hair as she jerked back. Her breaths coming fast, she dared a glance toward the advancing riders before facing the lone warrior. She couldn't leave the cover of the brambles, nor could she place herself in new danger.

The thrum of hoofbeats grew.

With a prayer and careful to keep her distance, she pushed her way beneath the brush.

The knights thundered past, their mounts' hooves casting dust, leaves, and sticks in their wake.

Through the branches, the stranger's gaze upon her never wavered.

Heart slamming against her chest, she edged back.

Leaves rattled. The stranger lunged toward her. With a groan, he crumbled to the ground.

Marie hesitated.

Another soft moan echoed into the night.

He was hurt! On edge she scanned the darkened woods where the riders had disappeared over the horizon. Mayhap she'd erred and the knights were hunting for this man? However much she wanted to believe that, she couldn't take the risk. Furious King Philip's bastard daughter had escaped from his imprisonment, naught would deter the English Duke of Renard in his quest to recapture her.

The injured man shifted to his back with a groan.

She should flee. Escape while she could.

Marie released a deep sigh. As if she could walk away from the wounded man without a care? The scent of earth melded with that of leaves and the warmth of the summer night as she edged closer. A hand's breadth away she halted.

An arrow extended from his left shoulder!

By his shallow breathing, he still lived, but the shaft must come out.

Go, her conscience urged. Even if afforded the luxury of time, this man was a stranger, nor did she know what had led him to this desperate end.

But what if he was innocent of a crime?

On a steadying breath, she pressed her fingers against the well-corded muscles of his neck. His strong pulse beat against her skin like a warm promise.

A warm promise? With a shake of her head, Marie withdrew her hand and dismissed the shimmer of heat to her overanxious state.

A wolf howled in the distance, another replied nearby.

In the silken moonlight, she touched the dagger secured within the folds of her dress, and then scoured her surroundings. A wolf could detect the scent of blood from a great distance. If attacked, the wounded man would stand no chance of survival. Unable to discern any immediate danger, she refocused on the stranger. Her whole life had been devoted to helping those in need. How could she leave him here to die? She couldn't. Nor would she linger. Once she'd determined his recovery was certain, she'd depart.

Satisfied with the compromise, Marie scanned the grass and tree shrouded landscape for a place where they both could hide. A dense blackness lay through the tangle of limbs ahead.

A cave!

Twigs snapped as she crawled behind the warrior. Careful to keep his left shoulder immobile, she slid her hands beneath his shoulders.

He groaned.

"I must move you, *monsieur*," she whispered. Sweat beaded her brow and every muscle rebelled as she dragged him through the brush. He was a goliath of a man, even taller and more muscular than she'd first believed.

After several brief stops to rest between tugs, she at last reached the entrance of the cave. Muscles aching, she collapsed against the rocky ledge and glanced skyward. The moon had set and the first rays of sunlight streamed across the heavens in a prism of blues and purples. Marie frowned. Moving him had taken longer than she'd expected.

Ignoring her body's protests, she dragged him inside, then rolled him onto his uninjured side. Opening her water pouch, she pressed it against his lips. "Drink."

With a soft groan, his mouth worked as he swallowed, then he shoved the water away.

Rubbing the fatigue from her eyes, Marie secured her pouch and set it aside. 'Twould hold him for now. "Rest. I will return shortly."

A quick sweep of their path with a pine bough erased any sign of their presence. Satisfied, she picked several herbs that she would need to treat the man's wounds, and then gathered pieces of ash, wood that would burn without a trail of smoke.

Sunlight trickled through the forest by the time Marie coaxed the first embers within the pile of dried moss and twigs into a flame. After feeding several larger branches into the fire, she turned.

Her breath caught.

Until this moment, the darkness of the night had shrouded the warrior. Illuminated by daylight, long, whisky-colored hair rested upon broad shoulders honed by muscle. Hard, unforgiving planes sculpted his face. Stubble darkened his square jaw.

He presented a formidable warrior for any kingdom. Irritated by her assessment, she frowned. Until she reached her father and informed him of the Duke of Renard's treachery, she could trust no one.

Marie knelt beside the stranger and clasped the arrow firmly in both hands.

His mouth tightened as he glared at her through half-raised lids. His gaze, even sheltered beneath dark lashes, burrowed deep into her conscious with a potent reminder of her foolishness. Nonetheless, the arrow must come out to allow him any chance at survival on his own. With a jerk, she snapped the shaft as close to the skin as possible.

He gasped, then slumped back.

Thankful when he remained unconscious, she divested him of his mail, gambeson, and undershirt, careful to avoid brushing the embedded arrow.

At the sight of his naked chest, she paused. Whorls of dark hair swirled around aged scars, unknown stories chiseled across a battlefield of sinewy muscle. As a healer, she'd aided many a man injured in combat, but this war-ravaged fighter exuded a dangerous edge. She eased further back. Only a fool would allow herself to offer this dangerous man trust.

Trust.

Her heart tightened as she recalled the price of allowing herself to trust any man.

A mistake she'd never make again.

Marie shoved her painful memories away. She must focus on the formidable task ahead, not wallow in the past.

After removing the arrow from his shoulder, she cauterized the torn flesh. Once she'd applied yarrow and toadflax over the wound, she secured the poultice with strips she'd torn from her undergown and prayed he wouldn't grow feverish.

With her body screaming its weariness, Marie lay back and closed her eyes. A warm haze fogged her mind. Images of her escape from Renard's guards, of the terror guiding her every step as she'd fled flickered through her mind. Exhausted, she shoved the images aside and fell into sleep's welcome embrace.

CHAPTER 2

Colyne MacKerran, the Earl of Strathcliff, shifted to his left side. Pain tore through his shoulder. On a curse he rolled onto his back, and his body nudged against a soft, pliable form.

What in blazes?

Groggy, he opened his eyes and sat up. Sunlight sifted into a cave he had nay memory of entering. Ashes of a recently used fire smoldered a short distance away. And at his side slept an incredibly beautiful woman.

A woman he'd never seen in his life.

Hair the color of warmed honey tumbled in a silken mass around her. And her full mouth was curved into a smile as her lithe body pressed against his. Christ's blood! He would have remembered bedding such an enchantress.

More importantly, who was she and how had either of them ended up here?

He shoved back the pain in his shoulder as he searched his blurred thoughts to remember. Like a merciless assault, images knifed through his mind. An oath sworn to Douglas, as his friend lay dying, that he'd deliver the writ to King Philip. Being pursued by the Duke of Renard's men. An arrow shot into his shoulder and his narrow escape.

Then blackness.

The writ! Like a madman Colyne grabbed his undershirt, skimmed his fingers over the bulge of the concealed document. Careful nae to make a sound, he withdrew the leather binding and removed the rolled parchment.

The blood-red royal seal remained intact.

Grief burned his throat at thoughts of Douglas. He hadna even had time to bury his friend. *Bedamned, his life wouldna be given in vain.* The writ to King Philip of France would be delivered!

The woman at his side released a long sigh.

He shot her a hard look. Had she seen the writ? If so, she'd left it untouched. Where had the lass come from?

Her simple garb attested to her life as a beggar. Or, mayhap a servant. From her healthy glow, he'd choose the latter. Had she stumbled across him while out gathering herbs for her lord and had saved his life? If so, he would thank her. But, before he allowed her to leave, he would discover if she had seen the royal document.

After concealing the writ, Colyne nudged the woman.

Her nose twitched in a delicate flare, then she shifted and continued her slumber.

"Lass," he whispered, nae wanting to frighten her.

"*Qu'est-ce que tu fais?*" she murmured.

Stunned, he stared in disbelief. What was a French woman doing in the dense forests of the Highlands? Disquiet edged through him. The French king's bastard daughter had been abducted by the English and hidden in the Highlands. This was the very reason he carried the writ to King Philip, to explain the Scots were nae behind this treachery.

Could this be Lady Marie Serouge?

Again, he assessed the dozing lass in mundane garb. He scoffed. Aye, as if the English duke would allow his captive to be roaming the hills without an escort dressed in little better than rags?

A wash of dizziness swept him, and Colyne struggled to clear his mind. Wherever Renard had King Philip's bastard daughter hidden, she was well guarded.

The woman's brow wrinkled in a delicate arch as she lifted her lids. Eyes the color of moss bewitched him as their gazes met.

"Lass," he said, irritated by his awareness. He sought naught but answers. Her eyes cleared. Surprise, then fear, widened them.

The woman started to scramble back, but Colyne caught her wrist. "I am nae going to harm you."

"Release me," she gasped, her words thick with a French accent.

"You have tended me?"

Shrewd eyes studied him as if deliberating the wisdom of a reply.

Fine then. "First, promise to nae run." His body trembled from his meager exertion. With legs as long as a king's prized filly, if she fled, Colyne doubted he'd be able to pursue her, much less remain conscious. Before he passed out, he needed to discover if she posed any kind of threat to his mission.

She angled her jaw. "I could have left you alone and injured."

Which spoke well for her character. Or indicated her presence here was planned. "But you did nae."

"*Non.*" Her gaze flicked to his fingers curled around her wrist. "Now release me."

"I will have your word that you will nae flee."

After a long moment, she nodded. "You have my word."

Colyne let her go. "Why did you stay and care for me?"

"You were hurt."

The sincerity of her words surprised him. "Most would have left a wounded man to die. Especially a stranger."

Her eyes narrowed. "I explained my reason."

A reason that invited more questions. The cave blurred around him, and he braced his hand against the dirt.

"You need to rest, *monsieur*. If you move about, you will reopen your wound. Please." She laid her hand upon his arm. "The arrow went deep. Your shoulder will take time to heal."

He stiffened. Time he didna have.

An angry mark across her cheek caught his attention. Colyne skimmed his finger atop the darkening skin, curious as she jerked back. "You have a bruise."

Her lashes lowered to shield her eyes, but not before he saw the fear. " 'Tis naught."

"You have been hit," he stated, furious any would dare touch this gentle woman who would offer aid to a stranger?

"I fell."

Fell his bloody arse. By her evasiveness, neither would she reveal more. He studied her a long moment, and his gut assured him that something was amiss. Long ago he'd learned to heed his instinct.

The woman started to rise.

He caught her arm. "What is your name?"

"You will release me!"

At the dictatorial slap of her words, he obeyed and she stood. What the devil? She'd spoken to him as if a woman used to giving orders, and having them followed without hesitation.

Was she in league with Roucliff? Colyne's suspicion grew tenfold. Had she turned against her king and joined England's fight to claim Scotland as their own? If so, why hadna she broken the writ's seal, read the contents, then carried it to the English duke while Colyne lay unconscious?

He shoved to his feet and loomed closer, dwarfing her in his shadow. "Who are you?" At her hesitation he scowled. "You will answer me!"

"I-I am a missionary," Marie blurted out. *Mon Dieu*. Though the warrior watching her was confused, from the intelligence in his eyes, he wasn't a fool. But a servant of God was the first logical explanation that had come to mind.

"A missionary?" the warrior repeated, his brogue rich with doubt.

"*Oui.*" *Please believe me!*

"A French missionary in the Highlands?" He shot a skeptical glance toward the exit, then back to her. "Alone?"

She fought for calm. What more could she say to convince him? Though he looked like a god, with his eyes the deepest blue of the ocean and the sides of his cheeks hinting of dimples, the warrior's sharp gaze assured her that he was not a man to trifle with.

"I am waiting," he stated, his tone dry.

"It is difficult for me." An understatement.

His expression darkened. "I am nae going anywhere."

Neither, it appeared, was she. At least not until he'd received an explanation that left him satisfied. Once she'd appeased him, she would allow him another day to recover. Then, that night while he slept, she'd slip away. Though with the men scouring the area to find her, travel would be difficult.

Through lowered lashes, she regarded the fierce warrior, a man with the power to intimidate and the strength to back his claims. His finely crafted mail that she'd set against the rocky wall of the cave bespoke wealth. Surely he carried the funds necessary to arrange for her passage to France.

Marie hesitated.

Was this man too dangerous to risk not only her life with, but the safety of Scotland as well? Perhaps 'twould be better if she traveled alone.

But as a Scot, he would know the terrain, and if necessary, places to hide. In addition, his presence would add another layer of safety. The knights searching for her sought a woman alone.

Unsure to what extent she could trust him, she decided it prudent to withhold the fact of her royal tie. Though a Scot, he could be an enemy of her country.

"While returning from Beauly Priory, our party was attacked, and our people were slaughtered." Marie closed her eyes, her pain real in that, if she failed to reach her father and tell him the truth of who'd abducted her, many Scots would indeed die.

Silence.

Marie lifted her lashes and found his gaze skeptical, though not totally dismissive. "During the attack, I escaped," she continued. "I was terrified."

He nodded. "Aye, you would be."

"I-I went back to . . ."

At her shudder, he lifted her chin, his eyes dark with regret. "Oh God, lass. 'Tis nae the likes of what a woman should witness."

Caught off guard by his solace, for a moment she leaned closer. What was she doing, they were strangers? Shaken to offer trust when he'd earn none, she stumbled back. "I am sorry," she said, fiercely regretting her lie. She despised untruths, but life had shown her the length people would go to, lying, cheating and murdering to achieve their goals.

"Do nae be."

The sincere concern on his face made her want to admit the truth, but she remained silent. She knew nothing about this Scot, except his actions deemed him a man of compassion. Did his conduct extend to honor as well? "I must return home and inform my father of this tragedy." Her quiet words echoed between them, and his gaze softened.

"I understand."

Hope ignited. "Then you will help me?"

The warmth in his expression faded to caution. "Help you?"

"*Oui.* As you are aware, travel for a woman alone is dangerous." She spoke faster as refusal crept into his eyes. "I would only need for you to escort me to the closest port. From there I—"

Coldness chilled his gaze. "Nay."

She touched his arm. "But you must."

Dry amusement quirked on his lips. "I must?" Deep blue eyes studied her with unapologetic interest. "Lass, you have a penchant of ordering people about."

"I do not . . ." She withdrew her hand. Heat swept her cheeks. He was right. The woman he believed her to be would focus on serving those in need. She glanced toward the opening of the cave. Roucliff's men along with miles of wilderness stood between her and a port city. "The last few days have been terrifying."

The truth. Her abduction, imprisonment, and learning of the English duke's plot to use her as a pawn in hopes her father would sever support to Scotland, had torn her life apart.

"I am distraught and am being impossibly rude." She paused. "Forgive me."

Mirth flickered through the tiredness in his eyes. "That is the second time you have apologized to me, and with nay reason. I am the one who is sorry that you have been subjected to such carnage."

"I . . . Thank you." Moved by his genuine concern, he fell silent. As much as she didn't wish to involve him, fate offered no other choice. Somehow she must convince him to escort her to the coast.

His brows furrowed in pain, the handsome man started to turn.

She bristled, caught his shoulder. "What are you doing?"

"As much as I wish to rest, I canna." Honed muscles rippled as he leaned over to pick up his undershirt.

Embarrassed to find herself staring, she turned away, but not before he caught her perusal. By the grace of Mary! "You need to rest." She tugged his gambeson from his hand and returned it atop his mail. "You are pushing yourself too quickly."

Mischief warmed his gaze as if amused by her show of will. "I always take care with what I do, regardless the task."

Heat stroked her body at his claim. Of that she had no doubt. "I am going to pick some herbs that will help relieve your pain." She walked toward the entrance of the cave.

"I have yet to thank you for caring for me."

The softness in his voice had her halting at the timeworn entry. She didn't turn, though he was a stranger, something about him invited friendship, akin to trust. Neither of which she was in a position to give. "You are welcome."

"You have nae told me your name."

Her entire body tensed. Her name? Drawn by a force she couldn't name, she turned and faced him.

A mistake.

A retired Navy Chief, AGC(AW), Diana Cosby is an international bestselling author of Scottish medieval romantic suspense. Diana has spoken at the Library of Congress, appeared at Lady Jane's Salon NYC, in *Woman's Day,* on *Texoma Living! Magazine, USA Today*'s romance blog, "Happily Ever After," and MSN.com.

After retiring from the navy, Diana dove into her passion—writing romance novels. With thirty-four moves behind her, she was anxious to create characters who reflected the amazing cultures and people she's met throughout the world. In August 2012, she released her story in the anthology, "Born to Bite," with Hannah Howell and Erica Ridley. At the moment, she is working on the third book in the bestselling The Oath Trilogy, *An Oath Sworn*. Diana looks forward to the years ahead of writing and meeting the amazing people who will share this journey.

Diana Cosby, International Bestselling Author
www.dianacosby.com

Love Diana Cosby?
Be sure to check out
The MacGruder Brothers series
Available now as a box set!

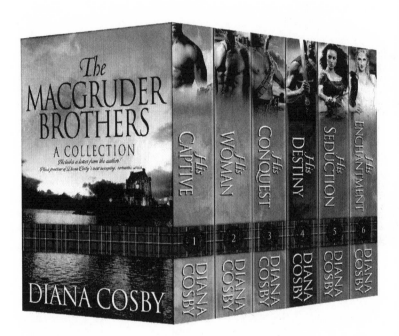

"Diana Cosby is superbly talented."
—Cathy Maxwell,
New York Times Bestselling Author

HIS
CAPTIVE

*Divided by loyalty,
drawn together
by desire...*

DIANA COSBY

HIS CAPTIVE

With a wastrel brother and a treacherous former fiancé, Lady Nichola Westcott hardly expects the dangerously seductive Scot who kidnaps her to be a man of his word. Though Sir Alexander Mac-Gruder promises not to hurt her, Nichola's only value is as a pawn to be ransomed.

Alexander's goal is to avenge his father's murder, not to become entangled with the enemy. But his desire to keep Nichola with him, in his home—in his bed—unwittingly makes her a target for those who have no qualms about shedding English blood.

Now Nichola is trapped—by her powerful attraction to a man whose touch shakes her to the core. Unwilling and unable to resist each other, can Nichola and Alexander save a love that has enslaved them both?

"Diana Cosby
is superbly talented."
—Cathy Maxwell,
New York Times
Bestselling Author

His
WOMAN

Some passions are too powerful to forget…

DIANA COSBY

HIS WOMAN

Lady Isabel Adair is the last woman Sir Duncan MacGruder wants to see again, much less be obliged to save. Three years ago, Isabel broke their engagement to become the Earl of Frasyer's mistress, shattering Duncan's heart and hopes in one painful blow. But Duncan's promise to Isabel's dying brother compels him to rescue her from those determined to bring down Scottish rebel Sir William Wallace.

Betraying the man she loved was the only way for Isabel to save her father, but every moment she spends with Duncan reminds her just how much she sacrificed. No one could blame him for despising her, yet Duncan's misgivings cannot withstand a desire that has grown wilder with time. Now, on a perilous journey through Scotland, two wary lovers must confront both the enemies who will stop at nothing to hunt them down, and the secret legacy that threatens their passion and their lives . . .

"Passion, danger, lush history and
a touch of magic."
—Hannah Howell,
New York Times Bestselling Author

His
CONQUEST
DIANA COSBY

HIS CONQUEST

Linet Dancort will not be sold. But that's essentially what her brother intends to do—to trade her like so much chattel to widen his already vast scope of influence. Linet will seize any opportunity to escape her fate—and opportunity comes in the form of a rebel prisoner locked in her brother's dungeon, predatory and fearsome, and sentenced to hang in the morning.

Seathan MacGruder, Earl of Grey, is not unused to cheating death. But even this legendary Scottish warrior is surprised when a beautiful Englishwoman creeps to his cell and offers him his freedom. What Linet wants in exchange, though—safe passage to the Highlands—is a steep price to pay. For the only thing more dangerous than the journey through embattled Scotland is the desire that smolders between these two fugitives the first time they touch . . .

DIANA COSBY

His DESTINY

HIS DESTINY

As one of England's most capable mercenaries, Emma Astyn can charm an enemy and brandish a knife with unmatched finesse. Assigned to befriend Dubh Duer, an infamous Scottish rebel, she assumes the guise of innocent damsel Christina Moffat to intercept the writ he's carrying to a traitorous bishop. But as she gains the dark hero's confidence and realizes they share a tattered past, compassion—and passion—distract her from the task at hand . . .

His legendary slaying of English knights has won him the name Dubh Duer, but Sir Patrik Cleary MacGruder is driven by duty and honor, not heroics. Rescuing Christina from the clutches of four such knights is a matter of obligation for the Scot. But there's something alluring about her fiery spirit, even if he has misgivings about her tragic history. Together, they'll endure a perilous journey of love and betrayal, and a harrowing fight for their lives . . .

DIANA COSBY
His SEDUCTION
"Medieval Scotland roars to life in this fabulous series."
—Pamela Palmer, New York Times bestselling author

HIS SEDUCTION

Lady Rois Drummond is fiercely devoted to her widowed father, the respected Scottish Earl of Brom. So when she believes he is about to be exposed as a traitor to England, she must think quickly. Desperate, Rois makes a shocking claim against the suspected accuser, Sir Griffin Westcott. But her impetuous lie leaves her in an outrageous circumstance: hastily married to the enemy. Yet Griffin is far from the man Rois thinks he is—and much closer to the man of her dreams . . .

Griffin may be an Englishman, but in truth he leads a clandestine life as a spy for Scotland. Refusing to endanger any woman, he has endured the loneliness of his mission. But Rois's absurd charge has suddenly changed all that. Now, with his cover in jeopardy, Griffin must find a way to keep his secret while keeping his distance from his spirited and tempting new wife—a task that proves more difficult than he ever imagined . . .

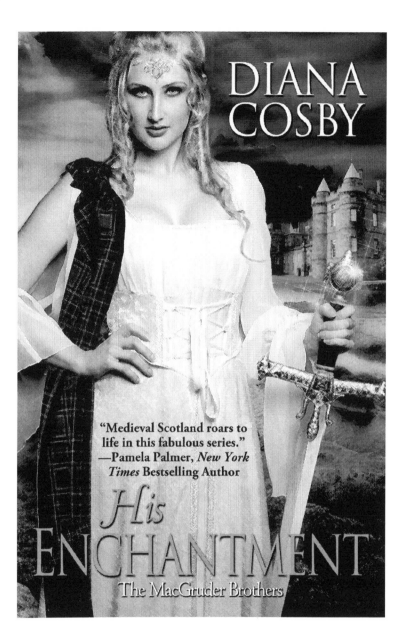

DIANA
COSBY

"Medieval Scotland roars to
life in this fabulous series."
—Pamela Palmer, *New York
Times* Bestselling Author

His
ENCHANTMENT
The MacGruder Brothers

HIS ENCHANTMENT

Lady Catarine MacLaren is a fairy princess, duty-bound to eschew the human world. But the line between the two realms is beginning to blur. English knights have launched an assault on the MacLarens, just as the families of Comyn have captured the Scottish king and queen. Now, Catarine is torn between loyalty to her people and helping the handsome, rust-haired Lord Trálin rescue the Scottish king . . .

As guard to King Alexander, Lord Trálin MacGruder will stop at nothing to defend the Scottish crown against the Comyns. And he finds a sympathetic, and gorgeous, ally in the enigmatic Princess Catarine. As they plot to rescue the kidnapped king and queen, Trálin and Catarine will discover a love made all but impossible by her obligations to the Otherworld. But a passion this extraordinary may be worth the irreversible sacrifices it demands . . .